Our
Red Hot
Romance
Is
Leaving Me
Blue

## Also by Dixie Cash

Curing the Blues with a New Pair of Shoes
Don't Make Me Choose Between You and My Shoes
I Gave You My Heart, But You Sold It Online
My Heart May Be Broken, But My Hair Still Looks Great
Since You're Leaving Anyway, Take Out the Trash

# Our Red Hot Romance Is Leaving Me Blue

## Dixie Cash

**AVON**

*An Imprint of HarperCollinsPublishers*

HarperCollins books may be purchased for educational, business, or sales promotional use. For information please write: Special Markets Department, HarperCollins Publishers, 10 East 53rd Street, New York, NY 10022.

FIRST AVON PAPERBACK EDITION PUBLISHED 2010.

*Designed by Diahann Sturge*

Library of Congress Cataloging-in-Publication Data
    Cash, Dixie.
        Our red hot romance is leaving me blue / Dixie Cash. — 1st ed.
            p. cm. — (Domestic equalizers ; 6)
        ISBN 978-0-06-143439-6 (pbk.)
        1. Chick lit.   I. Title.
    PS3603.A864O87   2010
    813'.6—dc22                                        2010002660

10 11 12 13 14   OV/RRD   10 9 8 7 6 5 4 3 2 1

Our
Red Hot
Romance
Is
Leaving Me
Blue

# one

*El Paso, Texas*

Sprays of fresh flowers blanketed the mound of dirt under which Sophia Paredes's grandmother lay. The tributes had wilted and were rapidly drying in the West Texas June heat. Sophia sank to her knees, bent forward and laid a fresh bouquet of yellow rosebuds among them. To her dismay, her gift, too, had already turned a darker shade within the last half hour.

Senora Isabella Paredes was the only parent Sophia had ever known. Gran Bella, as Sophia called her, had loved yellow roses and Sophia wouldn't think of bringing flowers made of plastic or silk. Artificial flowers were not a fitting memorial for a woman who had been loved by all who knew her and had lived every single day of her seventy-two years as if each were her last.

Though Sophia had cried so much she could scarcely breathe, she couldn't hold back tears as she straightened the sprays and removed the blooms that had turned brown.

A woman's soft voice interrupted her thoughts. "*Querida*, do not be afraid."

"I am not afraid."

"You cry as if you have no hope left in your life."

With her greatest supporter gone, indeed fear and doubt clouded Sophia's future. "That's how I feel. Hopeless and alone."

"But *querida*, do you not know you will never be alone?"

"*Si*. It's just that . . . nothing is the same. It will never be the same."

"There will always be changes in life, Sophia. How you handle them determines your happiness."

"*Si*. Of course. I know you are right."

"Good. So dry your eyes now." Sophia obediently wiped at her eyes with a crumpled tissue. "And Sophia?"

"Yes, ma'am?"

"Thank you for the yellow roses."

"You are welcome, Gran Bella."

*Two weeks later, 250 miles away . . .*

The only sound Justin Sadler heard as he approached his front door was the wind whistling around the corner of the house and the distant music of the aluminum wind chimes that hung from a branch of a spindly elm tree in the backyard. An icy shiver of dread crawled up his spine. He fumbled with his key, delaying opening the door.

If he hadn't broken into a cold sweat, the absurdity of his fear might amuse him. As a career firefighter, he entered burning structures with no hesitation. Yet here he was, taking his time, dragging out the moment before entering his own home. "Don't be stupid," he muttered, drew a deep breath and plugged his key into the lock.

Easing the door open, he craned his neck and scanned the small entry. No voice greeted him. He saw no sign of a person, heard no sound of somebody scurrying to make a quick exit. But he felt a presence. Was she here? Or had she been here? In his head, he knew it wasn't possible, but in the deepest part of his heart and soul, he longed for it to be true. "Rachel?" he said cautiously.

Once inside the house, Justin saw that his instincts had been right. Someone *had* been here. His wife's favorite afghan that had been neatly folded on the couch yesterday morning now lay in a disorderly heap. A copy of the latest *Western Horseman* lay on the leather ottoman, open to an article entitled "Life, Liberty and the Pursuit of Cutting." He didn't read the magazine himself, knew little of cutting horses and the finer points of the sport of cutting. Yet the magazine lay there, carelessly open, as if someone had paused to walk to the kitchen to freshen a drink.

Justin's jaw tightened and his pulse quickened. Was it Rachel? If not, then some earthly being was trying to drive him crazy. But who? Who would play such a cruel joke on him? This thing he had been dealing with for months was pushing him to a breaking point. He couldn't continue living this way.

Shaken, he returned to his truck, backed in an arc and hightailed it down the caliche road he had just crept up, a great white cloud of dust boiling up in his wake. Steering with his left hand, he used his free hand to dig through the duffel bag he had thrown onto the passenger seat. He found his wallet and fumbled with the leather folds until he came to a bent and worn business card. He had no intention of going back to that house until he talked to somebody who would help him find some answers.

Debbie Sue Overstreet, half owner and operator of one of only two beauty salons in Salt Lick, Texas, dried her hands and stared out the crosshatched window in the upper half of the Styling Station's entry door. Her partner, Edwina Perkins-Martin, busy unpacking a new shipment of nail polishes in spring colors, prattled behind her. "Ooo-whee, would you just look at these? They are *gorgeous*. They remind me of a bunch of jelly beans."

"Uh-huh," Debbie Sue answered, continuing to watch a newer-model pickup truck in the parking lot.

"You didn't even look. What's going on outside that's so interesting? "

"I'm watching this guy in this pickup, Ed. He pulled into our parking lot a few minutes ago and he's just sitting there.

Every now and then he opens his door, then he closes it again."

Edwina came over and stood beside Debbie Sue, both of them peering through the window. "Humph. My guess is he needs the Domestic Equalizers. Since we've been detectives, I've noticed that if men are looking for the truth about their lovers but not really wanting to know, they tend to drag in here like they're embarrassed."

Debbie Sue gave her partner's observation a few seconds of thought. "You're right. We have to pull the stories out of the men, but the women storm in, mad as hell, ready to kick butt."

These two comments were unassailable facts, Debbie Sue thought. And she and Edwina were qualified to draw this conclusion. Their second business, the Domestic Equalizers, specialized in following cheating spouses and significant others. They had formed the business soon after solving the mystery of Pearl Ann Carruthers' murder, for which they had collected a reward. Now, the private investigation agency had been in operation going on five years.

"But this guy's so cute," Debbie Sue said. "Even wearing that cap. Who'd cheat on him?"

Edwina's carefully tweezed and shaped black brow arched in a wise expression. "Husbands and wives don't cheat because of their partners' looks. It's some damned itch they gotta scratch and if hearts get broken while they're scratching, too bad. There's not enough calamine lotion in the whole friggin' world to cure it either."

Another indisputable pearl of wisdom from Edwina. Debbie Sue looked over and studied her friend's profile. After three failed marriages to men driven to scratch that itch, Edwina probably knew what she was talking about. Fortunately, Edwina had finally met Vic, her real-life action hero. Retired from the navy, these days his only goal in life was making Edwina happy. And God knew she deserved it.

"He's opening the door again," Edwina said, taking Debbie Sue's attention back to the pickup. "Okay, that's enough of this crap."

Before Debbie Sue could stop her, the skinny brunette opened the door and called out in a voice meant to draw attention, "Hey! My friend and I've got a bet on how many times you're gonna open and close that door. Do me a favor and come on in. I could sure use the money."

Startled, the man glared at her, but then he eased from behind the steering wheel and took a couple of steps in their direction. Apparently he knew how to take a joke, Debbie Sue thought.

He looked familiar, but Debbie Sue couldn't place when or where she might have seen him. She noticed the Equalizers' business card in his hand. Edging past Edwina she thrust her right hand out to him. "Morning, I'm Debbie Sue Overstreet and this is Edwina Perkins-Martin. We're the Domestic Equalizers. Is there something we can help you with?"

"Are you ladies . . . I'm looking for, uh, oh never mind. Sorry to have bothered you." He turned and started back to his pickup.

Achieving success and reputation as a legitimate investigator was Debbie Sue's fervent goal, though Edwina was more interested in the entertainment factor and nosing into other people's business. Debbie Sue had no intention of letting a potential customer escape. Moving with the agility and athleticism that had won barrel-racing championships back in her rodeo days, she darted past the new customer and planted herself against the driver's door of his pickup. "It doesn't take much of a detective to see you need help. Ed and I both know how hard it can be to start this off." She gestured from herself to Edwina. "Maybe we should ask you some questions. Would that be easier?"

Edwina came to her side and they stood as a fortress between the man and his pickup door. His gaze volleyed between them. "Uh, okay. Is there any charge for you asking questions?"

"Nope," Edwina said, leaning one hand against the door and propping the other fist on her hip. "Not until we decide if we can help you and you agree you want us to."

The man chewed on his lip. "Okay, sure. Go ahead and ask your questions."

Debbie Sue continued to study him, trying to decide if she knew him and from where. Formulating her questions carefully, she said, "Is that a wedding band on your finger?"

"Uh, yeah."

"Then I'd say you're having some problems with your wife." Debbie Sue perused the pickup's interior more closely. "There's no car seat in your pickup. You don't have any kids?"

"Uh, no."

"You've got that worn-out, dark-circle-around-the-eyes look. I'll bet you're not sleeping at night and this has been going on awhile. Am I right?"

"Uh, yeah."

"And being a firefighter, you're probably working everyone's shift to avoid going home."

The man's sky-blue eyes widened. "Wow, you are good."

Debbie Sue laughed. "Don't be too impressed. The kid's car seat part is fairly easy to see and as for knowing you're a firefighter"—she paused, flipping her hand toward his chest—"you're wearing your department's shirt. It's even got your name on it, Justin. From the dark circles around your eyes, it's obvious something's keeping you awake nights."

"And if you've come to see us," Edwina added, "it's a fairly safe bet that what's bothering you is something in the romance department."

"You're right," the man said, removing his cap and revealing thick hair the color of caramel. "It's my wife. She's trying to communicate with me, but I just can't, I mean . . . Man, I don't know where to begin."

"Communication's the most important thing in a marriage," Debbie Sue said with authority, believing she had learned that much the hard way. "If she wants to talk, what's stopping you?"

"She comes and goes and mostly . . ." His voice trailed off and his eyes took on a distant look. "Mostly she just leaves messages for me."

He had mumbled the statement, almost under his breath, but Debbie Sue heard him. What kind of woman only left messages for her husband? Frowning, Debbie Sue tried to look past the Matt Damon–like exterior standing in front of her to what might lie beneath. Why was his wife *coming* and *going*? Was she afraid to come around when he was home? Had he slapped her around to the point where playing tag and leaving messages was the only way she felt she could safely communicate with him? God, she hated that her thoughts immediately sprang to the worst-case scenario, but she had heard enough stories working as a hairdresser and seen enough abuse in her Domestic Equalizer role to know that in relationships, even loving relationships, no one was beyond doing anything. "When was the last time this happened?"

"Just a little earlier today, when I got home after my shift ended."

"And when did you actually *see* her last?"

The man stuffed his hands into his pants pockets and looked past Debbie Sue. "It's been a while."

"Can you be more specific? Exactly how long is *a while*?"

Justin looked Debbie Sue directly in the eye for the first time since their conversation started. "A year ago. At her funeral."

The man's words hung in the air like a curtain of ice. Edwina tried to speak. Well, not actually speak. In reality, she coughed and sputtered. Debbie Sue whacked her on the back, all the while watching their new prospect with a wary eye. Eventually, Edwina spit an enormous wad of chewing gum onto the ground.

Debbie Sue ran through a mental list of the funerals that

had occurred in Salt Lick over the past year, but nothing came to mind she could associate with this guy. "When you say 'at her funeral,'" Debbie Sue said, "you don't mean her funeral literally, right? You ran into her at a mutual friend's or maybe a family member's funeral?"

"God, don't I wish," the man said, combing his fingers through his closely cropped hair.

"So you do mean *her* funeral?" Edwina said.

The man's wounded demeanor tugged at Debbie Sue's heart. He must have lost the great love in his life. Could he be so deeply mired in denial he felt she was trying to communicate with him from the grave? He was either horribly heartbroken or crazy as a loon. Whichever, Debbie Sue now felt that help from the Domestic Equalizers was not a solution to his problem. But she would withhold her conclusions until she heard more. "Tell us your whole name," she said.

"It's Sadler, ma'am, Justin Sadler. You probably think I'm crazy."

*Sadler*. Debbie Sue slipped deeper into her own thoughts. His name rang a bell, but she still couldn't make a connection. "We don't think any such thing, Justin."

"Sure we do," Edwina said. "I mean, why wouldn't we? That's a pretty far-fetched story you're telling us."

Debbie Sue glared at her.

"Well, it is," Edwina said, her deep brown eyes wide and defensive behind a thick coating of black mascara on her lashes and a pair of black-framed glasses adorned with shiny rhinestones perched on her nose.

Justin looked at the ground, then back up to them. "I know. You're right, ma'am. I don't blame you for thinking I'm some kind of nut. That's why I've waited before saying anything to anyone about this. I thought my mind was playing tricks on me."

Debbie Sue couldn't remember when she had felt such conflict and confusion about a prospective client. He was so sweet and appealing, couldn't be much over thirty years old. He needed a hug and a gentle kiss on the cheek. . . . Or he needed a priest and a psychiatrist. He did *not* need a private detective.

As gently as she had ever approached anyone or anything, she said, "Justin, Ed and I are in the business of finding people who're cheating on their partners."

"Living, breathing, still-in-the-flesh people," Edwina said, now fully recovered from her choking spell.

Justin looked at them for a long time, his expression questioning. "But I thought you did surveillance work. I only want you to come to my house and set up some equipment. Some cameras or something. Somebody's doing this to me. I want you to see if you can find out who."

Debbie Sue felt tremendous relief that the guy sounded saner. "So you *don't* believe your wife's communicating from the grave?"

"My heart would love to think so. At first I tried to tell myself that's what was happening. I miss her so much. But my logical side tells me some living person's doing this, and I've had it. I want to know who and why."

"Well, we can sure find *that* out," Edwina said. "If there's anything we're good at, it's catching people in the act of making fools of themselves. We relate, if you know what I mean."

"Man, you had me going there for a while, Justin," Debbie Sue said. "I mean, we're good at what we do, but we're not ghost busters."

Justin's mouth tipped into a weak smile. "Sorry for the confusion. If it was really Rachel, uh . . . that's my wife's name, my ex . . . Hell, I still don't know how to refer to her."

*Rachel.* Debbie Sue zoomed through the halls of her memory. If a Rachel Sadler had ever been in the Styling Station for a hairdo, Debbie Sue would know it. But then, if Rachel was really from Midland, she probably didn't come in to Salt Lick to shop or get hairdos, either.

"If her name's Rachel, just call her Rachel," Edwina said soothingly. "We'll know who you're talking about."

"I really don't believe it's actually Rachel who's doing this. It's just that when I go into the house and see her rings on the table after I've just put them away a day or two before, or smell her perfume, it's just—"

"Her rings? Her perfume?" Debbie Sue gave him the squint-eye. "Who besides you would have access to her jewelry and perfume?"

Now wringing his bill cap, he continued. "Nobody. But I'm gone a lot. It's not impossible that somebody could come in the house and . . ." His voice trailed off again and his eyes took on a faraway look. "All I know is, somebody must have it in for me bad and they're doing things they know will get to me."

"You have no idea who could hate you so much?"

"Her family maybe. They're big-time wheeler dealers in Midland. They had higher hopes for her than marrying a city employee from Odessa. Rachel was brilliant and well educated. The world was her oyster."

"Hunh," Edwina said. "And you weren't her pearl. Been there! So how'd y'all meet anyway?"

"She was an attorney for a firm that specializes in casualty loss. She spoke at a state convention of the International Firefighters Union in Austin." A sheen of moisture appeared in his eyes and his face took on a wistful expression. "You should've heard her. She was something else."

This guy was breaking Debbie Sue's heart. "I'm sure she was," she said softly.

Edwina sniffed.

"After her speech I went up to her and told her how much I enjoyed it," Justin said, "and we got to talking. Turned out she was from Midland, grew up there and all her family was still there. We just kept talking until no one was left in the room but us. We went to dinner and pretty much never left each other's side for six years. Guess you ladies would call that a mushy love story, huh?"

Edwina sniffled again and Debbie Sue bit her lower lip.

"But I still don't understand why her family hated you so," Debbie Sue said. "I mean, in time families usually get over things like that. Y'all were happy, weren't you?"

"Oh, yeah. Rachel used to say we were crazy happy. Oh, we'd have our disagreements. After all, she was a lawyer and she loved a good argument. Things could get pretty heated, but we usually ended up laughing about it."

"If she's from Midland and you're from Odessa, how'd y'all end up living here in Cabell County?" Edwina asked.

"Cheap land that I could afford on my pay. She wanted a place for horses but we didn't want to ask her folks for money. She found our place for sale on the Internet."

"You still haven't said why her family hates you so, now that she's gone," Debbie Sue said. "Why would they carry such a grudge?"

Justin re-formed the hat he had been twisting and set it on his head. He shoved his hands deep into his jean pockets and gave her an intent look. "Because I killed her."

Debbie Sue caught a breath. She was married to a Texas Ranger. If a man had killed his wife within a hundred-mile radius, Buddy Overstreet would know about it. For the second time Edwina began coughing and sputtering. Debbie Sue gave her a daunting glare, then turned back to Justin. "Listen, we need to continue this conversation later. At this rate, Ed will be tossing her cookies. Neither one of us has time for her to be in the back room sick 'cause we've got customers arriving in the beauty shop any minute now. Give us directions to your house and we'll come out and look around. We can talk then."

"Sure thing," Justin said. "What time works for you?"

"We'll be done by three. We could meet you there around four."

"Four o'clock is great," Justin said. "I live about eighteen miles out, on the Odessa Highway. On the right side of the road."

Debbie Sue was shocked at herself for volunteering to show up at this guy's house when she really didn't know him. He had just announced he had killed his wife, forgodsake, and he hadn't disclosed the circumstances. The chill she had felt earlier was starting to creep back. "Even with cheap land, if you're an Odessa firefighter, why don't you live in Odessa or somewhere in Ector County?"

"I work three on and three off. I can live anywhere I want to on my days off. On my days on, I stay at the fire station."

"Right," Debbie Sue said, somewhat mollified.

"Listen, ma'am, I can't thank you enough," Justin said.

Debbie Sue was having a hard time believing he was a killer. She would talk to Buddy about it this evening. If this potential new client had been a suspect in a crime of any kind, Buddy would remember it.

But just in case Mr. Justin Sadler had done what he had just claimed and had somehow managed to escape detection, she said in her firmest, no-nonsense voice, "You need to know one thing, Justin. My husband is Texas Ranger James Russell Overstreet, Jr., and Cabell County is part of his territory."

"Yes, ma'am, I remember when Buddy was sheriff."

Not to be deterred, Debbie Sue continued, "And Edwina's husband is a retired Navy SEAL. You hurt either one of us and between the two of them they'll pound your head so hard you'll have to unzip your pants to blow out your birthday candles. *If* you live to see another birthday. Do we have an understanding?"

A frown of puzzlement formed a crease between Justin's brows. His gaze switched between her and Edwina for several seconds. "Oh, yes, ma'am. Absolutely."

# two

ebbie Sue, alongside Edwina, watched the Domestic Equalizers' new client climb into his pickup and drive away. Then she and her partner walked back into the salon. Edwina began busying herself with permanent rods, dividing them into groups by size and color, a task Debbie Sue knew was a stalling tactic. Waiting for Edwina's gripe to surface, Debbie Sue found a task of her own. She started straightening the objects that sat on her workstation. After several minutes, she could no longer stand the silence. "Okay, out with it. I know you're thinking something."

Edwina dropped a permanent rod into her tray and crossed her long arms over her flat chest, which was never a good sign. "We've never worked for a wife killer before. If he says he killed her, why didn't we ask him how? And when? And why? How come we've never heard anything about it? And how come you told him we'd meet him at his house?"

Good questions, all. "I'm almost positive Rachel Sadler died in a car accident. Hearing Justin say he had killed her had me so stunned I lost my train of thought. Meeting at his house just fell out of my mouth before I gave it thorough consideration." Debbie Sue's concern for her and Edwina's safety loomed in her mind, but unwilling to admit going to a wife killer's house might be a mistake, she planted a fist on her hip in her own show of defiance. "Why shouldn't we go to his house? We couldn't stand out there in the parking lot all day."

"But you don't like him. You don't want to do this."

Debbie Sue raised a palm in protest. "Whoa. I never said I didn't like him."

"That last remark you made to him wasn't exactly an invitation for a good time. Hon, you're easier to read than a newspaper. You do not like him and you don't trust him."

"Dammit, Ed, I don't know how I feel about him." Debbie Sue gave a deep sigh. "In the short time we spent talking to him, I went from disbelief, to pity, to suspicion and back to disbelief. I must be near my period. I just went through every emotion known to womankind."

"Not all of 'em." Edwina picked up a package of her favorite gum—Orbit Bubblemint—from her workstation, unwrapped a piece and popped it into her mouth. She plopped into her styling chair. "I can think of at least seven more."

"Whatever. So tell me, poker face, what did you think of him? And about taking him on as a client?"

Chewing, Edwina said, "A client's a client."

"That's right. Since when do we have to like everyone we say we'll work for? We wouldn't do much business if we took that attitude. But I have to admit, the whole conversation was a little bizarre."

Edwina lifted her foot, appearing to study the beaded red hearts that adorned her platform shoe. "You got that right. Everything he said just flat-ass weirded me out."

"You know what his story brings out in me?"

"What?"

"Curiosity. I mean, damn, Ed. Here we've got this cool-looking guy who's heartbroken over his dead wife. A wife he says *he* killed. What's not to love about that?"

"You left out the part about somebody trying to drive him crazy."

"Yes, and someone's trying to make him think he's bonkers. If that's not the makings of a good time for the Domestic Equalizers, I don't know what is."

"So you don't buy into that ghost-of-the-dead-wife BS?"

"Nah. There's got to be a logical explanation. I don't believe in ghosts. But if anyone ever would be a believer, *you* would, Edwina Perkins-Martin."

Edwina cocked her head, still studying her shoe. "Well . . ."

"I knew it!" Debbie Sue gleefully clapped her hands.

Edwina got to her feet and propped both hands on her skinny hips. "Just don't get too smug, Miss Priss. I've seen and heard a thing or two. Things that would make anybody think twice about the supernatural stuff. Even a hardhead like you."

Debbie Sue plucked a bottle of Windex from her bottom drawer and spritzed her mirror. "Oh, really? Like what?"

"You know my third husband, Jimmy Wayne Perkins? The one from El Paso? His mother—her name was Little Pearl Perkins—that woman either called or went to see a psychic in El Paso for every big decision she ever made. I mean, she—"

"Little Pearl?" Debbie Sue gave her partner an arch look. "You honestly knew someone named Little Pearl?"

"Little Pearl's mama was named Pearl too, so everyone called Jimmy Wayne's mother Little Pearl. Do you want to hear this story or not?"

Debbie Sue bent and returned the Windex to her bottom drawer. "Did they call her mother Big Pearl?"

"As a matter of fact, they did. Just so they could keep them sorted out when they were talking about them."

Debbie Sue straightened, a roll of paper towels in her hand. "Makes perfect sense." She began to wipe Windex off her mirror prepared to hear another one of Edwina's tales about her bizarre family.

"As I was saying," Edwina continued, "this woman could tell your future and she could communicate with the dead. If I hadn't witnessed it firsthand with my own beautiful brown eyes, I might not believe it either."

"And what'd she do firsthand, tell you Jimmy Wayne was gonna cheat on you?"

"Oh, hell, I didn't need a psychic to know that. But she did tell me he was hiding money from me. She even told me where to find it."

Debbie Sue set down the roll of paper towels, her interest piqued.

"Really?"

"Yep. Toward the end of that marriage-made-in-hell to Jimmy Wayne, he was gone more than he was home. Only passed through long enough to shower and shave. Half the time me and my girls didn't have enough food in the house to keep a person alive. Hell. If it hadn't been for Halloween that year, we might've starved to death. Me and the kids hit half the houses in El Paso, trick-or-treating. To this day I want to barf when I see a popcorn ball. That year caused me a bunch of cavities, but we made it."

Debbie Sue already knew Edwina had spent some hard times in her life. "Why haven't you ever told me that story before?" she said, contrite.

"No point in digging up bones," Edwina said absently, appearing to be lost for a moment in thought. Soon she resumed. "Anyway, that psychic told me to look in the toe of Jimmy Wayne's brown alligator boots. I did and I pulled out a roll of hundred-dollar bills. It was thick enough to choke a horse. That bastard had twenty-three hundred dollars hidden away for his drinking and partying."

Debbie Sue gasped. "The sonofabitch. I hope those were the same boots you poured cement in before you left him."

"The very same. And all his other fancy boots too."

"Finding that money might not have been something the psychic foresaw, Ed," Debbie Sue pointed out. "She could've made a lucky guess, based on what you asked her. It's not like people have never hidden anything in a boot."

"But I didn't ask her a single question. It wasn't even me who went to see her. I was just waiting. Here I am, sitting in this strange living room with this pretty little girl, playing checkers and killing time while Little Pearl got her reading. This Mexican woman I never saw before in my life walks in and tells me to look in the toe of my husband's alligator boot for the money I needed to feed my kids. It happened just like that. I was just sitting there waiting to have my king crowned and she says that."

"That's impressive," Debbie Sue said.

"Damn sure was," Edwina replied. "It changed my life."

"You remember her name?"

"I'll never forget it. It was Isabella Paredes."

For the second time in the same day, Justin crossed the cattle guard entrance to his home. He felt hopeful. He had made a move toward regaining control of his life. That knowledge alone gave him an enthusiasm that had been long absent. He could tell Debbie Sue Overstreet had mixed feelings about him, though. Probably because she was married to a cop.

In his driveway, Justin killed his truck engine and scooted out with more energy than he had felt in months when approaching his front door. Whoever or whatever was harassing him would soon be exposed. Of that he had no doubt. He unlocked and opened the door.

And stopped dead in his tracks.

The smell of roses was overwhelming.

He quickstepped to the living room and there in the center of the coffee table was Rachel's best Waterford cut crystal vase holding a bouquet of yellow roses. His heartbeat escalated, sweat broke out on his brow.

When Rachel was alive, when her family, or *any* company, was expected, she would pull out that vase and fill it with fresh-cut roses. If the yellow roses in the backyard were in bloom, she used them. Or she might buy a bouquet from the grocery store or a florist. She had always put them on the living-room coffee table in full view. Sunlight through the window behind the sofa would bounce off the vase's finely cut glass and send prisms of light through the room. The soft fragrance of roses would permeate the air.

Just like now.

Anxiety began creeping through him, dispelling the upbeat feeling he'd had after meeting Debbie Sue and Edwina. He stood perfectly still, re-gathering his emotions.

Then he was hit with a realization that made his knees almost buckle. Anyone who had ever visited in their home when Rachel was alive might know of her practice of putting out roses for company. But today, only *he* knew the Domestic Equalizers would be arriving here later this afternoon.

*Company.*

Was Rachel's Waterford crystal vase filled with yellow roses now sitting on the living-room coffee table for *company*?

He shook his head to clear it of those irrational thoughts zigzagging through his mind. He didn't know how those flowers got into that vase and onto his coffee table, but he was damn glad they were there, waiting for Debbie Sue and Edwina to see that he wasn't crazy or imagining things.

But whoever or whatever else the Domestic Equalizers might find lurking around his house, he wasn't entirely sure.

Sitting at the dining table in her small apartment, Sophia pushed away a stack of bills, propped her elbows on the table and dropped her face into her hands. So many bills, so little money.

During Gran Bella's illness, Sophia had put her own obligations on the back burner to concentrate on her dying grandmother's needs. She had readily reached into her own pocket to pay when the insurance company no longer would, making certain Gran Bella had been denied no treatment, necessity or comfort. The illness that had robbed her grandmother of her lust for life and finally, life itself, had wiped out both their savings.

But Sophia couldn't have done any less after all that Gran Bella had done for her. Senora Isabella Paredes's dream had been for Sophia to graduate from college. No member of their family had ever attended a single college class, much less graduated. Though a lofty desire, it became achievable because Gran Bella had worked and sacrificed and helped. Sophia had worked hard too, of course. And she had graduated with a degree in elementary education from the University of Texas at El Paso.

Sophia had no regrets about how she had handled her grandmother's last days, but she couldn't keep from thinking of the dilemma she now faced. The cost of the funeral and interment, even after the least-expensive choices the funeral home offered, had taken the last pennies Sophia and her grandmother had to their names. Now, besides being grief stricken, Sophia was flat broke.

The road going forward portended to be decidedly rougher. First-year, first-grade schoolteachers earned paltry salaries. Before Gran Bella's passing, Sophia's plan had always been to obtain her master's. Just a few additional letters after her name could add thousands to her paycheck. Now, a plan to continue her education would have to wait until she got back on her feet financially. The time she would have dedicated to evening classes would now have to be spent moonlighting.

She had to start by ceasing to dwell on the negative and turn her attention to the positive, even though at this moment, she was pretty positive her bank balance was a negative. She had to find a source of additional income. Being employed at a second job would be no different from holding down a full-time job while she had worked toward her college degree, she told herself.

She rose from her chair and pawed through the newspaper for the classified section. She carried it back to the table and in less than fifteen minutes, had scattered half a dozen red circles over the page in front of her.

While a student, she had held a variety of jobs. She already knew waitressing in a high-end eatery paid more than clerking in a retail store.

She had experience in both family dining and fast food. From that, she had learned that the real money in waiting tables came from tips. Good tips came in restaurants that served food on plates, on tables with linen cloths. No tips came from places that served food in Styrofoam carry-out containers, ordered from a menu where a number beside a picture defined an entree.

Besides that, Sophia knew she had to be discreet. The school district didn't forbid outside employment, but her employer might lose faith in her teaching ability if she spent part of her week wearing a paper hat resembling a chicken and asking, "Would you like to Super Cluck that order?"

Another thought lifted her mood. A second job would force her to get out of the house. She had virtually no social life and knew very few men. Among the patrons of an up-scale restaurant she might meet men. Perhaps she would meet someone she would fall in love with and marry. She might even meet bachelors who were rich. She didn't know how many women had met marriage-worthy men waiting tables, but surely there had been some. Wealth had never been at the top of her list of requirements in men, but after going through her stack of bills, money had jumped several notches.

She brought the phone to the dining table and pressed in the numbers from one of the ads. A male voice that made her think of silk answered the phone. After a brief conversation they agreed to meet at the restaurant at two o'clock for an interview. She had an hour to pull herself together.

Minutes later, she was at the bathroom sink brushing her teeth. Thanks to Gran Bella's investment in good dental care at an early age, Sophia had perfect, sparkling white teeth.

She washed her face, then freed her thick hair from the

elastic band that held it in a ponytail. She took pride in wearing her hair long and loose. A few strokes with a hairbrush and glossy ebony tresses fell around her shoulders. She had heard for her entire life that she was a natural beauty who needed little makeup, so with a swipe of coral blush to her high cheekbones and a touch of taupe lip gloss on full lips, she was finished.

She spent a moment studying her reflection. Her hazel eyes—her only feature that wasn't Mexican—were framed by long black lashes. People said her eyes were captivating. Now, if only they would help her capture a job.

# three

*D*ebbie Sue walked the Styling Station's last patron of the day to the door and locked it behind her. Edwina had moved to the payout desk and was already entering numbers into the calculator. "You don't have to do that now, Ed. We need to head out to Justin's place. It's almost four."

"Oh," Edwina replied. The calculator's whirr stopped as she looked up. "Don't you think I should finish this? Get the deposit ready, then sweep up a little?"

Those chores were part of the end-of-day routine in the Styling Station, but an appointment with an Equalizers prospective client had always taken precedence. Edwina was stalling again.

Debbie Sue reached into her purse and dug out a tube of lipstick. She returned to her workstation, leaned closer to the mirror and swiped a fresh layer of Coral Ice onto her lips, all the while watching Edwina in the mirror's reflection. The woman had moved from behind the desk to the front counter and was now intently occupied with putting pens in a coffee mug, ink tips up. Debbie Sue twisted the lipstick down and snapped the top back in place. "You gonna ride with me out to Justin's or do you want to follow?"

Edwina flopped her wrist in an exaggerated show of non-chalance. "Oh, I'll just go in my car. No need you coming all the way back to town just to bring me to my car. His place is the old Gill place. I know right where it is. After we look things over, I'll just hop on the butane route and be home before you know it." She didn't abandon arranging pens in the mug.

Debbie Sue heaved a sigh. "Okay, what's up? Why are you digging your heels in?"

"I'm not," Edwina said innocently.

"Ed, I've broken feral horses easier than I'm getting you to move. I thought we discussed the possibility of a ghost and we decided that it wasn't possible. There's an explanation."

"We didn't discuss it. Not really. We talked about psychics."

"Psychics, ghosts, monsters in the closet, it's all the same." Debbie Sue flipped the OPEN sign to the CLOSED side, then moved toward the back door, keys in hand. "Now, c'mon. We're gonna be late." She waited for Edwina to join her.

Edwina lifted herself from her chair as if she weighed three hundred pounds. Debbie Sue had never seen her so reluctant. Usually, she would jump in front of a tornado to prove her point. Yet from the second Justin told his story, a new side of Edwina had started to emerge.

The woman in El Paso—what had Edwina called her? Isabella something? She hadn't made just an impression on Edwina, she had scared the living shit out of her. Debbie Sue wanted to tell her longtime friend that her former mother-in-law had most likely been told about the money being hidden by Jimmy Wayne and dropping that bomb on the unsuspecting Edwina drummed up business for the crystal-ball reader. But intuition told Debbie Sue to let it go. Edwina could take a joke as well as anyone, but teasing her at this point would be a bad idea.

Outside in the parking lot behind the salon sat Edwina's royal blue 1968 Mustang. As she began to paw inside her purse for keys, it occurred to Debbie Sue that she could end up at Justin Sadler's house alone while her partner went on her merry way home. "Why don't you ride with me, Ed? With the price of gas, we'll save a buck or two by taking one rig."

"Well . . . I guess I could . . . but I should call Vic and tell him where I'm going."

"Why?"

"In case he needs me for something. He's due home in a couple of hours."

Debbie Sue knew that Vic, who now owned his own big rig and worked as a long-haul trucker in his retirement, had been on the road for a week. "So call him on your cell."

"Well . . . I guess I could . . ." But Edwina made no move to make the call.

"Ed, call him. We need to get going."

"Oh, hell, Debbie Sue." Edwina dug her cell phone from her purse and speed-dialed a number. Debbie Sue listened as Edwina explained to Vic where she was headed and added she should be home in approximately an hour and a half. Debbie Sue had to admit letting someone know where they were going could be a good idea, and she didn't know where Buddy was at the moment. "Look, Ed, there's no such thing as dead wives coming back from the grave."

"I know that." Edwina hoisted her chin and dropped her cell phone into her purse. She strode to Debbie Sue's red pickup truck and climbed into the passenger seat.

Twenty minutes later, they rumbled across the cattle-guard entrance to Justin's place. As they approached the house they saw that it was a sixties-vintage rambling ranch-style house. An air conditioner unit underpinned by cinder blocks jutted from a window. Trees so large they had to have been planted twenty or thirty years ago shaded the home. A yard with big trees other than mesquites was a rarity in Cabell County.

The horse corrals and two sorrel mares caught Debbie Sue's attention. To an untrained eye, they would be nothing special, but to Debbie Sue, who had spent most of her life on horseback, they were spectacular. This pair had cost someone a lot of money. Justin hadn't impressed her as being a cowboy, so had these obviously highbred horses belonged to his deceased wife?

Braking to a complete stop, Debbie Sue sat and studied them. She could see they were restless and tense. Too bad they were being treated as if they were house pets. They needed exercise and grooming. From the looks of them, Justin wasn't the only one missing Rachel. Debbie Sue had even more questions than before for this young man.

Justin walked out on the porch. His chocolate lab, Turnup, got to his feet and met him. "Get back, boy. We've got company."

He watched as a red Silverado crew-cab truck came to a stop in his circular drive. Shoving his hands into his pockets, he called out to the two women inside, "Y'all have any trouble finding the place?"

Debbie Sue climbed out of the truck. "Nah. Richard Gill and his brood used to live here."

"His mama was an invalid, bless her heart," the woman named Edwina said. "Years ago I used to come out here every week or so and fix her hair."

"You make house calls to fix people's hair?"

"Not as a rule. But Mary Gill was bedridden. She always took pride in her looks. It picked her spirits up to have her hair done. Don't guess anyone ever saw it, but it made her feel better."

Justin took an immediate liking to Edwina. He could tell she had a kind heart. He had always felt the world could use more kind hearts, especially women's. He smiled, shielding his eyes from the afternoon sun.

Turnup pranced over to Debbie Sue, his tail whipping as he begged for attention. She reached down and stroked his head. "Turnup, get down," Justin ordered.

"He's all right," Debbie Sue said, crouching to a squat. She cradled the dog's snout in her hand. "He's just happy to see someone. Why do you call him Turnip?"

"Rachel named him that because he just turned up on our doorstep one day. 'Turn up.' Get it?"

Debbie Sue laughed for the first time since he had met her, a warm laugh that lit up her face. She was tall, not as tall as her partner, but taller than Rachel had been. And she had green eyes like Rachel's.

Setting the dog away, Debbie Sue rose, straightened her clothing and became serious again. She strode toward him, all business. "Justin, our normal procedure before we agree to do surveillance work is to take a look around. Sort of do an assessment. Then Ed and I discuss it. We get back to you in a day or two and tell you if we can help you and what we'll charge."

"Wow, you're ready to just jump right in, aren't you?"

Edwina lowered her huge sunglasses to the tip of her nose and looked over the top edge. "She takes our work very seriously."

"Yes, well I guess that's what I want. Somebody to do a serious job. Uh, sure thing, ma'am. Take a look around. Am I supposed to go somewhere or do you want me to stay here?"

"These incidents that have been bothering you, we'll need

you to show us where they've taken place," Debbie Sue answered. "I'll get my camera and be right with you." She walked back to her truck.

"I always thought this was a nice place," Edwina said. "You keep it real clean and neat, just like the Gills always did."

"Thanks. Rachel and I bought it right after we got married. It's more house than we needed, but at the time we figured on having some kids someday. And she wanted a place for her horses. This house came with the six hundred and forty acres and some good outbuildings. Rachel always had a way of making me give in to whatever she wanted."

Debbie Sue returned, camera in hand, "I couldn't help but notice those mares you've got penned up. Did I hear you say the horses were your wife's?"

"Yes, ma'am, you did. I think she loved those horses as much as she loved me."

"They're beautiful animals, but they need some exercise."

"I know they need to be ridden, but I've seldom been on a horse. Don't even know much about them. I grew up in the city."

"You don't have to ride them, though it would be good for them. Just turn them loose in the pasture so they can run around a little. They look like they've been penned up for weeks. It's not right to treat horses like that. They need exercise."

Justin heaved a breath, and looked down, contrite. "You're right. Truth is, it's been hard to be around them."

"You aren't the only one that misses her," Debbie Sue said sternly. "They lost someone they loved too. It's cruel what you're doing to them." She walked past him into the house, leaving him and Edwina to stand and stare.

"There are some areas of Debbie Sue's life you don't mess with," Edwina said, removing her sunglasses and shoving them onto the top of her head. "The treatment of animals, horses in particular, is one of them. She's funny that way."

Justin was more than a little wary of Debbie Sue after the warning she had delivered back at the beauty shop. "Yes, ma'am. I can see she is."

He trailed the two women into the house, stopping in the foyer. "Uh, see those yellow roses? They weren't here when I went to town earlier. But they were here when I came back. That's just one of the things."

Edwina cocked her head and gave him a strange look. "Oh, yeah? You mean you didn't put 'em there?"

"No. I don't know how they got there." Justin saw Edwina's eyes flare, but she said nothing.

Debbie Sue rubbed one of the rose petals between her thumb and fingers, leaned in and smelled them. "They're real," she said.

"Yeah, we've got some yellow roses growing in the backyard," Justin said.

"Did you check to see if someone had cut any today?"

"I didn't have to. I think they came from one of our, uh, my bushes."

"Well, let's be sure. Ed, you want to check the rosebushes? See if there are fresh cuts."

"I think *you* should check the rosebushes," Edwina said. "I don't know a damned thing about flowers."

Debbie Sue sighed. "Okay."

Justin showed them the patio door leading outside from the dining area and followed them to Rachel's rose garden, where several varieties of roses grew. Sure enough, fresh cuts showed on the stems of the bushes that produced the yellow blooms. "Damn," Justin said when he saw them. He was starting to get that crawly feeling up his spine again.

"Hmm," Debbie Sue said.

"Shit," Edwina mumbled.

Debbie Sue raised her camera and snapped a picture. "And you have no idea who might have cut roses from these bushes? Or when?"

"No," Justin answered, slowly shaking his head. "Honest to God."

"Shit," Edwina mumbled again.

"What other unusual things have happened?" Debbie Sue walked around the rose garden, snapping pictures, while Edwina stayed a few feet away.

"Out here, not much," Justin said. "Most of what I've noticed has been inside the house."

Debbie Sue started back toward the house. Inside, she circled the coffee table and snapped more pictures of the roses in the vase from every angle. Edwina looked under lamps and behind furniture.

"That blue afghan on the sofa was Rachel's," Justin said. "She liked to curl up under it and read. Several times a week I fold it up and put it on the end of the sofa. But sometimes, when I come home from work, it's moved and heaped in a pile, like someone has used it."

"The hell," Edwina said. She walked over to the sofa, lifted the cushions and peered under them.

"Hmm." Debbie Sue fingered the afghan and snapped more pictures.

Justin wasn't sure what they expected to find, but since they were the professionals, he decided to just let them work.

Edwina moved from the living room to the dining room and disappeared into the kitchen. "Well would you look at this?" she called out. "I haven't seen these in a hundred years."

Debbie Sue followed the voice and Justin trailed behind. "What is it?" she asked.

Justin was curious, too. He and Rachel had no hundred-year-old antiques that he was aware of.

Passing through the kitchen doorway just behind Debbie Sue, he saw Edwina studying the refrigerator door where Rachel had placed magnetized alphabet letters. "My kids used to have these when they were little," she said. She set her purse on the counter and plucked a letter from its place. "My oldest would sit on the kitchen floor and practice her ABC's while I cooked."

"It must have been a hundred years back," Debbie Sue quipped. "Because I don't believe I've ever seen you cook."

Justin smiled. "Rachel told me she'd done the same thing as a little girl. She saw these at a garage sale and bought them. She was hoping our little one would do the same one day. But a few letters are missing."

A profound sense of loss threatened to overpower Justin,

as it sometimes did when the future without his wife and the hopes and dreams they had shared became even more starkly clear. An uncomfortable, almost unbearable, silence fell. He returned to the living room and sank to the sofa, staring at the vase of yellow roses, regretting all that would never be.

Debbie Sue and Edwina came back from the kitchen. "Hey, you okay?" Edwina asked.

"I'm fine," Justin said a little too brightly. "Sometimes things just—" He shook his head and blinked away moisture, certain these two women didn't want to see a grown man break into tears. "Yeah, I'm fine."

Debbie Sue and Edwina took seats in the wingback chairs opposite him. Debbie Sue was studying her notes when Turnup began to pace and bark insistently.

"Excuse me," Justin said, rising from the sofa. "I wasn't expecting anyone. I'll just go see who's outside."

He walked out onto the porch and watched as his brother-in-law, John Patrick Daly, drove into view, his black Porsche Cayenne SUV ginning up whorls of white caliche dust.

Justin normally welcomed the occasional visit from Rachel's brother, John Patrick. He was the only person from the Daly family who treated him with decency. But Justin had never mentioned the strange happenings in his home to his brother-in-law and he sure wasn't ready to admit to anyone that he had enlisted the aid of detectives to unravel mysterious happenings.

After the Cayenne stopped and the driver's window quietly slid down, Justin approached it. "Hey, J. P., how's it going?"

John Patrick eyed Debbie Sue's red truck with interest.

"Damn, man. Am I just in time for the party or am I too late?"

John Patrick was known for his carousing ways. In his mid-thirties, unemployed but married to wealth and long-bored in that union, if a party was going on, he wanted to be included, especially if women were present.

Justin believed his brother-in-law became a hard partier to compensate for his small frame and short stature. He was five feet six and probably didn't weigh a hundred thirty pounds. The guy suffered a Napoleon complex in a big way. Knowing his appearance wouldn't win him favors, John Patrick talked loud and long about his family's money and power in Midland, as well as that of his in-laws, though he had neither money nor influence of his own. Still, he had been good to Justin, more like a brother than an in-law, and Justin was grateful. He could overlook John Patrick's flaws.

Justin laughed, glancing at the red truck parked in his driveway. "Naw, that's just a couple of folks from Salt Lick. They, uh . . . they came to look at Rachel's horses."

"You're not selling them, are you?"

"Oh, I'd never sell those horses." Remembering Debbie Sue's scolding, he said, "These folks are going to exercise and groom them for me. It's not right keeping them penned up and I can't keep depending on the neighbors to do it."

"Oh, sure, yeah. They do need the attention. Well, if you're busy, I'll go. I was headed home and just stopped by to check on you." After Rachel's passing John Patrick and his wife had moved to a vacant house about five miles up the road, ostensibly to be near Justin for moral support.

Justin smiled and hooked his thumbs in his belt loops. "Everything's fine, J. P. Thanks for asking. I'll holler at you later."

"One more thing," John Patrick said. "Did you ever hear any more from that oil and gas company, the one that left the business card on your screen door?"

"Lone Star Oil and Gas? Nah. They were probably just fishing around. I figure if they'd been really interested in drilling on this place, they would've gotten back in touch by now."

"Right," John Patrick said. "You're probably right . . . Well, I'd better go."

He backed in an arc and drove away. Justin walked back to the house, feeling guilty for the lie by omission to his brother-in-law.

# four

*G*lancing in his rearview mirror, John Patrick Daly watched as Justin's house grew smaller. He agreed it was about time Justin got someone to look after those damned horses, because John Patrick knew Justin had little knowledge of taking care of horses. Rachel had always done it.

John Patrick hadn't recognized the red truck parked in the driveway. For some reason he couldn't shake a bad feeling about it and what really was going on at Justin's house. The truck looked like dozens in the area. Nothing unusual about the make or model. John Patrick did note that no petroleum company signs were affixed to the doors, no tools or equipment rode in the bed. All he had seen there were some hay remnants.

John Patrick had no reason to think his brother-in-law wouldn't confide in him or that he would tell him a lie about being contacted by Lone Star Oil and Gas. Hell, Justin Sadler was pure as the driven snow. John Patrick doubted the man had ever told a lie in his entire boring, wholesome life.

But still he felt uneasy.

A thought zoomed into his mind and made him slam on the brakes, sending the SUV into a skid. This was perfect. Fuckin' perfect. His plan had been to sneak onto Justin's place some evening within the coming two or three weeks and turn those horses loose, but he had worried about being discovered. But now he could suggest the blame lay with the people Justin had enlisted to help care for the horses. He could hear it now: *"Gee, they must have left a gate unlatched, Justin. Tough luck, buddy."*

John Patrick was almost giddy with relief. With the horses gone, Justin would have no reason to stay in a big-ass house with so much acreage. With no reason to stay, selling the place to his brother-in-law, the only Daly who had ever treated Justin like real family, would be as natural as nodding off in church. And Justin, being Justin, would sell it cheap, too.

John Patrick thought about the business card he had removed from Justin's screen door. Somebody from Lone Star Oil and Gas had come back just a few days after leaving the first business card and left a second one. So the oil company must have a serious interest in negotiating with Justin to drill on his land. And why not? John Patrick knew from reliable sources that Justin sat on top of one of the largest untapped gas reservoirs since the boom of the fifties and sixties. The very thought of a well or two or three being put down on that section of land made John Patrick giddy all over again. Luckily, he had found the second business card before Justin did and had promptly disposed of it.

Haunting Justin with Rachel's afghan, her magazine, her wedding rings and perfume had cracked John Patrick up when he thought of them, but the pièce de résistance was the roses. Whenever he and his sexless wife, Felicia the Non-nympho, as he preferred to call her, had been invited to Rachel and Justin's home, fresh roses had always been sitting on the coffee table. It was just Rachel's added touch, something women did. So going to Justin's house earlier today before Justin finished his shift, cutting a few roses and putting them on the coffee table had been a snap.

John Patrick chuckled at his own cleverness. He couldn't believe how well his luck was running. It was all so easy, he almost felt guilty. Almost, but not quite. He whooped out loud and pressed the accelerator, reveling in the immediate response of the Cayenne's big engine. He liked when things responded—man, woman or machine.

Still grinning, he reached for his cell phone. So much success had left him feeling smug and sure of himself. And horny as hell. He pressed a number and waited. A sweet voice, husky and seductive, greeted him.

"Hey, Priscilla, how are ya, darlin'? . . . That's good, that's good. Listen, dumplin', how 'bout I go by the store and pick up a couple of bottles of champagne? We can have a party in your pants tonight."

★ ★ ★

Re-entering his house, Justin mustered a smile. "Sorry, ladies. That was my brother in-law. He comes by from time to time. He's been a good friend to me."

"Thought you said Rachel's family hated your guts," Edwina said.

"They do. John Patrick's the only one who doesn't hold a grudge after . . . after what happened to Rachel."

"Speaking of grudges," Debbie Sue said, "we need to know just exactly what did happen to Rachel, Justin."

"Yeah," Edwina said. "That's pretty much gonna decide whether we accept your business or Debbie Sue runs over you with her truck when we leave here."

For the next few minutes Justin told a story of how one fateful evening a year earlier, he and Rachel had spent an evening at her parents' house in Midland. Things hadn't gone well and had ended worse. Tempers flared, harsh words were exchanged. Justin and Rachel argued on the drive home. Her defending her parents made him feel she was showing disloyalty to him and disrespecting their marriage. Distracted from the road and his driving, too late he saw a speeding car weaving in and out of lanes and closing on them. The car swerved to dodge a truck and crashed directly into them on the passenger side, killing Rachel on impact. At the time, Justin had been too shaken to realize immediately what had happened, but drivers behind him had verified the facts to the DPS troopers who investigated the accident.

Other than a cut on his forehead, which the EMTs covered with a butterfly bandage, Justin had been spared injury.

Knowing he hadn't suffered physically and had only his heart and mind to nurse back to health had only made him feel worse.

"Oh, my God, Justin, that was you?" Debbie Sue said. "I remember when that happened."

Silence filled the house for several seconds. Finally, Edwina spoke up. "Hon, that must have been hard for you to tell us and I can see where you'd feel some guilt. But there's always gonna be stuff that happens in life that we can't control. You just have to keep on living."

"I know this is no consolation, Justin," Debbie Sue said softly, "but my husband was one of the troopers who investigated that wreck. I do remember him saying the blame lay squarely on the drunk driver."

Justin cleared his throat, trying to dislodge the lump that had stuck there. "He plea-bargained," Justin said bitterly. "Pled guilty to manslaughter. He's serving time in Huntsville, but he'll soon be out."

Debbie Sue sat straighter, pushed her hair away from her face and continued, her tone serious but friendlier than it had been earlier. "You mentioned your wife's perfume and her wedding set. Where do you normally keep those things?"

"The rings are in a velvet box on the dresser. The perfume is there too."

"So they're accessible to anyone that enters the house?"

"I suppose so."

"Has there ever been a forced entry into your house, broken windows, jimmied locks?"

"No, nothing like that."

"But the locks look pretty old," Debbie Sue said. "I noticed them when we came in. They're probably the original ones from when the house was built. Let me show you something." Among the many things Debbie Sue had learned since she became a detective was breaking and entering. She fished around inside her purse and came up with a metal nail file. At the front door, she pushed the button that locked it, approached the lock from the outside with the file and in a matter of two seconds of maneuvering the nail file, popped the lock.

"Good Lord," Justin said, awed. "I guess I need to get some new locks."

"And these things that have happened in your house," Debbie Sue said, "they've always occurred when you're gone? Nothing strange or out of the ordinary has occurred when you're home?"

"Yes, I've always been gone," he answered, still studying the door lock.

"That says the person doing this doesn't want to be seen," Edwina said. "If a ghost was doing it, being seen wouldn't be a real problem, would it? A ghost wouldn't care if you were gone or not. I mean, who can see a ghost?"

Justin swung a look from one woman to the other. "But today, these roses, when I came home these roses were in this vase on the coffee table. I didn't put them there. Rachel was the one who loved roses. She always put them out when company came over."

"You want it to be Rachel, don't you, hon?" Edwina said.

"The Styling Station is on the main street in town, Justin," Debbie Sue said. "Anyone could have seen you talking to us in the parking lot. Most of the people in town know what we do. They could've guessed we'd be coming out here to your house."

Both women were now staring at him, waiting for a reply. He was startled that he felt a sudden drop in his stomach, like being in an elevator that lurched unexpectedly. He had never admitted to himself how desperately he had hoped Rachel was trying to reach out to him from the grave, and the reality that she wasn't left him feeling empty and inexplicably saddened.

Debbie Sue rose and hung her purse on her shoulder. "We've got enough information, Justin. I'll get back to you this evening. Is it okay if I call you around nine?"

Edwina rose also.

"Sure, nine would be fine," he said, his tone dull and lifeless.

He stood and dragged behind the two women out of the house and to the driveway, where their rig was parked. No one spoke. Debbie Sue reached into her purse for her keys and moved items around. "Dammit, I must have left the camera in the kitchen. I remember laying it on the counter."

"I'll get it," Justin said.

"I'll go," Edwina offered. "If you don't mind, Justin, I'd like to stop off in your bathroom."

"Sure, first door on the right as you go down the hallway."

Edwina disappeared into the house. As Justin and Debbie Sue spoke about the horses and the care that they needed, a bloodcurdling screech came from inside the house.

In unison, Justin and Debbie Sue bolted for the front door. Before they reached it, it flew open and whacked against the wall. Edwina, legs churning, arms windmilling, barreled through. Debbie Sue blocked her path and grabbed her by the shoulders. "Ed, forgodsake! What's wrong?"

"The kitchen," she wailed. "The kitchen."

Justin and Debbie Sue exchanged looks. Debbie Sue released Edwina and charged through the doorway, headed for the kitchen. There she skidded to a stop, staring at the refrigerator door. "Oh, sweet Jesus. Oh, sweet Jesus."

Justin came up behind her. "Oh, God . . ." He leaned against the cabinet for support as he too stared at the refrigerator door.

There, on its slick surface, spelled out with the alphabet letters that were available, was a message that had not been there earlier:

*D E PLZ HLP JUSTIN.*

A chill raced up Debbie Sue's spine. She dashed from the house as if the devil himself chased her. Justin came up behind her and they joined an ashen-faced Edwina, who was pacing back and forth in the front yard. Breathing hard, Debbie Sue bent forward, her hands braced on her knees, waiting for her pounding heart to slow. "Fuck!" she gasped.

She gathered her wits. Someone or some thing had damn sure been in Justin Sadler's kitchen since they had walked out of it just a few minutes earlier. At last she straightened and glared at him. "Are these the messages you were talking about?"

Justin looked back at her, confusion and desperation in his eyes.

Debbie Sue turned to her partner, who had inched closer to the pickup's passenger door. "Ed, when you went back inside, which did you do first, go pee or go into the kitchen?"

"Straight to the kitchen." Edwina flapped a hand toward the front door. "That's when the pee got scared clean out of me. It's a wonder we don't need a mop."

"Tell us exactly what happened," Debbie Sue said, still pondering how and when those letters could possibly have been moved.

Edwina swore she hadn't seen or heard anything she hadn't revealed.

"I can't believe I ran out here," Justin said, an expression of bewilderment on his face. "I've been dealing with these signs and messages for months. I must have been reacting to you, Edwina. I've seen that happen in firefighting—the man on your right goes into hysteria and others around follow. It's called group panic reaction."

"Well, you almost *saw* panic reaction run down my leg," Edwina said warily, stealing furtive glances at the house's front door. "I don't suppose you're a smoker. Or I don't suppose you'd have any cigarettes in the house. I quit smoking a couple of years ago, but for the life of me, I can't think of a better time to start again."

"Cigarette, hell. I could use a drink," Debbie Sue said.

"Would you like to go back inside?" Justin asked. "I've got—"

"Not me," Edwina said firmly.

Still confused and nervous, Debbie Sue directed her attention to Justin again. "I think we've seen all we need to, Justin. Ed and I need to get home. I've still got a husband and animals to feed and Ed's husband is coming in off the road tonight. Look, we need to give this whole thing some thought. I'll . . . or we'll . . . oh, hell, one of us will call you this evening."

"I'll be here," Justin said, looking over his shoulder at the front door. "I hope you won't let what just happened scare you off. I think whatever is going on is harmless. I mean, I've been seeing this kind of stuff for months and nothing's happened to me."

"Don't worry," Debbie Sue said. "We aren't scared." *And she really wasn't*, she told herself. She started toward her truck again, but stopped. *Oh, hell*, they hadn't retrieved the camera. "Oops. I still don't have my camera. Could I ask you to go back inside and bring it out to me?"

"Sure," Justin said, and re-entered the house. Soon he returned and handed over the camera. "You're the only people I've talked to about this," he said. "I trust you ladies. And I sure hope you can help me."

Debbie Sue saw a sincere plea in his eyes. "I don't know

if we can be of help, Justin. The only thing I can promise is Ed and I'll talk about it." She climbed behind her pickup's steering wheel.

Edwina seated herself on the passenger seat, latched her seat belt and stared straight ahead. Debbie Sue cranked the engine, backed up and drove away, leaving Justin standing at his doorstep.

Edwina remained wordless until Justin's house was well behind them. "Just look at my arm." She stuck her left arm out for inspection. "Those goose bumps won't be gone for days. Maybe never. If I shaved my legs right now I'd bleed to death. But I'm in no frame of mind to talk about it, so just keep driving."

Not talking suited Debbie Sue fine for the moment. She needed time to mull over what she had seen. At the cattle guard she started to turn left, but Edwina grabbed the wheel. "Don't go back to Salt Lick. I don't know when Vic will be home and I'm not going home alone. Take me home with you."

"Ed, you can't seriously believe a ghost changed those letters around."

"What else am I supposed to believe? That they just magically moved themselves to form a message? And a message directed at us at that? "

Debbie Sue didn't have an explanation, and for her, being unable to explain was as bad as discovering what the answer might be. "You don't know that it was directed at us."

"I sure as hell do. What do you think D E stands for?"

*Domestic Equalizers.* Debbie Sue stopped that thought, though the very idea made the hair stand up on the back of her neck. She simply would not buy into this ghost crap. "I don't know."

"Well, I know. D E stands for Debbie Sue and Edwina."

*Yikes!* Debbie Sue hadn't thought of that. A creepy feeling snaked through her. "Look, Ed, I know it's a little eerie, but—"

"*A little eerie?* No, girlfriend, a magician pulling a live rabbit out of a hat is a *little* eerie. A tornado destroying everything in a house and leaving a cup and saucer untouched on a table is a *little* eerie. That message on Justin Sadler's refrigerator was *off-the-chart* eerie."

"Okay, okay." Debbie Sue reversed, then turned her pickup in the opposite direction. "It was more than a little eerie. It was weird, but there has to be a logical explanation."

"Why? Why does there *have* to be a logical explanation? I'm telling you, Debbie Sue, there's shit in life that has no explanation. We have to accept some things on faith."

"But I need an explanation, Ed." Debbie Sue thrust out her palm for emphasis. "I can't, just can't, believe that some ghost came in and spelled a message on a refrigerator door while we sat in the living room ten feet away."

"Keep your hands on the steering wheel," Edwina said. "You think some human snuck in and did it, right under our noses? Is that what you think?"

"No. But someone could've been hiding in the kitchen."

"Well I'll be damned. You won't even consider that a

lost spirit could be trying to communicate with us, or with Justin. But you'll accept that a micro-midget was hid out in those three-foot high kitchen cabinets and waiting for a chance to send us a message with magnetic letters? Now that's real logic."

Debbie Sue knew she was losing this argument, not a position in which she often found herself. She heaved a sigh. "But, Ed, I've never seen anything remotely close to something like this before. I guess I'm at a loss for logic."

Silence. Debbie Sue glanced across the pickup cab at Edwina, who was sitting there with her arms crossed and intently studying her. She knew from experience that her old friend and partner would have the last word as soon as she could come up with a good one.

"I've never seen God before, neither," Edwina groused, "but I believe He's up there."

"Dammit, Ed, that's not fair. And it's not exactly a new idea. You're playing the religious card. You're an asshole to do that. You know it always makes me fold. You know I'm afraid that if I'm wrong, lightning will strike me or something."

"Don't cuss when we're talking about heaven and hell. It's sacrilegious."

Debbie Sue sighed again and for the next ten minutes they rode in silence. As she neared the home where she had grown up and now shared with Buddy, she made a left turn and crossed her own cattle guard. "So I say we set up surveillance equipment and find the bastard that's pulling this crap on Justin."

Edwina shifted in her seat. "Or we could call up that Isabella Paredes in El Paso and ask for her help. She's personally acquainted with ghosts."

"Oh, forchristsake, I'm being serious."

"So am I. Why couldn't we do both? I'll help with the surveillance and you agree to call the psychic. That way, if it turns out that a ghost is raising hell in Justin's life, we could meet it on equal terms."

"Hunh. I'll let you explain that one to Justin. He's the one who's footing the bill."

Debbie Sue came to a stop under the covered car shed and killed the motor. She looked earnestly at her friend. "I'll go along with you, Ed. We're partners. And I can see you've got your mind made up, but I can't keep the goose bumps off your body. You're the only one who can do that."

Debbie Sue opened her door, slid out of the truck cab and started for the house. Edwina opened her door and yelled at the top of her lungs, "Don't leave me out here! It's getting dark!"

Justin sat on the sofa in his living room, fingering the blue afghan beside him. Rachel's afghan. He had been sitting here ever since Debbie Sue and Edwina left. The idea his conscious mind had resisted, the hope he had pushed to his subconscious and never allowed to surface, was now full frontal, demanding his attention.

More than fear, he felt puzzlement and awe. He had no clue about the world beyond. Until the last few weeks he hadn't believed it existed. Now he wondered, did spirits come and go at will? Were they on a timetable that allowed only so much *earth time* before being required to check back in to wherever ghosts reside? Could his sweet Rachel have been trying to reach out to him from the other side?

He left the sofa, stood in the middle of the living room and made a slow circle. "Rach? . . . Honey, is that you? . . . Is there something you want to tell me, babe?"

The only sound he heard was the mantel clock's ticking. No voice. No whisper. Nothing. If Rachel wanted to reach him, if she thought he needed help, why didn't she answer him now?

Should he call his brother-in-law and tell him that his kid sister might be trying to talk from the grave? John Patrick had always been supportive and understanding, but how would he react to hearing that information?

These were the kinds of thoughts, if revealed, that could leave people whispering about you and your sanity all of your life and beyond. Justin thought of his parents in Midland. How would they react to a rumor that their only son, their pride and joy, was a kook who talked to ghosts?

The one thing supporting this extreme notion was that two women who were professional detectives had seen the same thing he had. They wouldn't, couldn't discredit him without casting a shadow on themselves. He would wait for their phone call tonight and hope they wanted to help. At this point, what other option did he have?

He walked back into the kitchen and looked again at the

refrigerator door. The message was still there. Not a letter out of place.

*D E PLZ HLP JUSTIN*

D E. Domestic Equalizers? Was the message directed to the two women detectives? "Damn, Rach," he half whispered, moisture stinging his eyes. "You always thought about what was best for me. Are you still doing it?"

# five

Inside Debbie Sue's kitchen, she sat at her yellow, cracked-ice Formica kitchen table, phone in hand, trying to locate Isabella Paredes, whose last known whereabouts, according to Edwina, was El Paso. A hastily thrown together tuna casserole baked in the oven. Buddy would be home soon and Debbie Sue was mindful that he might have had nothing to eat all day but fast food.

Edwina sat on the opposite side of the table with a game of solitaire laid out before her. She sharply snapped three cards from the deck that rested in her palm, careful to protect the stars-and-stripes paint job on her talon-like acrylic nails. As many years as Debbie Sue had watched Edwina at work in the beauty salon, she still hadn't figured out how she ever got anything done with those fingernails.

"Can you spell that, please," a voice in the phone said, re-capturing Debbie Sue's attention. Debbie Sue was more impatient than a hornet in a bonnet, but she managed to speak slowly, "P-A-R-E-D-E-S." Covering the receiver with her hand, she said to Edwina, "Where in the hell do they get these people? I can't understand her, she can't understand me. I might as well be calling Yugo-fuckin'-slavia."

The operator came on the line again and glory be, she had the number for Isabella Paredes.

"Yes, ma'am," Debbie Sue said, turning her attention back to the business at hand and jotting the number on a notepad. "Thank you. Yes, you have a good day too." Disconnecting, she waved the piece of notepaper in the air triumphantly. "Got it!"

Concentrating on her game, Edwina barely looked up. Her lack of enthusiasm was damned annoying. "Ed, did you hear me?"

"I'm not deaf," Edwina said, moving cards from one stack to another with the tips of her fingernails.

"She's there. In El Paso. Or at least, she has a number there.

"That doesn't mean she's still alive. Even if she is, she must be in her eighties."

"Calling her was your idea, wasn't it? You keep running hot and cold on this. Why *is* that?"

Edwina looked up from her card game, an earnest expression on her face. "I don't know. I get excited thinking about the case, but then I start worrying."

Debbie Sue knitted her brow. She left her chair, moved to a chair adjacent to Edwina's and took the cards from her hand. "Look at me, Ed. Are you afraid she might tell you something personal again?"

Edwina returned her gaze. "Maybe." She relaxed against her chair's padded back and sighed. "My life's never been as good as it is now, Debbie Sue. You know that better than anybody. And you know what I've been through. Hell, if the women in my family weren't stronger than bleach and if I hadn't inherited their genes, I'd probably be locked up in some asylum by now."

"I don't think they have asylums anymore, Ed," Debbie Sue said.

"Whatever. Isabella Paredes told me something before that changed everything for me. What if she does it again?"

Debbie Sue bit back the urge to repeat what she had already said: that the money in the boot toe had been a lucky guess or maybe the Paredes woman had capitalized on something mentioned to her in an earlier session with Edwina's mother-in-law and it most likely wouldn't happen again. "But don't you see, Ed? What she told you before *did* change your life, but it was for the better. If the woman really has psychic powers, she would've known that. She probably doesn't make it a practice to just blurt out bad news unsolicited."

Edwina seemed to be working that idea through her head as Debbie Sue waited and watched. "I think you're right," she finally said. "If I don't ask her any questions, she won't tell me any bad news."

"Perfect." Debbie Sue slapped Edwina's shoulder. "Now, here's the plan."

She spent the next hour discussing the plan for helping Justin with his problem. They would install cameras and listening equipment in strategic places. They would operate and oversee surveillance of his home and its surroundings. And since Edwina feared a ghost might be the culprit, to appease her, they would go ahead and call the psychic in El Paso to tie up any loose ends—all with Justin's approval and agreement to pay for a psychic, of course. Debbie Sue picked up the phone again and started pressing keys.

Edwina's hand came out and clutched her forearm, stopping her before she finished the number. "It's six thirty. You're calling her now?"

"I have to, Ed. I have to find out how much she'll charge before I can pitch the plan to Justin, don't I?"

Edwina released her grip "Yeah, yeah, I guess so. But listen, don't tell her I'm here."

"Hell, Ed, after twenty years, she probably won't even remember you. But if she does and if she's even a half-assed psychic, she'll probably know you're here." Debbie Sue pushed the last digit and looked at her friend.

"Super," Edwina muttered. "Now all I have to worry about is what she's *not* telling me."

As Sophia wrestled with the antiquated lock on the front door of the modest home she had shared with her grandmother, she heard the phone ringing inside. She had just returned from a couple of job interviews. Maybe one of the interviewers was calling her back. Part of her hoped that was the case, but another part wished it wouldn't be. The interviews had gone well enough. She had been confident, but soft-spoken and polite, emphasizing that she wanted employment for the summer only. The need for extra income had been an acceptable explanation for why she wanted the job.

Only one thing was wrong. Instead of looking at her as a job applicant and a prospective employee, both interviewers had leered as if she were a dessert item on their menus. They had been so obvious she was embarrassed for them. She liked men and their company a lot, but she didn't enjoy feeling like the flavor of the day.

Pushing the front door open at last, she grabbed for the receiver on the fourth ring, answering breathlessly.

A woman's voice came across the line. "Is this the home of Isabella Paredes?"

Sophia found going into the details of her Gran Bella's demise with a total stranger over the phone too painful. Easier to just agree.

"May I speak to her?"

A tingling sensation crawled across Sophia's scalp. A twitch in her left eye gave her a clue that this was something she needed to take care of. "Uh, she's out right now. I can speak for her." Sophia told herself this wasn't really a lie. "I'm her granddaughter, Sophia Paredes," she added.

The voice on the other end of the line hurried on, leaving

no openings for a response. "Ma'am, my partner and I run a private investigative service out of Salt Lick, Texas, called the Domestic Equalizers. We understand that Senora Paredes is a psychic. We have a complicated case we think she could help us with."

The caller knew of Gran Bella and her reputation? Sophia's grip tightened on the receiver.

"I was hoping to speak to her about her services," the woman on the phone continued. "We'd like to know her fee for traveling to Salt Lick for a few days."

Sophia knew her grandmother's fee for a lengthy involvement, and it was as much or more than she would make waiting tables part-time through the summer. Sophia possessed the same psychic powers as her dear departed grandmother, but only Sophia and Gran Bella knew it. Her eye twitched again, a sure sign that her financial troubles might be reaching a resolution, that her prayers might be answered.

Possibilities began to filter through Sophia's mind. Having long kept her own psychic powers under wraps, she wouldn't consider using them except under dire circumstances. From her bank balance to the stack of unpaid bills on her dining table, she could think of nothing more dire than her current situation. She had no choice.

"Hello? You still there?" The caller's voice brought her back from her thoughts. "Hello? Hellloooo." The woman's tone held a sharper edge. "Hell," she said away from the receiver but still audible to Sophia, "I think we got disconnected."

"No," Sophia said quickly. "I'm here. Please don't hang up. I'm here."

"Oh, I thought I'd lost you."

"No, I'm sorry. Uh, my grandmother just came in and I was explaining the call to her."

There, it was done. The lie had begun. Sophia was committed to the decision she had hastily made.

"Maybe I should speak to her directly," the voice on the phone said.

"Oh, that is not necessary. Gran Bella is, uh, she has gone to the bathroom." On a shaky breath Sophia took the plunge. "Senora Paredes's fee is three hundred and fifty dollars a day. Or two thousand dollars for a full week of her service. The fee is non-negotiable. The money must be paid up front. Also, she would need to have her round-trip airfare paid as well as have transportation and lodging provided."

Sophia heard no response. For a moment, she considered that they had been disconnected or the caller had hung up in disgust. She heard distant conversation, as if the caller were speaking to someone else, a different voice with a pronounced West Texas twang. "Damn, she gets three fifty a day? We charge fifty and feel bad about it."

Sophia held her breath. At least the caller was interested enough to discuss it with someone. Then the voice came back on the line. "Look, let me talk to our client and see if he's willing to pay that much. May I call you back tomorrow?"

"Absolutely. I'll, uh . . . I mean, we'll be here."

"Super. I'll call you tomorrow."

"Oh, thank you, Debbie Sue. I hope we can do business together. "

Sophia hung up, her thought pattern veering off in a new direction.

It was amazing how when you thought you saw no prospect in sight, life could turn a corner. Gran Bella had told her that many times. She had also said, *"Be careful what you pray for, Sophia."*

Stunned, Debbie Sue turned to Edwina, the receiver still in hand.

"What'd she say?" Edwina asked. "Did she say she'd come? What's the fee you were talking about?"

Debbie Sue found herself blank for a moment.

"What's the matter with you?" Edwina asked, moving closer, peering into Debbie Sue's eyes. "Lord, woman, you look like you just saw Jesus."

"She appears to be willing. So I told her I'll call her tomorrow after I talk to Justin." Debbie Sue's voice sounded distant and dreamlike in her own ears. "I was talking to Isabella's granddaughter. Her name's Sophia. She sounded real nice."

Edwina thrust out her left arm and rapidly rubbed her forearm up and down. "Dammit, those goose bumps are back. Just look at my arm. I'll bet I just put on twenty pounds' worth of goose bumps."

"Ed, don't you get it? She called me Debbie Sue."

"So? That's not exactly earth-shattering news. Everybody I know calls you that."

"I didn't tell her my name, Ed. I didn't mention my name at all. All I said was the Domestic Equalizers. How could she know my name?"

"Geez, this is creepy," Edwina mumbled, rubbing her forearm again. "You know, I heard somebody say once, 'Be careful what you pray for.'"

# six

*$3,000, give or take . . .*

Justin disconnected from the call from Debbie Sue and drew another block around the note he had written on the scratch pad by the phone on the end of the kitchen counter. He had traced it so many times his pen had cut through the paper to the next page.

He hadn't expected to hear from Debbie Sue and Edwina so soon. They had been gone from his house no more than a couple of hours. He tried to decide if Debbie Sue calling back this quickly meant they were a little bit *too* eager to take the case.

She had explained what the Equalizers could offer and *their* fee, with which he had no problem, but she had added an unexpected expense—the services of a woman in El Paso who had "powers." And Debbie Sue had even personally vouched for her. Compared to the El Paso woman's fee, the cost of the services of the Domestic Equalizers was small potatoes.

Justin was happy Debbie Sue had agreed to help him, but a psychic? Communicating with the dead? The whole thing was creepy. But was it possible? And if it were, what would he say to Rachel's, uh . . . *ghost*?

He remembered horror stories he had heard around a campfire as a boy. Movies he had seen came to mind. *Poltergeist* had scared the bejesus out of him when he was a kid.

He knew reams of articles had been written about extrasensory perception, but he had read few of them. He had seen news stories and TV shows about charlatans who had taken advantage and collected enormous amounts of money from people whose common sense had been overpowered by profound grief. He knew of reported cases of people who claimed to have ESP, but he didn't know anyone personally. Nor did he know anyone who had even relied on someone with this so-called God-given gift.

Yet, for all of his skepticism, something from a mysterious place deeply buried within him told him the unexplained message on his refrigerator called for something beyond simple surveillance. Maybe hiring someone who claimed to be able to communicate with unearthly types could explain it for an earthly type like him.

But spending so much money on something like a fortune-teller still gave him pause. It wasn't the money, not really, because he had money to spare. He never discussed—and tried hard to not think about— the money that had been awarded to him by Rachel's insurance company. His deceased wife had been insured by the law firm that employed her by a $250,000 double-indemnity life policy. The proceeds came via certified mail six weeks after the accident. Though he was the beneficiary, he hadn't even been the one to make the claim. He assumed someone where she worked submitted it. That money, more than he had ever seen or hoped to see in his life, now lay untouched in several banks. The cost of the medium would scarcely make a dent in the total.

He had to do it, didn't he? What better option was there? But if he said he would pay for this, he could be cautious, couldn't he? He could agree to bring the person claiming to have mystic powers to Odessa, spring for a nice hotel room and meals. He could even establish up front that before she and the Domestic Equalizers got their hands on any part of the proceeds from his dear Rachel's death, they had to prove themselves to him.

He turned away from the phone and started for the refrigerator for a Coke, but was stopped in his tracks. To his shock and astonishment, a new message glared from the refrigerator door.

*E P CAN HLP*

"Oh, my God," he whispered as a shudder passed over him. He had just told Debbie Sue he would call back tomorrow, but he walked back to the phone. Holding the business card in his trembling left hand, he punched in the number and waited only two burrs before he got an answer. "Okay, I'll do it," he said. "Surveillance and the fortune-teller. But I've got conditions." He outlined his expectations, then hung up.

He returned to the table, picked up the pen and drew another box around *$3,000, give or take.*

Debbie Sue disconnected and turned to Edwina.

"What'd he say?" Edwina asked.

"Not much. But he's going for it. Surveillance and the fortune-teller. Those were his exact words."

"No shit?" Edwina said slowly. "I didn't think he'd agree to it."

"I didn't say he's enthusiastic about it. He just said he agrees to bring Isabella and her granddaughter here. He'll pay their room and board, but he's got one condition."

Edwina huffed. "What does he want, a money-back guarantee?"

"Sophia said her grandmother's fee had to be paid up front, but Justin isn't willing to do that. He wants her to prove she's really got psychic powers before he pays her anything. He wants to, you know, kick the tires, take it for a test drive."

Edwina shot straight up from her seat. "Holy shit, Debbie Sue. Don't you dare let Isabella Paredes tell me anything about *my* future. I said already, I do not want to know a damned thing about it. I do not want to worry about things before they happen. I'd rather handle them as they come. Don't you dare use me as a guinea pig. And I'm as serious as a heat rash about that."

Debbie Sue patted the air with her palms. "Settle down, oh great one. You act like you've got a two-way radio plugged in to the spirit world. *I'm* the one she singled out and called by name, remember? How do you explain that?"

Edwina dropped to her seat again and covered her face with her hands. "Hell, I can't even explain why rap music is so damn popular. Or why boys are wearing the crotch of their pants down to their ankles. How can I explain how a psychic knows stuff?"

Debbie Sue laughed. "When she gets here, maybe you can ask her about the rap music and the baggy pants. Then we'll all know the answer to that. The point is, Ed, that she might be able to tell Justin something that will make him believe in her."

"You vouching for her wasn't enough for him?"

"Apparently not. But you heard me. I didn't exactly give a glowing endorsement. Three thousand dollars plus expenses is a lot of money. I don't blame him for being cautious."

"Oh, hell, me neither," Edwina said.

"I'll work with him tomorrow on the details. And a room somewhere nice in Odessa." Debbie Sue bit down on the tip of her nail, deep in thought. "Can you think of anything else?"

"I'm *afraid* to think of anything," Edwina said.

The sound of an approaching car and the frenzied barking and whining of Jack, Jose and Jim, the Overstreet dogs, interrupted. "Buddy's home," Debbie Sue said and headed for the back door.

Stepping out the back door, she let the screen door close

behind her as she watched Texas Ranger James Russell Overstreet Jr.'s black-and-white cruiser creep up the quarter-mile caliche driveway. Her memory didn't travel back far enough to recall when she hadn't loved Buddy Overstreet. He had been in her existence for as long as she could remember. Sometimes she wondered if her life could go on if he weren't a part of it. Not that their relationship didn't require work and patience—more so on his part than hers, she readily admitted. She was stubborn and willful, even when she didn't know it. And those were just the traits she would openly acknowledge. Her poor good-natured Buddy endured much from her.

He came to a stop under the shed. He gave her a smile and a wink as he opened the car door and began gathering papers from the passenger seat. "Hey, Flash. I love it when you meet me."

Her being home and out of mischief was his preference, but not necessarily hers. Still, she loved being home before him. It gave her a feeling of being a pioneer woman greeting her man home from a hard day of hunting and warring. She smiled. "Hiya, Wyatt"—she often lovingly called him Wyatt Earp—"I've got beer in the fridge and a casserole in the oven."

"Good Lord. A welcome home and cooked food to boot. I must've done something right today." He unfolded his solid six-foot, two-inch frame from the car's interior. Lord, he was handsome in his starched white shirt and khakis. He wore his white Stetson at just the right set on his head.

She walked to him, wrapped her arms around his neck and

hungrily kissed him. Oh, yeah, she could pass up a supper of tuna casserole and feast on her husband's kisses. That is, if Edwina were not inside the house.

"Hmm, I like this," Buddy said, one hand squeezing her bottom. "But I have to admit, it scares me a little. What's up?"

Debbie Sue pushed him away and gasped with feigned indignation. Just then, Edwina came out of the house and called out, "Hey, good-looking." She walked toward them.

"Well, hello, Ed. I didn't see your car out front."

"I rode out here with Debbie Sue. Vic's supposed to pick me up in about half an hour. He's coming in from the West Coast. Man, have we got a new case to tell you about."

Debbie Sue shot her partner a murderous look, but the woman was paying her no attention.

Debbie Sue preferred briefing Buddy in advance on the activities of the Domestic Equalizers. He wasn't crazy about the detective agency and was quick to either declare that something she and Edwina had committed to do was "too dangerous" or "over their heads." She tried not to lie to him directly about the cases they took on, although she sometimes didn't tell him everything she knew. In her mind, she always debated if a fib by *o*-mission was equal to a lie by *co*-mission. In Debbie-Sue logic, choosing to omit every detail usually won the argument and unfortunately, this caused her no inner conflict, though it sometimes caused great outer conflict between her and Buddy.

Indeed Buddy had divorced her once for her hardheaded ways, and now that she had him back, withholding facts here and there seemed to make things go more smoothly between them. His learning of some of her and Edwina's escapades and unintended consequences upset him much less after the fact than if he knew of them beforehand.

"I'll tell you all about it over supper," Debbie Sue said, taking his arm. "Ed, why don't you call Vic and tell him to come over here when he gets to town? Y'all eat with us tonight."

"Thought you'd never ask," Edwina said. "I'm about one burned-to-a-crisp meal away from losing that man altogether."

"Thought Vic did all the cooking," Buddy said.

"He does when he's home. But when he's coming back off the road, I make an effort. It's hard because I have to start by dragging all my shoes out of the oven."

Buddy laughed. "You kill me, Ed."

Edwina took Buddy's other arm and the three of them walked toward the door.

"I'll wait until Vic gets here to tell you everything," Debbie Sue said. "I don't want him to miss it and I'm not sure I'd believe it if I had to repeat it."

Vic arrived on schedule and he and Edwina had such a charged homecoming, Debbie Sue was almost embarrassed. Through the meal, Debbie Sue, with Edwina's help, explained the mysterious events in Justin Sadler's house. Buddy's comments amounted to mostly *Hmm*'s, a few *Really?*'s and twitches of his thick black mustache. Throughout the discussion, Debbie Sue stole glances at Vic. He didn't even say *Hmm* and *Really?* She felt he was holding something back.

After the meal, she and Edwina began clearing the table

and carrying the dishes to the sink. Vic parked his massive hulk in the kitchen doorway, arms crossed over his barrel chest, shoulder braced against the doorjamb. "Anyone, living or dead, who would carry on this campaign of harassment against this Justin guy for months is either desperate or extremely pissed off."

"Oh, absolutely." Debbie Sue looked at Edwina with a wink and mouthed *campaign of harassment.*

"And experience has taught me that situation can cause someone to get hurt," Vic added.

Debbie Sue's scalp tingled. *Shit.* She knew where Vic was headed and Buddy would jump right on that wagon with him before it even had time to leave tracks.

As if acting on cue, Buddy closed the refrigerator door and said, "I couldn't agree more. That's why I want you two to back out of this one, Flash."

"Good idea," Vic said.

"But, Buddy, I've already made a commitment," Debbie Sue pleaded. "Justin's depending on us to help him. That's what the Equalizers are all about—not *causing* pain by uncovering secrets, but *helping* people with real-life problems."

To Debbie Sue's astonishment, Edwina said, "I agree with Buddy and Vic. I don't like getting involved with ghosts."

Debbie Sue turned on her partner. "Ed! You traitor."

Buddy leaned against the cabinet and heaved a great sigh. "Flash, there's nothing about this that could be defined as a 'real-life' problem. It's weird to the point of being ridiculous. It could make you two a laughingstock all over Texas. Remember how pissed off you got when that sheriff in Haskell called y'all clowns? I refuse to allow you to get involved in it."

"Yeah," Vic put in. "Can't you girls find something else to do?"

*A laughingstock? Something else to do?* Debbie Sue gasped. These were the three people she dearly loved and who were supposed to love and support her. She couldn't believe that after all the cajoling and reasoning she had done with Edwina, the woman had sided against her. And after all the talking, negotiating, begging and downright knock-down, drag-out fighting she had done with Buddy over his "forbidding" her to do something, she was stunned that he was taking this obstinate position.

Oh, well, she could easily twist Edwina's arm and make her change her mind. It was Buddy's attitude that stung the most and he didn't respond very well to arm-twisting. Planting her right fist on her hip, she looked up at him with the squint-eye and spoke slowly. "Clowns? You think what Ed and I do is laughable?"

"That's not what—"

"You know what, Buddy Overstreet?" In spite of herself, Debbie Sue's voice elevated a decibel. "If I end up wearing face paint, a fuckin' rubber ball on my nose and juggling horse turds, I wouldn't back out of this now." She turned to Edwina. "You know damn well my word is my bond. You're my partner. You're supposed to support me."

The room fell silent. Debbie Sue swung her gaze to Buddy, her eyes boring deep. Vic cleared his throat.

"Well, it's been lovely, kids," Edwina said breezily. "We

should do it again sometime." She picked up her purse and started for the door. "Vic, you ready to go, sugar buns?"

"You don't have to leave," Debbie Sue said, not veering her eyes from Buddy's.

"I'm tired," Edwina said, "and Vic's been on the road for a week. We're going home. Y'all have a good time. I'll see you tomorrow."

Backing away from the argument momentarily, Debbie Sue and Buddy walked their guests to the door.

"Y'all drive careful going back into town," Buddy called out as Edwina and Vic reached Vic's pickup.

"Drive careful," Debbie Sue echoed. "Enjoyed y'all having supper with us."

As soon as the door closed, Debbie Sue turned to her husband, one hand on her hip. "Now, where was I?"

"You were on your way to bed." Buddy scooped her into his arms and carried her toward the bedroom.

She clung to his shoulders. "No fair," she wailed. "You're bigger and stronger. You're taking advantage."

"I know," he replied. "But I promise this conversation will have a better outcome if we're naked."

# seven

*T*he next morning, Justin walked out of his house, into the cool pleasance of the early hour. The rising sun showed as a bright orange ball hovering just above the horizon. Layers of mauve, lavender and gold swept the sky like brush strokes. He liked rising early and enjoying the quiet beauty as well as a brief respite from the unyielding heat that would come later in the day.

He ambled toward the barn, a place he had largely avoided for a year. Debbie Sue had been wrong, accusing him of keeping Rachel's horses penned up and *never* letting them graze. Sometimes he had done the perfunctory chores— feeding, watering and turning them out to pasture and returning them to their stalls at night. He had hired a farrier to come by periodically and check their feet. But most of the time, he had hired the teenager up the road to do the chores. He knew he should do more. Rachel had spent hours with the two horses.

All this talk about the animals and Debbie Sue scolding him for neglecting them had made him feel guilty. He chastised himself for not paying more attention to them. Rachel had loved them so much and Debbie Sue was right. They too had lost someone they loved. What if he and Rachel had had a child? Would he have avoided it and neglected it in the same way just to avoid his own personal pain?

A sliding bar secured the gate to the corral. Slipping it to the left, he opened the gate just wide enough to squeeze through, crossed to the barn and the two horse stalls. He filled a bucket with oats and dumped them into feeding troughs in the corner of each stall. The horses watched him with bored detachment, obviously understanding the routine and their roles better than he did. He couldn't even remember their names. He had to admit he had never bothered to learn. His firefighting career and horse ownership didn't complement each other.

Inside the eight-by-eight tack room, a bucket of grooming tools sat on a shelf to the side of the door. Justin didn't know the purpose of each tool, but he did know what do with the one he had seen Rachel use most frequently. He carried the curry comb back to a stall and started on one of the reddish-colored mares, talking in low, comforting tones. The mare's ears pricked forward, her eyes wary. Rachel had said the ears and eyes of a horse were their most effective means of communication. He couldn't keep from wondering what these animals would say to him if they could talk.

He brushed the mare in earnest, dislodging weeks of dirt and debris. Her muscles rippled and twitched and she looked at him with huge, soft brown eyes. As he brushed, he began to feel better, doing something Rachel would want him to do. He didn't know what had come over him. He had never been unkind to animals. From the time he was a small boy, he had always been the first to jump to the aid of a help-less creature. His mother had delighted family and friends with tales of how he saved a kitten that had fallen into an irrigation ditch and how once he had taped an entire box of Band-Aids on a scratch on his grandparents' milk cow, that had promptly slobbered them off. He remembered lying in bed when storm clouds rolled through and crying for all of the animals left out in the open with no shelter.

He labored vigorously, brushing the mare and concentrat-ing only on the task at hand. When he finished one horse, he moved to the second. Debbie Sue had been right about one thing. He should have done this long ago. Not just for the benefit of the horses, but also for the release of his own pent-up emotions.

Not until he finished the grooming did he realize that the tightness in his neck and shoulders with which he had lived for months was gone. Stopping to wipe his brow and catch his breath, he stepped back to admire his work. The horses weren't exactly ready for a show ring, but they looked 100 percent better. He wondered if regularly taking care of them could actually be therapeutic for him.

"I promise to do this more often, girls," he said. "I won't ignore you anymore."

He had barely uttered the words when he heard the distinctive sound of an approaching car. He recognized the engine sound immediately. John Patrick.

Glancing at his watch, Justin was stunned to see that two hours had slipped past and it was mid-morning. Early by John Patrick's clock.

As the Cayenne neared, Justin stepped up on the bottom rail of the fence and let out a loud whistle, waving his arm to draw his brother-in-law's attention. John Patrick looked in his direction. He braked his high-powered SUV into a caliche-grinding halt and sent up a cloud of dust that hung over the corral like a film.

John Patrick was laughing when he opened the door. He turned in the driver's seat and planted his feet on the ground. "Man, I almost didn't see you. I was haulin' ass. What're you doing in the corral? Thought you'd hired somebody to take care of these horses."

Justin couldn't help but notice that the rotund man, balding despite the fact he had yet to see his thirty-fifth birthday, was still wearing the same clothes as yesterday. The surprise at seeing him so early gave way to understanding. John Patrick was out and about at this hour because he hadn't been home yet and was most likely killing time before going.

Justin didn't understand this behavior. John Patrick's marriage was more like having a roommate who shared all your stuff and your money, except in John Patrick's case, he had been the one who married for money. He had come from a wealthy family, but his father had believed in a man earning his own way. John Patrick's solution to that dilemma had been to marry rich.

"You got any coffee on?" John Patrick asked.

"Sure," Justin answered, shaking his head but laughing. "Go on up to the house. I'll be there in a minute."

Justin watched his brother-in-law park and enter the house. It was pure irony that a marriage like John Patrick's would probably last forever, while his own, as perfect a union as there ever was, had ended suddenly and tragically.

John Patrick Daly parked his SUV and strode into his brother-in-law's house, salivating for a cup of hot black coffee. After a night of partying hard, he dreaded the icy stare and caustic comments from his wife when he went home, so he had detoured by Justin's place. He supposed one day he would push Felicia too far and she would kick him out, but he was willing to take the gamble. Life as a kept eunuch wasn't his long-term plan.

And if things progressed as he hoped, he would be escaping sooner than he had expected. He believed Justin was at a breaking point, and selling this house and land to his departed wife's brother at a good price would be the most Christian thing he could do. After all, he was John Patrick Daly, Rachel's brother and Justin's "best friend."

Setting up mysterious happenings inside Justin's home

hadn't been his plan this morning, but hell, the opportunity was too blatant, thus tempting, to resist. And Justin was so naive. John Patrick walked to the sofa and as he had done many times previously, mussed the neatly folded throw on one end, as someone lying in repose might do. He tossed the stupid horse magazine casually on the floor as someone might do if dropping off for a nap. Today, the roses would have to wait until another time when he was more prepared and had more than a few minutes. Justin could walk in at any time.

Moving to the kitchen, he found the coffeepot, dragged a mug off a cabinet shelf and poured it full. As he sipped, he scanned the room for something he could move, something that he hadn't relocated before. Or perhaps something he could break. The clatter of ice cubes falling from their tray into the ice receptacle inside the refrigerator's freezer took his eyes to the white appliance's door. Magnetic letters were scattered on it in no particular pattern. He pondered using the letters to make a message that would scare Justin shitless.

He turned back to the coffeepot and warmed up his coffee, then swung his attention back to the refrigerator door. Stunned at what he now saw, he gasped and the coffee mug slipped from his fingers to the floor.

Justin started for the house, but he had taken only a few steps when the front door flew open. Turnup, sleeping on the porch, jumped to his feet and scatted, tail between his legs. John Patrick came out the door, scurried to his SUV and climbed in. He cranked the engine, backed in an arc with the door still open and roared down the driveway toward the county road.

Justin felt his brow tug into a frown. What the hell was going on now?

He jogged to his house, but stopped at the front door and took a few seconds to gather himself. Finally, he drew a deep breath and entered. In the living room, Rachel's afghan was spread haphazardly across the couch. Her magazine lay on the floor. *Whoa!* That afghan was neatly folded this morning. That magazine was neatly placed on top of a stack of others on the side table. Justin's heartbeat picked up. Had J. P. seen someone or some *thing* move them? Was that what had sent him racing from the house as if chased by demons?

Moving to the kitchen Justin saw a mug on the floor, coffee spilled over the vinyl flooring. Nothing else was amiss, nothing out of place. He looked around again. And his gaze froze on the refrigerator door.

Nearing the junction with the county road, John Patrick let his foot relax on the accelerator. The Cayenne purred in gratitude. Its air conditioner was cranking at full blast and icy air filled the interior of the rig, yet sweat covered John Patrick's brow, trickled down the sides of his face to his collar. Glancing in the rearview mirror, he noticed that the few hairs remaining on his head were visibly spiked. He took his pudgy hand from the steering wheel and smoothed them down. "Fuck!"

What in the hell had happened back there? He ran through his memory bank again, replaying what he had seen on the refrigerator door, spelled out with kids' magnetic letters. It was a message that had to be meant only for him:

*JP U R N ASHOLE*

While Debbie Sue waited for Edwina, though she was low on energy, she vigorously swept a mound of gritty sand toward the Styling Station's back door. The business day had yet to begin and the floor was sandy already. Sweeping it was a never-ending job. The unpaved road that ran beside the beauty shop was the source of this annoyance and she couldn't count the number of dirty names she had labeled that road over the years.

She had plenty to get off her chest this morning. Last night, thanks to Edwina taking Buddy's side, he had spent hours trying to persuade her to abandon Justin Sadler's case. Midnight had come and gone before the two of them fell asleep exhausted.

Just then the back door opened, letting a gust of wind blow the swept-up sand back into the shop and bring with it a new supply. Behind it, Edwina appeared, rhinestone-encrusted sunglasses covering half her face, Dr Pepper and a package of animal crackers in hand. She looked over the top of her sunglasses. "Oops, sorry."

"Ed, we need to talk," Debbie Sue said firmly.

"Well good morning to you, too." Wearing her typical platform shoes, Edwina clomped to her workstation, set her drink and animal crackers on the counter and dropped her purse onto her hydraulic chair seat. "Chilly this morning, isn't it?" She peeled off her sunglasses and stuffed them into her purse. "Damn, girl, I'm guessing you and Buddy didn't settle your differences last night."

"It isn't Buddy I need to talk about."

"Don't tell me Quint Matthews is back in town." Edwina tore open the package of animal crackers and popped one into her mouth.

Edwina bringing up Debbie Sue's former boyfriend and fiancé, world champion bull rider Quint Matthews, was a low blow. Debbie Sue thrust the broom out to her side at arm's length and planted the opposite fist on her hip. "You are changing the subject, Edwina Perkins-Martin. You know damn well I'm talking about you siding against me last night over taking Justin's case."

"Debbie Sue, I love you like you're one of my own kids, but I'm entitled to have an opinion. That's what being partners is all about."

"But you took Buddy's side."

"I gave my *opinion*," Edwina said, punctuating her sentence with an animal cracker. "And my *opinion* hasn't changed, Debbie Sue. Vic agrees with me too. He thinks this could get crazy."

"So what if it does? It couldn't get any crazier than things got in New York. And if you felt so strong about it, why didn't you say something to me privately, when Buddy wasn't present?"

"I think I did."

"Him knowing you agreed with him just made him tor- ment me that much more. You should've seen him last night. Here I was trying to put up a good argument and every time I opened my mouth he kissed me in a ticklish spot. I ended up with two big hickeys on my stomach." She resumed her sweeping, not wanting to look Edwina in the eye. "And one on my thigh."

From the corner of her eye, Debbie Sue caught a grin starting to sneak across Edwina's bright red lips. "Inside or outside?"

*Shit!* Edwina thought sex was more important than any- thing and after last night with Buddy and this morning in the shower, Debbie Sue thought she might have a point. But Debbie Sue would never admit it aloud. "Cut it out, Ed. I'm serious."

"Inside, I'm guessing," Edwina said, now cackling like a witch. "And I'm guessing he won the argument."

Debbie Sue stopped her sweeping and glared at Edwina. "Don't you dare laugh, Ed. That's one of the problems with being married all these years and sleeping with the same guy every night. He gets to where he knows all of your ticklish spots and he isn't afraid to strip off your clothes and go for them just to win an argument."

Edwina's head slowly shook. "You know what, sweetie? Probably most of the woman in Cabell County would just love to have Buddy Overstreet strip off their clothes and look for their ticklish spots. Lord, why you continue to battle what you've got at home beats me. So did you and Buddy settle things or not?"

"Oh, they're settled all right. The Domestic Equalizers are helping Justin, Ed. Just like I promised. And if you're scared, you need to just cowboy up and be my partner. And Buddy will just have to get over it. I told him if he doesn't, we're never again playing that kissing-each-other-all-over game. And I told him I would never again let him . . . well, you know."

"Oh, I'll bet that got his attention."

"It didn't make him change his mind. That's when I got the thigh hickey. I didn't even know I had until we showered this morning."

Debbie Sue continued sweeping, still avoiding looking Edwina in the face. She pushed her little mound of sand to the back door again, opened the door, swept the sand outside and tossed the broom outside behind it. She walked back toward Edwina, dusting her palms. "That's the last time I sweep this damn floor with a broom. I'm buying an electric broom and I'm making a special trip to Odessa to do it."

"Hurray!" Edwina pumped a fist. "That's one for the girls. Now what?"

"Now, oh great one, just to satisfy you, I call this psychic or medium or whatever she is and get things moving. If I'm going to have to endure Buddy's torturing me, I might as well make the most of it."

"Torture. Hmm," Edwina said. "Like I said, most of the women in—"

"Cut it out, Ed." Debbie Sue moved behind the receptionist desk and placed her hand on the receiver. "Remind me again. Is El Paso one hour behind or one hour ahead?"

"Oh, hell," Edwina grumbled, her brow knit. "You'd think after a lifetime I'd have that down pat. But I have to stop and think every single time. Mountain time is one hour ahead. No, wait, it's an hour behind. It's the way I taught my girls. Time goes *behind* the mountain."

"So that means I have to wait an hour."

Just then, before she could pick up the receiver, the phone warbled.

"Let the answering machine get it," Edwina said. "We're not open yet."

Debbie Sue stared at the persistent phone. "And what if it's opportunity calling?"

"I've always heard opportunity knocks."

Sending her an arch look, Debbie Sue picked up the receiver. "Styling Station, this is Debbie Sue."

For a few seconds, she heard only dead air, then a hesitant voice said, "Uh, Mrs. Overstreet, please?"

Debbie Sue's mind did a split-second inventory of her bills. She wasn't delinquent on any of them that she could recall. Once she had struggled to make ends meet, but these days, she had no trouble paying her bills. "This is Debbie Sue Overstreet."

"Oh, Mrs. Overstreet. Hi." The voice brightened noticeably. "This is Sophia Paredes from El Paso. We spoke last night?"

Debbie Sue recognized the Spanish accent at once. Sophia Paredes spoke perfect English, but her speech still had a Spanish lilt. "Why, hello. I was just thinking about calling you. And listen, please call me Debbie Sue."

"Thank you, I will. I hope I'm not calling too early. Sometimes the change in time zones confuses people."

"Oh, not me. I was just going to wait an hour and call you."

Sophia laughed. "I'm an early riser. Even with us an hour behind, you'd have to call very early to wake me. I want to speak to you about coming to Odessa."

"Super."

"My car, uh, *our* car is old. It has a lot of miles. I'm thinking of taking the bus."

"Airfares are cheap these days. You could fly into Midland, which is only thirty miles from Odessa."

"There's no flight from El Paso to Midland. I checked. Southwest flies to Midland eventually, but they have to go all the way to Dallas first, then loop back."

"But that doesn't make sense," Debbie Sue said. "We're only four hours from El Paso."

"I know. But I don't mind taking the bus. I checked the fares and it's fifty-six dollars one way, directly to Odessa. Do you think your client would mind paying that?"

"Fifty-six dollars is really cheap for two people. You aren't sending your grandmother alone, are you?"

"Oh, uh, my goodness, what was I thinking?" Sophia laughed. "That's for *one* person. Yes, it would be double that."

"I'm sure he wouldn't mind that. It's probably cheaper than gas for the car with the prices being what they are. But wouldn't a bus ride be hard on your grandmother? They might not make stops when she needs them. She might need to get off the bus and move around."

"You'd be surprised how resilient she is. We're thinking

we could leave today around noon and be there about five o'clock, your time. Can someone meet us or should I rent a car? I know there's an Enterprise rental across the street from the bus station."

"There is? You've been there before?"

"No, never."

The hair stood up on the back of Debbie Sue's neck. "Then how do you know about it?"

"Uh . . . my grandmother knows. She knows many things. If you'll give me the address for the hotel where we'll be staying, we'll call you from there."

This was certainly a take-charge person. Debbie Sue was impressed. Weak, helpless women had a tendency to bring out the worst in her. She liked Sophia Paredes immediately. "Hey, that would be great. We don't finish up in the shop today until almost five. Call here or call the cell number I gave you."

"Okay. I will talk to you later."

"Sure thing," Debbie Sue replied.

"Who was that?" Edwina asked as Debbie Sue hung up.

"That was the woman in El Paso's granddaughter, Sophia. She's bringing her grandmother today. They'll be in Odessa around five. You know, I really like her."

"I wonder if she could be the same little girl I played checkers with. She would be grown by now. Damn, I feel old."

"Well, you're not old," Debbie Sue said, her mood elevated. "But you *are* booked solid today, so you better get your young ass in gear."

"Oh, it's in gear," Edwina said. "In fact, if it gets any more in gear I'm liable to throw a rod."

"I'm not *even* touching that one," Debbie Sue said. "Unlock the door. The day awaits."

Sophia returned the phone to its cradle and lifted her suitcase to the bed. She didn't know how much to pack, because she didn't know how long she would be gone. She'd seen her grandmother involved in cases from as little as a few hours to all the way up to a week or more.

*Better to take too much than too little*, a soft voice in her head interjected.

"That's true," Sophia replied.

For the next twenty minutes she busied herself packing. Speaking again to the empty room, she said, "I think I'll stop at the store and get the latest *Cosmopolitan* to read on the trip."

*Best to read the Holy Bible*, the voice replied.

# eight

The Styling Station's main wall clock, a freebie from Grissom Farm Equipment in Odessa, was the size of a big skillet. A cartoon image of a green tractor rode atop the green hour hand and a bale of hay ticked off the minutes. Over the course of a few hours, Debbie Sue and Edwina continued working side by side and not talking about the visitors coming in from the west at 5 P.M. Debbie Sue must have looked at that bale of hay passing up that tractor a hundred times. She couldn't help but notice that Edwina was as interested in the clock as she was.

Debbie Sue had always been excited about the cases the Domestic Equalizers took on, but this one had a totally different appeal from their previous adventures. She had absolutely no logical, plausible explanation for the goings-on at

Justin's house or the message that had appeared on his refrigerator door. Though she held a huge bit of skepticism about the supernatural, she might—emphasis on *might*—consider it if surveillance revealed no clues. And to appease Edwina.

Debbie Sue had watched tales of the paranormal on TV. She had even caught a couple of Montel Williams shows when guest Sylvia Browne had given psychic readings to a hushed audience. When it came to the afterlife and those who claimed to communicate with the ones who had passed over, she had to admit she was intrigued and was willing to be open-minded.

With the last person paid and out the door and less than an hour left to keep the doors open, Jolene Wiley, great-granddaughter of their favorite octogenarian, Maudeen Wiley, bounded in. Jolene had just completed her senior year at Salt Lick High. With her flaming-red hair and bubbly personality, she literally lit up the room.

"Hey, Mrs. Overstreet. Mrs. Martin."

"Hey, yourself," Edwina said, placing her hand on her hip and giving the girl a playful once-over. "Just look at you. What are you doing with yourself now that school's out? Chasing boys or being chased by boys?"

The teenager laughed. "Neither one. I don't have time." She began to tick off on her fingers. "Between working the morning shift at Hogg's, getting ready to go to college in the fall, babysitting Karla Kennedy's kids in the evening and running errands for Mama and Great Gram, I don't have time for boys."

"Lord-a-mercy," Edwina said, "what has gone wrong with

this country? You're only young once, honey-child. Believe me, you'll find in your lifetime there's more need for work than play. Use that youth before you lose it is what I say."

Debbie Sue shook her head and gave Jolene a wink, sensing that Edwina was fired up and on the verge of one of her speeches.

"The price of gasoline is high, groceries are high, utilities are high and sex drives are low," Edwina said. "We're all going to hell in a handbasket."

"You sound just like Great Gram," Jolene said, giggling.

"Speaking of that dear little lady," Debbie Sue said, "how's she doing?"

"That's why I'm here. She's in the car out front." The teenager motioned to the front parking lot of the salon. "She wanted me to ask if you'd come out and talk to her outside. She wants to ask you something."

Alarms went off in Debbie Sue's head. She loved Maudeen Wiley like the grandmother she had never known. Was she ill? Had time finally taken such a toll on her frail body that she wasn't able to even leave the car?

"Is she okay?" Edwina asked.

"She's fine. She's just too embarrassed to come inside is all."

Debbie Sue didn't know which was more disturbing—her first thought that Maudeen was ill or the news that she was embarrassed. As far as Debbie Sue was concerned, either one was reason for worry.

Leaving Ed to start the end-of-the-day cleanup, Debbie Sue walked out to the parking lot. She could see a diminutive figure outlined against the high-back passenger seat, her head barely visible over the dashboard.

As Debbie Sue opened the door, the tiny woman turned toward her and gave her the usual big smile. "Why, hello, honey. Thanks for coming out to the car."

Maudeen was wearing a pair of huge black sunglasses with lenses so dark her eyes couldn't be seen, the type an eye doctor had once given Debbie Sue's mother after her eyes had been dilated for an exam. Debbie Sue was puzzled. Surely this wasn't cause for embarrassment by a woman who wasn't bothered by an opinion from one single individual other than herself.

Taking Maudeen's birdlike hand in her own, Debbie Sue squatted beside the open door. "What in the world is wrong, Maudeen? Jolene said you didn't want to come in. Are you all right? You know how much I worry about you."

"That's sweet of you, honey. It really is. But I'm fine, if doing something stupid is being fine."

"Stupid? What in the world are you talking about? I've never heard anyone call you stupid."

"Well, I have been this time, honey." Maudeen freed her hand from Debbie Sue's and removed her sunglasses. "Who else but a stupid old woman would do this to herself?"

At first glance, half an inch above Maudeen's eyebrows, a couple of fuzzy black caterpillars appeared to be crawling across her wrinkled forehead. Debbie Sue gasped. She reached to touch, but drew her hand back. "What *is* that?"

"I got to looking in the mirror, honey," Maudeen said.

"And that right there isn't a smart thing to do at my age. I noticed my eyebrows were nearly plumb gray. They had practically disappeared. I decided they needed dyeing."

"Sweetheart," Debbie Sue said gently, "me or Ed would have been happy to do that for you. Why didn't you come see us?"

"It was one of those Saturday night spur-of-the-moment things, honey. My life's pretty much been ruled by Saturday night spur-of-the-moment things, if you get my drift."

Debbie Sue got it. She nodded. The only person who had always enjoyed her sex life more than Edwina Perkins-Martin had to be Maudeen Wiley. "You tried to dye them yourself?"

"Well, that was the plan, honey, but I never got that far."

"But—"

"I was using a pen to practice the shape I was going to make 'em. That's why they're perched above my own eye-brows. But when I started practicing, I didn't know I was using a laundry marker."

"Uh-oh. That's permanent," Debbie Sue said.

"When I realized what I'd done, I tried to wipe it off."

"And that's how you got the fuzzy look?" Debbie Sue looked at the ground, biting her lip and not wanting to make Maudeen feel worse by laughing.

"Oh, go ahead and laugh," Maudeen said. She began to chuckle and was soon into a breath-grabbing laugh. Debbie Sue joined her.

Wiping a tear from her eye, Maudeen said, "At my age, honey, you never know if you're going to wake up in the morning. And here I've made such a mess of myself I might have to meet my maker with a just-been-goosed-from-behind look on my face."

Debbie Sue went from squatting to sitting on the ground, legs extended, laughing harder. Finally, she wiped her eyes with her shirtsleeve. "Speaking of meeting your maker, Maudeen, do you believe in ghosts?"

"Heavens, yes. When you've lived as long as I have, you're surprised by very little. Why, honey, I could tell you stories that would rearrange your DNA."

Debbie Sue stretched her hand out to her friend. "Come on inside and tell me more. We have some lotion that helps take hair dye stains off our hands. It doesn't work one hundred percent, but we can try it on your, uh, eyebrows."

"That's okay. It doesn't have to be a hundred percent. If you just get a little of this black off, I can spackle my face up good enough with some pancake makeup. And while we're at it, maybe you could go ahead and dye my real eyebrows. Give me a professional job."

Debbie Sue smiled and took Maudeen's hand again. "We can do that." She assisted Maudeen from the car and walked her into the salon.

"Jolene," Maudeen called out from the shop's front doorway. "Honey, you can run on and do what you need to get done. Debbie Sue and Edwina are going to work their magic on me." The octogenarian glanced up at Debbie Sue and patted her arm. "Aren't you, girls?"

Edwina walked over to them. "You bet we are," she shouted.

Debbie Sue cringed. Edwina always yelled when speaking to Maudeen, but as far as Debbie Sue knew, nothing was wrong with Maudeen's hearing.

"Why you got them big-ass black sunglasses on, hon?" Edwina yelled as she walked the elderly woman across the room and seated her in Debbie Sue's hydraulic chair. "You look like you're wearing manhole covers."

Maudeen eased the sunglasses from her face and looked up at Edwina.

Edwina slapped her own cheek with her fingers. "Great day in the morning!"

"Where's that lotion that takes hair dye off our hands?" Debbie Sue said. "It might work on her face."

"In the storeroom. I think that stuff would remove a tattoo if we let it set long enough." Edwina leaned down closer to Maudeen's ear. "I said it's in the storeroom," she shouted.

Debbie Sue rolled her eyes. "Ed, would you please get it for us?"

Edwina disappeared behind the floral curtain that covered the storage-room doorway. Maudeen looked at Debbie Sue in the mirror. "Why does Edwina insist on yelling at me? Does she have a hearing problem?"

Debbie Sue chuckled. "What she has is a comprehension problem. She can't comprehend that aging and being hard of hearing don't necessarily go hand in hand."

"Why did you ask me about ghosts?" Maudeen said, smoothing the nylon cape that Debbie Sue had placed around her small neck. "Have you got a stubborn dearly departed who's refusing to move on?"

"Not me. It's a client. So you believe there really are ghosts?"

"Honey, when you've lived as long as I have, you get to a place where you've done things you swore you wouldn't, and you believe in things you didn't think existed. It's one of the perks of old age."

"I guess," Debbie Sue replied.

"Have you called in a professional? You know, someone to speak to the spirits for you? You need to get a professional, honey. Don't try to do it on your own. Spirits make sport of watching mortals make fools of themselves. Guess they've got little else to do."

Edwina returned from the storeroom and handed a bottle of white lotion to Debbie Sue. "We called a woman in El Paso. Her name's Isabella—"

"Not Izzy Paredes," Maudeen said with a start.

Debbie Sue and Edwina looked at each other, mouths agape.

"*You know* Isabella Paredes?" Debbie Sue asked.

"I lived in El Paso for four years. During the big war, my first husband, Homer, was in the army. He was stationed at Fort Bliss. Everybody knew Izzy Paredes. Back in those days, she was a celebrity."

"People called her Izzy?" Edwina asked.

"Just her good friends," Maudeen replied.

"You were good friends with Isabella Paredes?" Debbie Sue asked, incredulous.

"I'd like to think so. At any rate, she was sure a good friend to me. She helped me tell Homer good-bye."

Debbie Sue felt a sting behind her eyes. She glanced over at Edwina, whose chin had a quiver to it. "You mean Homer went into the light?" Debbie Sue asked softly.

"As fast as he could, honey," Maudeen said.

"What did Isabella Paredes do to help?" Edwina asked.

"She loaned me her pickup."

"What?" Debbie Sue and Edwina chorused.

"To move after Homer met a stripper from Vegas and went AWOL. She loaned me her pickup. Even helped me carry the heavy stuff."

Debbie Sue stomped her foot. "Dammit, Maudeen, I thought you meant he died."

"Oh, he did, eventually. But not before he spent thirty years with the meanest woman that ever drew a breath. That's the sort of thing that kind of compensates an old woman for outliving everybody. You get to see them that screwed you over get their just rewards."

A faraway look came into Maudeen's eyes and she chuckled. "The day I found out what Homer done, me and Izzy sat at her kitchen table and killed a bottle of tequila. She held my hand while I cried. Yes, honey, that crazy Izzy was a good friend to me. I can't wait to see her.

# nine

*J*ustin arrived at home after four in the afternoon. He was beat. He had spent the entire morning working with the horses, followed by a trip into town to run errands and buy groceries.

Even before he put his grocery sacks on the kitchen counter, he checked the refrigerator door for a new message. Before leaving for town, he had rearranged the letters on the refrigerator door back to alphabetical order. Nothing had changed. This left him with mixed emotions. On the one hand he was relieved; on the other he was disappointed because he was now starting to believe Rachel was truly communicating with him.

He played his voice-mail messages and listened to one from Debbie Sue, informing him that the psychic from El

Paso would be arriving in Odessa this afternoon and would be at his place tomorrow. "Maybe your questions will be answered then," Debbie Sue had said.

Justin hadn't expected all of this to happen so soon. He had thought the Domestic Equalizers would put listening devices and cameras in the house before they relied on the supernatural and caused him to risk $3,000.

He intended to be in his home every minute the psychic was present. With his work schedule, that would be impossible unless he put in a request for vacation time. Because of his regular schedule, a week of vacation worked out to be two full weeks off. How long could the woman be in town—a few hours? Two weeks was more time than necessary, but he needed the break. He would make use of the extra days. Those thoughts prompted him to call to his captain to ask for some vacation time.

"If it was anyone but you, Sadler, I'd say not just no, but hell no," Captain Baugus groused.

"Thanks, Cap, I really appreciate it," Justin told him. "I know how you hate last-minute requests. If it wasn't important, I wouldn't ask."

"You've been working doubles and filling in every vacant slot for more than a year. It's time you took some days off. Hope you're going somewhere to raise hell. Run down to Mexico. Lie on the beach and get yourself laid."

Justin had more important things to think about than deepening his tan or ending his long stint of celibacy.

Avoiding giving his captain the answer Justin knew he wanted, he said, "My plans right now don't include any of those things, but if something happens I think you'd want to hear about, I won't hesitate to call you."

Justin dragged a frosty glass from the freezer, grabbed a beer and carried them outside to the front porch. A strong breeze from the north gave a welcome reprieve from the heat. Easing himself into one of the two matching rocking chairs, he poured his beer and tried to relax.

*So she's really coming*, he thought. He still found the whole thing a little hard to grasp. He was certain he wouldn't be condoning this, or even allowing it, if Debbie Sue and Edwina hadn't promoted it.

Well, this psychic woman would have to prove to him that she possessed extrasensory perception or whatever. With the unlimited capabilities of the Internet to uncover his life from beginning to the present—his date of birth, his parent's names, when he married, what he did for a living—a computer in the hands of any charlatan could pull up that data. He wouldn't settle for just any old facts, either. Nor was he worried about *how* she might convince him she was legit. That was her problem, not his. She would have to knock him off his feet before he would fork over the money he had agreed to pay.

Beyond that, what should he say when meeting a person who could look at you and possibly tell you your future and your past? What if she looked at him with a perplexing expression on her face? Would it mean she was just tired? Or would it mean she had a headache or was suffering from constipation, for chrissake? How would he keep from overreacting to her human actions?

Turnup had been sleeping peacefully at the side of Justin's rocking chair, but suddenly he raised his head and stared at the front screen door. Whining pitifully, he tilted his head to the left, then right, clearly listening to something Justin couldn't hear. Apprehension began to sneak through Justin. He followed the dog's gaze but saw nothing through the screen door's haze except the living area of his home. "What's the matter, boy?" He reached to touch Turnup's head but the dog rose, his tail tucked between his legs.

Before Justin could react, Turnup's behavior changed as quickly as before. The dog began to prance around, never taking his eyes off the front door.

"What the hell . . ." Justin muttered.

Suddenly Turnup bolted from the front porch, ran into the yard and picked up something in the grass. With the object secured in his mouth, he returned. Ignoring Justin, Turnup placed the object in front of the door and rose on his hind legs, begging. Begging who? No one was present but Justin.

Justin looked at what the dog had brought and his blood chilled. It was a ragged tennis ball. The same tennis ball Rachel had thrown a thousand times and laughed with delight when Turnup raced for it and brought it back to her. Justin hadn't even known where it was.

Rachel would sit on the porch in one of the rocking chairs and call out to him, "Baby, look at how smart Turnup is. He brings the ball right back to me every time."

Justin stared at the empty doorway for uncountable seconds. Finally he swallowed hard and softly said, "Rach? Honey, is that you? Are you here?"

No reply. No sound. Even the wind seemed to have stopped. Justin looked at Turnup, who had given up on his pleading and now lay quietly again. Reaction burned in Justin's chest. Adrenaline rush was something he recognized. But this time it wasn't the life-saving response his body called for in his job. It was more primitive than that. It was anger.

He sprang to his feet, the force of his sudden movement knocking the rocking chair backward. Turnup jumped, ran from the porch and sat in the grass, watching his master warily.

Justin opened the screen door and slammed it with all his might. "Why are you doing this to me?" he bellowed to the air. "If you've got something to tell me, just say it! I'm not taking any more of this shit!"

Overcome with emotion Justin dropped to the porch, hard. He buried his head in his hands. His stiff upper lip quivered and he wept, releasing a deep reservoir of sorrow and anger into his hands. The tears that he had held back for so long flowed. No one placed a comforting hand on his shoulder, no familiar voice soothed. No one and nothing made a sound. Beyond his angst, his only awareness was the faint scent of roses.

Nearly to Odessa, Sophia sat back and watched the arid West Texas landscape speed past her window. *Domestic Equalizers*, she thought, curious about the origin of the name and the two women who had claimed it. She had spoken by phone only to Debbie Sue, but she knew the other partner from a voice in the background. Sophia hoped to be around them long enough to get the full story of their business. She knew a little of their reputation and couldn't wait to meet them.

She drew a deep breath in an effort to calm herself. This would be the first time she had ever publicly demonstrated her abilities. To say she was nervous was putting it mildly.

Because she had seen clients demand proof from her grand-mother, Sophia had no doubt the client in Salt Lick would also. And she didn't know at the moment how she would manage that. Most people thought a psychic could call up visions like using the TV remote control, going from one premonition to another. But it wasn't like that. She didn't know how her visions came; they just did. She couldn't nec-essarily predict their arrival. Sometimes a scene formed in her mind. Another time, holding an object would prompt a flashback and cause her hand to shake. One occurrence had never been the same as another, and it wasn't just one thing in particular.

The only thing she knew for certain was that the Domes-tic Equalizers and their client expected to meet her grand-mother. Sophia showing up instead probably wouldn't be welcomed. They might even think she was crooked. "Gran Bella," she whispered softly, "I am going to need your help. Please don't let me fail. Please help me help these people. Are you with me?"

A voice came into her ear. "I am right beside you, *querida*. We will not fail."

Sophia smiled and finally relaxed into her seat, but a gravelly male voice interrupted her rest. "Excuse me, miss."

Sophia looked up. A tall, swarthy man loomed over her. She had been aware of his eyeing her ever since she boarded the bus. He gave her a tobacco-stained leer. She scooted as far away as she could, until she was pressed against the window. He pointed to the empty seat beside her. "Mind if I sit here, pretty lady?"

Sophia visualized her Gran Bella demurely sitting there, hands crossed on her lap. "No, I'm sorry. The seat is taken."

The man looked at the seat, then at her and backed away. But not before eyeing her up and down one more time. From where she sat, she couldn't see where he went, but she hoped it was all the way to the back of the bus.

Time passed. Between reading *Cosmo* and catnapping, before Sophia could believe it, the driver announced their arrival in Odessa.

Sophia gathered her purse and magazine and made her way off the bus, looking around at her new surroundings. Except for the outline of El Paso's Franklin Mountains, which ran north and south, dividing the city almost in two perfect halves, the scenery was the same. Flat land, few trees, lots of open, uncluttered skies. And heat.

Stepping into the air-conditioned bus terminal, she shivered at the sudden change in temperature, but the chill was a welcome reprieve from the ninety-plus heat outside. She scanned the room, noticing travelers of every age, size, shape and color. Several people, men and women both, appeared to be trying to blend into the walls. She recognized them as being the homeless, seemingly ignoring the NO LOITERING signs that were posted everywhere.

Sophia's heart went out to them, especially the elderly, the women and the children. She believed that homeless able-bodied men had choices and many of them had opted to be where they were. But as a teacher of young children, Sophia couldn't accept that sleeping in a bus station was what the woman who held a small child's hand had in mind. A twist of bad luck or bad choices had detoured their lives.

What immunity did she have from that same fate? She wasn't that far from being homeless herself, as her recent financial challenges had shown her.

A clattering sound pulled her attention to the doorway through which she had just entered. The driver, sweating profusely, struggled to pull a luggage cart indoors.

Sophia was unsure how to go about claiming her bag but quickly saw that, apparently, a numbered ticket attached to her travel voucher was the claim check for it. Still, she hung back and let the more-seasoned bus travelers take the lead.

After waiting patiently for her opportunity she presented the ticket to the driver, who promptly handed her suitcase to her. She pulled up the retractable handle and rolled it toward the front door, already seeing Enterprise Rent-A-Car's sign across the street.

As she neared the exit, the man who had asked if he could sit next to her during the bus trip jumped from his chair near the doorway and opened the plate-glass door wide for her. She gave a tight, quick smile and started through the doorway. Once outside she realized he had followed her and was startled when his hand covered hers and he reached for control of her suitcase. "Why don't you let me help you, sweetheart? A pretty thing like you shouldn't have to carry your own bags. That's a man's job."

His touch spurred a disgusting film clip in her mind of his life and the way he had chosen to live it. "No, thank you," she said, shifting her bag to her other side and giving him a long, hard look. "I've got it."

The man, undeterred, stepped in front of her, halting her progress. "How about I go with you? You might find something you need help with later on." He slid his tongue around his mouth in an attempt, Sophia supposed, to look sexy.

His approach didn't scare her as much as it steeled something in her she'd never felt before. She was struck with the knowledge that she had the upper hand, and the feeling of power brought a smile to her lips.

The man apparently mistook the smile for an invitation and moved closer to her, looking her up and down as if he were appraising a banquet table. Smile still in place, she said, "Here's what I think you should do, Bob. Or are you going by Jack now? I'd think if you wanted to use an alias you'd choose one you hadn't used before."

Multiple expressions zipped across his face—shock, fear, mistrust and anger. All that she had hoped for.

"How the hell—"

"Don't worry about it, Bob. It's *way* over your head. And I'm *way* over the age you prefer. How old was the last girl you molested? Seven or eight? I teach small children. I've often wondered about men like you. Do you make victims of babies because you know you'd never have a chance with a grown woman?"

Shaken, the stranger puffed up with bravado. "Who the hell are you? How do you know—"

"It doesn't matter who I am. What should matter to you is that I know your probation officer's name is Phil Casey in El Paso and he would like to know where you are. I've never met him, but I know he would like to hear from me. I'll have no trouble finding his phone number. You either get back on the bus and head back to where you came from in El Paso or I'll call him right here and now and you'll be returned to prison." She leveled a glare at him, while reaching inside her purse for her cell phone.

At that moment an Odessa police officer rounded the corner of the building and stopped, observing the scene. He was a mountain of a man with a weathered face. "Ma'am, are you in trouble here?"

Sophia looked at the policeman and gave him her most sincere smile. "I'm so happy to see you, officer. This man is trying to pick me up. He's also proud he's putting one over his parole officer in El Paso." She glared at her tormentor again. "Aren't you, Bob?"

The man licked his lips and laughed nervously. "I was just trying to be nice to her. I didn't—"

In a flash, the officer grasped the man's upper arm. "Come with me, sir. My cruiser's just around the corner. You can sit in the backseat where it's nice and cool while I run a check on you. If it comes back clean I'll stay with you and make sure you get on that bus back to El Paso." He returned his attention to Sophia. "Miss, are you gonna be all right?"

"Yes sir, I'm going to be just fine. Thank you so much. And officer, regardless of what alias he gives you, his real name is Robert Alan Chandler."

Sophia had no idea how she knew Bob Chandler's real name or that of his parole officer and his police record. The information had just come to her. That's the way her visions always were. Only in recent years had she learned to trust them.

In less than half an hour she drove a Chevy Aero from Enterprise's parking lot. As she passed the officer's police cruiser, the child molester was leaning against the car while the officer handcuffed him. This incident was definitely one where having the ability to see the future, and especially the past, had been beneficial.

Just as she had requested, the rental car was equipped with a GPS. Debbie Sue had told her the client had made a reservation for her at the Blue Mesa Inn. Leaving the rental car parking lot, she stopped at the YIELD sign and carefully entered the address of her destination into the computer. She followed the commands dutifully and couldn't help but think how easy life would be if everyone was equipped with his own personal navigation device. Turn left, don't turn left, stop ahead, keep going.

In time she found herself at the hotel. She had to laugh at the irony of a satellite in outer space giving her guidance. She had come here to help someone with voices from the spirit world while relying on an object in space to guide her in the right direction.

The Blue Mesa Inn wasn't the nicest hotel she had ever seen, but it wasn't the worst, either. A room had been reserved for her, just as promised. Opening the door and seeing two double beds was a painful reminder that she was truly alone.

# *ten*

*D*ebbie Sue pushed her body deep into the tangle of bedsheets. She sighed and moaned, languishing in the pleasure only Buddy and his nimble fingers could provide. He knew the right spots and wasn't selfish with his time and attention. "I know you're tired, sweetheart," she purred, "but would you do that spot again?"

Smiling, Buddy reached for the squatty jar on the bedside table and scooped out a generous glob of soy body whip. He warmed the silky cream between his large palms, then began massaging her right foot again, squeezing and slowly manipulating her ankle.

"Man, after standing on my feet all day, you cannot imagine how good that feels," she told him.

Buddy chuckled. "I sat on my ass in front of a computer for eight hours today. You willing to return the favor?"

Debbie Sue raised her head and gave him a seductive smile. "Anytime, sugarfoot. I'd rub soy body whip on your bottom anytime."

"The Eyes of Texas" blared in a staccato beat from Debbie Sue's cell phone, shattering the tranquility and intimacy of the moment. If the call had come on the house phone, she would've gladly let it go to the answering machine, but given the fact that she could count on less than two hands the number of people who had her cell number, she caved and dragged her purse from the bedside table. But not without firing off a string of expletives.

"Humph," Buddy huffed. "Haven't heard you use *those* words before. Where'd you learn 'em?"

"I made 'em up." Debbie Sue plowed through the purse for the phone. Looking at caller ID, she didn't recognize the number. She frowned and grumbled, "Damn telemarketers. How'd they get my cell number?" She flipped open the phone and slapped it against her ear. "Hello," she snapped.

Silence. Good. Maybe her abrupt answer had dissuaded the caller. She was in no mood to hear about refinancing her home or signing up for termite inspection or investing in a burial plot.

"Uh, Debbie Sue?"

The hesitant voice wasn't entirely unfamiliar, but Debbie Sue couldn't quite place it. "Yeah, who's this?"

"Uh, uh, this is Sophia Paredes. Did I call at a bad time?"

*Oops.* Debbie Sue rolled her eyes. This wasn't the first time she had jumped to the wrong conclusion. And if the past was a harbinger of the future, it wouldn't be the last. Glancing at the clock on the bedside table, she said, "Oh, heavensake, no. You just caught me trying to sound tough."

"You thought I was a telemarketer?" Sophia asked on a small laugh.

Debbie Sue felt her stomach knot up. How did Sophia Paredes know that? "Well, uh, yes. I have a tendency to sound mean when people I don't know call me at suppertime."

"I do the same thing," Sophia said. "I think everyone does. My job as a first-grade schoolteacher can be hard at times, but I wouldn't be a telemarketer for anything." Sophia laughed another nervous laugh.

Debbie Sue laughed too, watching Buddy rise from the bed and pad barefooted into the bathroom. He had changed into old jeans and a T-shirt when he came home from work, clothing that showed off his perfect body. Eye candy, for sure. He would hate it if she called him that aloud. She giggled inwardly.

She leaned back against the pillow, returning her attention to the call. "I hope the trip wasn't too much for your grandmother."

"Oh, uh, no, not too much at all. She's resting just fine. Thanks so much for asking."

An awkward silence. Debbie Sue still wasn't sure if she was supposed to play the role of hostess or facilitator. Should she make an attempt toward friendship or just keep things on a business level? She asked a question she would have asked anyone. "Is your room all right? I'm sorry to say I don't know much about the Blue Mesa Inn."

"The room is fine. It's very clean and they offer a complimentary breakfast in the morning."

Debbie Sue slapped the side of her forehead. *Food.* Of course. The ultimate icebreaker. "I haven't even asked if you and your grandmother have had supper yet." She glanced again at the clock on the bedside table. "If your grandmother's on a special diet, I could recommend—"

"Thanks, but we're really just fine. I noticed several fast-food places around the hotel. I'll run out and get something. I only wanted to check in with you and tell you I, uh, we've arrived and see what the plan is. Justin is the client's name?

"Yes. Justin Sadler."

"I assume Mr. Sadler wants to meet tomorrow and not tonight?"

*Mr. Sadler.* Not once since Debbie Sue had met Justin had she thought of him as *Mr. Sadler.* "I told him we'd come out to his place tomorrow morning around ten o'clock, if that's all right with you. He's located between Salt Lick and Odessa. Did you rent a car with GPS?"

"Absolutely. I've never been in the area before. I don't think even psychic help could keep me from getting lost. There are so few landmarks."

"I know. Just lots of blue sky. The GPS will help you get to Salt Lick, but I doubt it'll find an unmarked country road.

Got some paper handy? You need to write these directions down."

Debbie Sue spoke slowly, allowing Sophia to write and read back the instructions. "You can't miss the turnoff. Coming from Odessa, it'll be on your left. The cattle guard has a rock stanchion on each side. One has an American flag on top of it and the other has a Texas flag. Like I said, you can't miss it. The house is a ways back from the gate."

"Super. Will you and Edwina be meeting me, er, us at the gate?"

"We hadn't planned on it. Do you want us to meet you there?"

"If you don't mind I'd rather talk to the two of you first . . . alone."

*Uh-oh.* Why had she added the last word as an after-thought? "Uh, sure, we can do that. Nine thirty?"

"Nine thirty is perfect. See you then."

Sophia disconnected. Debbie Sue glanced up at Buddy as he re-entered the room.

"You look confused," he said. "Is something wrong?"

"That was the granddaughter of the woman who's gonna meet with Justin Sadler. She wants to talk to Edwina and me first. Alone. I've got a funny feeling."

"Really?" He slid toward her atop the bed covers, encircled her in his arms and pulled her close to him. "Maybe you've developed ESP yourself."

Debbie Sue giggled and combed her fingers through his thick black hair. "Maybe I have. For example, right now, I can't explain it, but I can tell you what you're up to." She pressed her body against his.

"You can?"

"You're gonna have your way with me, aren't you?"

"That's amazing. I thought I was gonna keep rubbing your feet, but now that I think about it, you're right. You're just amazing, my sweet girl." He nuzzled her neck and said softly, "Amazing."

The gray of dawn lightened Sophia's hotel room. All night, every one hundred and twenty minutes, she had awakened worrying over what it would mean for her if this Justin Sadler decided to send her packing. She had no contract with him, real or implied. She hadn't even spoken directly to him. When he discovered she was not her grandmother, he could easily tell her to take a hike.

And if he did, hike was frightfully close to what she would have to do—right back to El Paso. She had no guarantee of the support of the Domestic Equalizers either, once they discovered she was an imposter. She could only hope Mr. Sadler, or someone, would reimburse her the expenses she had incurred to date.

This trip could have a grim outcome, very grim indeed.

She surrendered the fight for sleep. It wasn't going to happen. She feared if she let herself finally doze, she would sink into the deep sleep she had wished for all night and miss her appointment with the two detectives. The green digital number in the clock radio showed 6:00 A.M. Close enough to her meeting time to give in and just get up. Frustrated, she threw back the covers.

With the luxury of extra time and no worry about the cost of utilities, she pressed the down arrow on the air conditioner even further and moved to the shower. A long, warm luxurious shower with complimentary soaps and shampoos was just what she needed.

Twenty minutes later she emerged from the bathroom wrapped in a towel. She pawed through her makeup bag and found a bottle of after-shower lotion, then sat on the edge of the bed, slathering the rich cream on her brown arms, legs and feet.

She was lucky, so her girlfriends at home told her repeatedly. She had an effortless year-round tan, courtesy of her father's genes. Even on the rare occasions when she sunburned, the discomfort was gone the next day and she had an even deeper golden color to her skin. Though her friends told her they envied her, she viewed the ivory-skinned princesses with the same envy.

She put on her underwear, then took a wide-tooth comb to her thick mane. It would be hours drying on its own, but she decided to let it do that. She had forgotten to pack her Sedu hair dryer, an expensive accessory someone with her thick, coarse hair couldn't afford to be without. The alternate choice was the hotel's wall-mounted dryer, which would leave her with not only a tired arm for her effort, but hair that expanded in volume to the point of being comical.

Besides jeans, she had brought a blue denim skirt and a

simple white scoop-neck T-shirt with her. The skirt hit just above the knees. Not too short, but short enough to be cooler than long pants. A few swipes and brushes of cosmetics and her makeup was done. She hooked thong sandals between her toes and studied herself in the mirror. A half-Mexican, half-Anglo, demure, non-threatening young woman was what she saw, which was what she strived for, for that was what she was.

Last, she put on her jewelry, something she loved and took great pride in wearing. Gran Bella, in her youth, had acquired wonderful antique sterling-silver pieces from the Mexican mining town of Taxco. Upon Sophia's graduation from college, Gran Bella had given her the jewelry.

A well-meaning friend, upon hearing Sophia lament the desperate state of her finances, had suggested she sell the jewelry. The Southwest style was high fashion and some of the jewelry pieces were originals signed by the artist. No doubt they would bring a premium price. But Sophia would never sell her grandmother's jewelry, no matter how desperate things became.

Shiny, hammered silver hoops hung from her earlobes. Two large silver-and-turquoise rings circled the ring fingers of each of her hands, and half a dozen silver bracelets with textures from rough hewn to smooth as glass ringed her left wrist. A silver Virgin Mary dangled from a thread-thin chain of tiny turquoise stones around her neck. The details of the pendant had been worn almost smooth by years of Gran Bella's fingers rubbing it.

Everything in place, she looked again at the clock on the

bedside table and groaned. Not much more than an hour had passed. She thought she had surely drawn out the morning routine beyond that.

Her room reeked of Mexican spices and onions, thanks to her run to Taco Bell the evening before. The sack of food had met her hunger needs last night and this morning the smell aroused her appetite again. Her thoughts turned to breakfast. She would take advantage of the free meal off the hotel's tiny lobby. Maybe she would find a newspaper someone had left behind with an unfinished crossword or a sudoku puzzle. She could spend time on that, then she would drive slowly and take in the city of Odessa. And if worse came to worse, she would simply go to the meeting place and wait at the gate for the Domestic Equalizers.

*See, querida?* a voice said inside her head. *There is a solution for even the smallest of problems.*

Sophia left the hotel room in good spirits. The breakfast was passable, but there was no newspaper. Even driving slowly she figured she could kill maybe half an hour. Accepting that she would just have to arrive early and wait, she again read the directions Debbie Sue had given her and turned the car southwest toward Salt Lick.

Before she knew it the two stanchions with the flags mounted on top came into her sight. The drive on a sunny morning in virtually no traffic had relaxed her and after having little sleep she began to nod. She came to a stop on the side of the road, buzzed down the windows and turned the engine off. She leaned her head against the driver's seat headrest and drifted to sleep in seconds.

★ ★ ★

Justin hurried from the convenience store a couple of miles from his house with the coffee filters he had bought in case Debbie Sue and Edwina and the psychic wanted coffee. A tiny white car he didn't recognize was parked near his gate on the shoulder of the county road.

He could see the silhouette of a person inside.

He came to a stop behind the car, but the person didn't move. He stepped out of his truck and walked up to the door. The window was open and he saw a woman asleep behind the wheel . . . And she was young and beautiful.

She appeared to be Hispanic, just what his captain had suggested he seek on the sunny beaches of Mexico. But what was she doing here, parked on the side of the county road? Maybe she had run out of gas, but then why would she be sleeping?

He leaned closer to assure that she was breathing and took a few more seconds to just look at her. Then he stopped himself. What was wrong with him? Less than twenty-four hours ago he had been crying out to his departed wife to re-enter his life and make him whole again. This woman being parked here and annoyance at his own thoughts turned his mood to downright surly.

A rapping against her car door and a male voice startled Sophia awake. "Hey, lady? Miss, are you all right? Ma'am?"

Raising her head from its resting spot, Sophia peered at dark sunglasses on the face of a man. Her first impression was that he was handsome. "I'm waiting for someone—"

"Parking here like this is dangerous," he said sternly. "What if I'd been a hitchhiker and liked the looks of your, uh . . . your, uh, car? . . . Have you been drinking?"

His attitude brought her defenses forward. "Excuse me? You are *not* the law, are you?"

"Indirectly, yeah. I'm a firefighter and EMT."

"I haven't broken any laws. I don't think you have any right to ask me questions."

"Look, you're a beautiful woman. God knows who you might attract sitting here alone like this on the side of the road. Beyond that, I've gone to plenty of accident sites where people were parked on the side of the road and got rear-ended. Just a whole lot of them have been killed or crippled."

"I only closed my eyes for—"

"A few minutes," he said finishing her sentence for her. "Yeah, I hear that all the time too."

"You're being very—"

"Rude? Mean? Nasty?"

Sophia's seldom-aroused temper began to rise. "Sir, why do you keep interrupting me and putting words into my mouth?"

"If I don't wake you up and shock some sense into you, me or somebody else could be putting a *breathing* tube into your mouth."

The message hit home and Sophia softened. After all, he was only trying to help and his advice was wise. "I'm sorry. I wasn't thinking."

"Apparently not. Do me and yourself a favor. Pull your car inside that gate and wait for your friends." He gestured toward the other side of the cattle guard. "You'll at least be off the road."

Without another word he turned and stomped back to a pickup parked behind her rental car. He drove around her, through the gate and up a long caliche road without a backward glance, churning dirt and caliche behind him. Sophia watched him in stunned silence. In a matter of seconds he was out of sight.

"Jerk," she muttered, but she started the engine, obediently eased across the cattle guard and parked just inside the gate.

His display of anger continued to disturb her. She should have offered her right hand. People rarely rejected a handshake. Touching him might have at least given her some insight into his psyche. There was a reason why this handsome-looking man was so mean inside. But he had hardly given her the opportunity to shake hands or even say much. She sighed, willing the incident out of her mind. She doubted she would ever see him again.

But as her eyes focused on the road the stranger's pickup had taken, a familiar voice came to her: *Do not be so quick to judge, Sophia.*

*He did call you beautiful.*

Justin watched in his rearview mirror. He couldn't tell if the woman had moved her car as he had instructed, but there would be a rise in the driveway soon that would give him a perfect view. If he saw she hadn't left the county road's shoulder, he might just go back and move her himself.

His reaction to the potential danger wasn't out of the ordinary for him. Jumping into the role of mega-hero wasn't new for him either. But what *was* new—and unsettling—was how the young woman in the car had affected him. His reaction had been sexual and raw and he felt ashamed. He smacked his head with the heel of his hand. *God, did I just call her beautiful? What would Rachel think?*

# eleven

*F*orgodsake, Ed," Debbie Sue grumbled, "we're gonna meet an old lady from El Paso, not the Pope." Sitting in her pickup in front of Edwina and Vic's cream-with-powder-blue-trim mobile home, big engine idling and wasting gas, she tapped her horn for the second time.

It was Saturday morning and they had accomplished a miracle in re-scheduling their salon customers for the day. Debbie Sue had already wasted enough of the bonus time squeezing into her Wranglers; she wanted to waste no more.

She still hadn't figured out the necessity for her and Edwina to meet with Isabella Paredes and her granddaughter, but she was willing to go along rather than make waves. Besides, they were killing two birds with one stone, so to

speak. They had already told Justin they would install surveillance equipment today.

Toward the end, in the backseat of the pickup were a
couple of motion-sensitive cameras that could blend into any
décor and capture a picture of any human who crossed its
eye, as well as an innocuous hardbound book that was, in
reality, a motion-activated DVR. The book's title, *How To
Do Home Plumbing Projects*, was sure to be ignored by most
people who saw it.

Over the past few years, as their funds had allowed, the
Domestic Equalizers had accumulated gadgets of varying
levels of sophistication, including an eavesdropping device
they had acquired in New York City. Some of their equipment was already outdated. It seemed that one device had
no sooner been paid off before another came on line with
the promise of being better, quicker, quieter and unfortunately, most times, cheaper. Debbie Sue longed for newer
and better equipment, but as difficult as keeping up with
current technology was, neither she nor Edwina was excited
about spending Styling Station funds on equipment for the
Domestic Equalizers to use. The beauty salon was still their
bread and butter.

Debbie Sue kept her complaints about their equipment
to a minimum. Even outdated stuff beat none at all. And it
sure beat sitting and waiting for hours on end eyeballing a
subject or the haphazard method of putting a watch under a
tire to be crushed when the vehicle moved, forever freezing
the time of its departure.

After agreeing to work for Justin, Debbie Sue had done her homework online and learned the devices ghost hunters used—infrared thermometers, ion counters and/or electromagnetic field detectors, things that were too costly to consider. She was glad to leave ghosts and the spirit world to Sophia and let the Domestic Equalizers concentrate on earthbound subjects known as humans.

The double-wide's screen door opened and closed again, giving her hope that Edwina was on the way out.

Minutes later, Debbie Sue had her hand on her pickup's door latch, set to march into the mobile and hurry Edwina up, when the skinny brunette appeared wearing bright yellow jeans and some kind of white, floaty tunic top with a huge turquoise-and-yellow floral pattern. She was typically accessorized—enormous earrings, a black-and-white cowhide purse the size of a third-world country, half a dozen bangle bracelets clicking on each wrist, makeup worthy of a beauty pageant queen and in one hand, a Sonic Route 44 Dr Pepper. If the locals who knew her saw her any other way, they would think she was ill. Debbie Sue sighed and watched her gingerly make her way down the five wooden steps that led from a small wooden porch attached to the double-wide.

To take those steps any way other than carefully would be irresponsible, because the woman was wearing three-inch wedge heels on size-ten feet. The shoes could easily be described as her trademark since she was rarely seen wearing any style but that one.

Edwina climbed into the pickup and plopped onto the passenger seat. She deposited her belongings, reached for the seat belt, buckled it snugly and heaved a great breath. "What are we waiting for, Dippity-Do? Let's get this show on the road."

Debbie Sue knew debating the number of minutes she had been waiting would be pointless. She rarely won an argument with Edwina. Not because she was always wrong, but because she usually wearied of trying to sort out some of Edwina's logic and gave up.

She slowly backed out of the caliche driveway to avoid spraying the area with dirt and dust. "What's Vic doing today, working on his bike?"

"Lord, yes. Since he got that damn motorcycle he's become obsessed with getting it in top shape and meeting his old navy pals at Terlingua again. What about Buddy, is he home?"

"He started work on the deck on the back of the house. He was so eager to get at it, we didn't even eat breakfast. I'm surprised at how well he's doing. He's never built anything in his life."

"Wait!" Edwina threw her arm across the cab and struck Debbie Sue's shoulder. "I forgot something!"

"No. You. Did. Not." Debbie Sue put firm emphasis on each word. "I've used a quarter tank of gas waiting for you."

"Well you could've turned off your motor."

"Ed. Whatever it is, if you don't have it now, you're not going to." She cast an eye at Edwina's purse. "Besides, you've got everything in the world in that overnight case you call a purse."

"But—"

"Forget it, Ed. We're already late. I've gotta drive like a bat out of hell to get to Justin's on time." Debbie Sue steered her pickup toward a left entrance to the Odessa highway. Looking over her shoulder, she pressed the accelerator and the pickup's engine responded. "I'm starving. I was hoping we'd have time to run through Hogg's drive-thru and grab some breakfast, but too late for that."

They rode without talking all the way through Big & Rich booming from the radio with "Save a Horse (Ride a Cowboy)." When the commercials began, Debbie Sue turned down the radio. "What were you doing, anyway? I was beginning to think you'd backed out on me, that you'd changed your mind about meeting this psychic."

Edwina crossed her arms over her flat chest, lifted her nose and sniffed as if she were offended. "I was fixing your breakfast. Unlike some people I know, Vic and I *did* have breakfast. Sausage patties and Vic's homemade biscuits and cream gravy. I was putting a sausage patty dipped in gravy between a biscuit for you. And a Styrofoam cup of fresh-brewed coffee. I was putting it all in a sack, but I set it down when I had to hurry up and grab my purse. I didn't pick it up again."

Debbie Sue gasped and stared agape at Edwina's profile. She really was hungry and no one made better biscuits or gravy than Vic. "Ed, dammit, why didn't you tell me?"

"I just did tell you."

They made the rest of the trip without talking, with Edwina staring straight ahead, arms crossed over her chest and Debbie Sue mentally snarling and gnashing her teeth. She turned up the radio, needing to be calmed by George Strait's sweet voice crooning "How 'Bout Them Cowgirls."

As they approached Justin's cattle guard, Debbie Sue saw a white economy car parked just inside the gate, to the side and away from the driveway. "Guess that's them."

"I only see one person," Edwina said, leaning forward and squinting.

"Me too. And she looks young. Didn't you say Isabella Paredes is old?

"Older than I am. Hell. She's older than my mother.

"Maybe she's laying down in the backseat."

"What backseat? Hell. Maybe she's dead."

"Ed, don't say that."

"Sorry. You know I'm kidding. What I can remember about her is that she's a pretty small woman. That was fifteen or so years ago. Maybe she's shrunk some more."

"Now that's entirely possible. Just look at Maudeen. If she gets any smaller she'll just disappear."

"Oops, I think she's spotted us." Edwina hunkered down. "Don't pull up beside them on my side. I don't want to be the closest. She might remember me. You talk to them."

"Oh, Ed, she isn't gonna remember you after fifteen years. You said you only saw her the one time. But I don't mind doing the talking."

Stopping within a few feet of the car, Debbie Sue killed her pickup motor, slid out of the cab and started walking toward the white car. "Sophia?"

The driver's door opened and the woman got out. "Yes. Debbie Sue?"

Sophia was a girl, almost a kid, Debbie Sue determined. Couldn't be more than twenty-five years old. "Nice to finally meet you." Debbie Sue glanced into the car's interior, but spotted no other occupant. "I don't see your grandmother."

Sophia shifted her stance, pushed her hair back and bit her lower lip.

Debbie Sue was proud of the fact that since she had become a hairdresser, she had also become "bilingual." Thanks to her experience listening daily to women and their ups and downs—and a few men—she understood body language as well as she understood English. She had no trouble translating that this girl was nervous. Something was terribly wrong. Maybe the older woman was sick. Hell. Maybe she *was* dead, just like Edwina had said. "I hope she isn't ill."

When Sophia didn't reply, Debbie Sue tilted her head and narrowed her eyes, studying the girl's face. "Sophia?"

Sophia began talking in a gush, spilling a story of the recent loss of her grandmother. She wept intermittently, stopping occasionally to dab at her eyes with her fingers.

*Fuck!*

As Sophia talked, concern for Justin Sadler and his money grew in Debbie Sue's mind and she hated that she had recommended to him that he pay this woman's travel expenses. Debbie Sue listened without interrupting, mostly because her brain was scrabbling for what to do next. She glanced over her shoulder once to reassure herself that her partner was still seated in the pickup. If Edwina heard what was going on with Sophia, she might have one of her fits. Dealing with one person having a meltdown and bawling was hard enough. She didn't need one of Edwina's fits on top of it.

Debbie Sue dug deep and struggled for genuine sincerity. "I'm sorry for your loss, Sophia. But why didn't you tell me this when I called you the first time?"

"I was looking for a second job when you called," Sophia said. "I'm broke. It took every cent I had just to make this trip. I don't want to sound like I'm whining, but Gran Bella was ill for such a long time. Between the medical bills and the funeral expenses—"

"And now you want to pass yourself off as a physic," Debbie Sue said dully. "And you expect me and my partner to back you up."

The girl's eyes widened, as if she was alarmed. "Oh, no. I'd never do anything deceitful."

Debbie Sue's mouth twisted into a horseshoe scowl. "With all due respect to your grandmother's departure, that's exactly what you've already done."

Sophia broke into tears again. "I knew if I told you over the phone, you wouldn't give me the chance to prove myself." She walked over to the car, reached inside and brought out a purse. She dug inside it, came up with a tissue, blew her nose and dabbed at her eyes again. "I swear, I have the same psychic powers my Gran Bella had. I've just never used them, uh . . . *commercially* before. I do need the money, but it's more than that. I honestly believe I can help your client."

Debbie Sue had never trusted a liar. That fact alone had done more to destroy her former engagement to Quint Matthews than any other. She couldn't keep from shaking her head. "Well, I don't know. I probably should consult my partner."

"Please, Debbie Sue. I'm begging you to just give me a chance."

"I don't know," Debbie Sue said again. "Justin Sadler's already skeptical. He agreed to this because my partner and I recommended it. It's a lot of money."

"Debbie Sue, please. It took every cent I had to make this trip. But look, if he doesn't think I can help, I won't ask him to reimburse me a dime."

Debbie Sue tilted her head and studied Sophia's face. Except for her swollen eyes and reddened nose from crying, she looked innocent enough. "You're that sure of yourself?"

"Yes, I am," she said firmly.

"What's going on?" A voice behind them called out. Debbie Sue turned and saw Edwina's head poking out the pickup's window. She opened the door and stood on the running board, holding on to the door for support and at the same time trying to tie a scarf over her beehive hairdo.

Debbie Sue walked back to the pickup and spoke quietly to Edwina. "Ed, the grandmother really is dead, just like you said. We might be fucked."

Edwina's stare came at Debbie Sue like a heat blast. A full thirty seconds passed. "Well, do-dah, do-dah," she finally said, a singsong inflection in her tone. "I hope there's another chorus to that song."

A gust of wind yanked the scarf from her hand and sent it airborne. Edwina grabbed for it but missed, hooking her other arm over the door frame to keep from falling off the running board. "Well, shit. There goes my good silk scarf."

Sophia couldn't hear the conversation between Debbie Sue and Edwina. As she watched and waited for Debbie Sue to return, the partner's scarf floated toward Sophia. The wind abated for a moment and the scarf fluttered to the ground at Sophia's feet. She bent and picked it up and rubbed the cool fabric between her fingers. Instantly a vision appeared in her mind, like a photo plucked from the pages of a family album. A dark-haired child sat opposite a grown woman, with a checkerboard between them. Sophia saw that she herself was that child and even more remarkably, the woman playing checkers with her was none other than the one who had lost the scarf, Debbie Sue's partner.

Startled by the information, Sophia swung her attention to the partner. She had looked almost exactly the same in Sophia's vision from fifteen years ago as she looked today. Coal-black hair in a beehive hairdo, cat-eye glasses, flamboyant dress. She was tall and thin as a rail. Time had neither subtracted nor added much to her appearance.

Smiling, Sophia called out, "Edwina, hi. Do you remember that day years ago when we played checkers? You never did let me put a crown on your king. I hope Vic treats you better than your husband did back then."

Sophia had expected a reaction. Who wouldn't in the same situation? But she had not counted on the racket that came. The scarf's owner let out a shriek that could wake the dead and drive dogs into frenzy throughout the surrounding area. Then she ducked back into the big red pickup and slammed the door with a loud *whump.*

A shiver zoomed up Debbie Sue's spine. "Jesus Christ," she whispered. She shot a stunned look toward Sophia, her mind scrambling for a logical interpretation of what Sophia had just said. She tapped on the pickup window. "Ed, buzz down the window."

The tinted power window slid down three inches. All Debbie Sue could see was Edwina's eyes.

"Let's get out of here, Debbie Sue," Edwina said, her voice coming through the window with a quiver. "I told you earlier—"

"Now you listen to me," Debbie Sue stage whispered. "You're the one who thought we should call this psychic person to come here. Far be it from me to point out that you're making an ass of yourself."

"I don't care," Edwina said. "I deny everything."

Debbie Sue pointed toward Sophia. "That girl *remembered* you, Ed. That's all. She *remembered* you from fifteen years ago. Hell. Maybe she's just got a good memory." But as Debbie Sue said that, she wondered if it was even possible. "You probably haven't changed one damn bit," she continued. "Not to mention that if you took the news from her grandmother about Jimmy Wayne and that money in his boot as well as you've taken what you *think* you heard just now, I'd say you made a definite impression on her."

The window lowered another three inches. "Okay," Edwina whispered, "I'll admit she might remember me, but how did she know about Vic?"

"I don't know. But I'm sure there's a perfectly logical explanation." But Debbie Sue continued to wonder.

"Bullshit," Edwina said. "That kid must've inherited that mystic shit from her grandmother."

Debbie Sue sighed heavily. "You don't have to whisper, Ed. She can't hear you."

"How do you know? I'm not budging from this pickup, Miss Smarty Pants, until you give me a good explanation for how she even knows Vic's name."

"Hell, I don't know, Ed. Maybe she Googled the Domestic Equalizers on the Internet. I don't doubt she did because she would've wanted to check us out. I'm sure she found our bios, which include who we're married to. Especially the one you submitted. You told everything about yourself. You practically told your and Vic's favorite sex position."

"I did not. What I said was—"

"Stop." Debbie Sue lifted a palm. "I don't want to talk about it. The point I'm trying to make is it's not hard to find out information about us."

"I'm not buying it. What if she doesn't have access to the Internet?"

"Well I'm pretty sure she reads, Ed. She *is* a schoolteacher and *Texas Monthly* did do a real nice article on us, if you recall, including the mention of Buddy and Vic. And it *is* on the Internet."

Debbie Sue expected more of the window would slide down but instead she heard the pop of the door latch releasing. Edwina gingerly opened her door and looked at Debbie Sue sheepishly. "I feel like a turd."

Debbie Sue reached out and rubbed her friend's right arm soothingly. "Aw, I'm sorry. Would it make you feel better if I said you *look* like one, too?"

The beginning of a grin twitched at the corner of Edwina's mouth.

Finally she broke into laughter. "Oh, hell, yes. Please do."

"Great. Now let's go see if we can salvage this situation before it turns into a regular goat-fuck."

# twelve

Sophia mustered what she hoped was an engaging smile as the two women came toward her. In her vision, she hadn't seen exactly how tall and slender the one named Edwina was. Five ten, Sophia guessed. Sometimes the visions were a little scarce on detail.

At this moment, she deduced that Edwina was psychic-phobic. Many were and it was best to know that up front. Sophia would have to be mindful of Edwina's fears. Gran Bella had taught her to never reveal unsolicited information unless a person's well being was at stake. So Sophia saw no point in telling Edwina all she had seen in that brief moment when she had held Edwina's scarf in her hand. Truth be known, Sophia was having some trouble believing it herself.

Debbie Sue started by introducing her partner. Sophia didn't let on that she already knew Edwina in ways Debbie Sue probably didn't.

"Look, Sophia," Debbie Sue said. "I've said all I'm going to on your behalf to Justin Sadler. I warn you, he's gonna be a hard sell."

"Right," Edwina said from behind Debbie Sue's shoulder. "Justin doesn't believe in psychics."

Sophia almost sighed with relief. At least they weren't telling her to get in her car and go back home. "Oh, we aren't called psychics these days. That's a word that conjures up images of mysterious women wrapped in head scarves and speaking mumbo-jumbo over a crystal ball."

"You mean you don't do that?" Edwina asked.

"These days, those of us who have the gift prefer to be called mentalists. My grandmother was called all kinds of things, many of them disrespectful, but she paid them no mind. I would like it if you call me a mentalist."

"Okay," Debbie Sue said, ignoring her partner and raising her palms in a gesture of surrender. "Mentalist. Call yourself anything you want to. All we care about is your being honest. We have to think of our client's best interest. But I'll keep my mouth shut and give you a chance to convince him you're the real deal."

Sophia realized her honesty was questionable, since she had already lied to them. "Oh, thank you so much. I promise I am honest."

"Okay, then. I guess we can go on up to the house. Justin should be expecting us." Debbie Sue turned and started back to her big red pickup. Even psychic powers wouldn't permit Sophia to imagine how it would feel to drive such a huge pickup truck.

"You go first," Debbie Sue said over her shoulder. "If you follow me you won't be able to see for the dust. Just drive on up this road. It really isn't a road. It's really Justin's driveway."

Sophia felt her stomach dip. Was Justin the man who had scolded her earlier?

"After about a mile there'll be a split in the road," Debbie Sue said, gesturing with her hands. "Stay to the left and you'll drive right up to the house. We'll be behind you."

"I understand," Sophia called back to her and slid into her car.

Debbie Sue watched and waited for Sophia to slowly move forward. "You can come out from behind me, Ed," she said.

"I wasn't behind you," Edwina snapped indignantly.

"Let's go." Debbie Sue climbed behind the steering wheel. Edwina fumbled into the passenger seat and settled and adjusted the floaty garment she was wearing. "I don't know about you," Debbie Sue said, following Sophia's car, "but all of a sudden, I've got a bad feeling about this."

"I'd just as soon not talk about feelings, thank you very much. I'm more nervous than a surprise guest on *The Jerry Springer Show*."

"But it's not about you, Ed. Not everything in life is about you, you know?"

"No, I don't know. I surely don't. And furthermore,

I'll have you know everything in *my* life *is* about me. If I can hear it, see it, smell it or touch it, it's about me. If it brings a reaction *from* me, it affects *me*. So you see, it is all about me."

In some weird, convoluted way Edwina was right, Debbie Sue thought, so she didn't argue. "I feel kinda sorry for her. She's so young to be in her situation. She told me she didn't have any living relatives that she knew of or a penny to her name."

"Bless her heart. Broke and alone. That's a road I've been down so many times I've worn the rubber off my tires."

"At least she's got a good education," Debbie Sue said. "That's something no one can take away from her. She's lucky that way."

"What she needs is a good man," Edwina said. "She's heartbroken, Justin's heartbroken. What a great reason for a relationship."

Except for the fact that she was closely following Sophia to their destination, Debbie Sue would have hit her brake. She stared at her partner, making no attempt to hide her incredulity. "Good God almighty, Ed, you can't be serious. We're taking her to communicate with Justin's dead wife who he's still in love with."

"Dead wife," Edwina said. "D-E-A-D. It's not like the woman's gone shopping in Abilene or taking a long vacation in Fort Worth. She's out of the picture, Debbie Sue, permanently."

Debbie Sue frowned and bit down on her lower lip.

"God rest her soul," Edwina added.

"Ed, don't you dare try any of your matchmaking tricks with these two. You just mind your own business and let nature take its course."

"I'm a firm believer in that," Edwina said.

Sophia's car came to a stop in front of Justin's home and Debbie Sue stopped behind her. She turned to Edwina. "Well, partner, here goes nothing."

Debbie Sue slid from her seat and walked up to Sophia's car. The girl didn't seem to notice her. She sat intently staring at the black Toyota pickup parked to the side of the house. Was she in a trance? Debbie Sue wondered. She tapped on the window.

Startled, Sophia jerked her head toward her and buzzed down the window. She killed the ignition and opened the door. "Sorry, my mind was elsewhere."

"I'll say," Debbie Sue said, unable to mask the sarcasm. "I was afraid you were going to drive off. Are you nervous?"

"Very. As I told you back at the gate, I've never done this before. I've seen things in my mind all my life and I've watched my Gran Bella, but I never thought I'd step into her shoes."

"Well, look on the bright side. If things work out for you on this job, maybe you'll want to do more work as a, uh, mentalist."

"Goodness, no. The responsibility is too much. And it can be very painful. My grandmother saw to it that I got a good education to prevent this very thing from happening."

Edwina walked up. She was removing the wrapper from a piece of gum. She folded it into a compact square and popped it into her mouth. Between smacks she asked, "What's up? We going in or not?"

Debbie Sue turned to Edwina. "You're the one who's been dragging your feet all along. Now you're anxious to go?"

"I never said I was anxious to go. Just ready. There's a big difference."

Before Debbie Sue could say more, Justin's front door opened and he walked out onto the porch. "Hi, Debbie Sue, Edwina." He said nothing to Sophia, only looked at her with a puzzled expression. The slightly elevated porch gave him a height advantage and he scanned both Sophia's car and Debbie Sue's pickup several times. "Where's the older woman from El Paso?"

Smiling weakly, Debbie Sue glanced at Edwina, then Sophia, then back at Justin. "Justin, what do you say we all go inside and have a talk?"

Justin reached behind for the door handle and opened it wide for all three of them. Edwina urged Sophia to take the lead with her following. Debbie Sue, then Justin brought up the rear. Catching Debbie Sue's arm, Justin leaned toward her and whispered, "Who's that other person? I'm confused."

Debbie Sue patted his hand reassuringly. "That's okay. We're all a little confused right now. But I promise we'll get it all ironed out."

Once they were in Justin's living room, Debbie Sue said, "Justin this is Sophia Paredes. She's from El Paso. She's the granddaughter of the woman you were expecting."

Justin's upper body leaned back, his distrust blatant. "I saw her earlier on the road when I was coming back from EZ Stop. What's going on?"

"You wouldn't happen to have some coffee or some iced tea, would you?"

"Sure. Please sit down. What would everyone like? Coffee, iced tea?"

"You got any tequila?" Edwina said.

Debbie Sue shot her a murderous glare. "Ed, for chrissake, it's still morning."

"Well my nerves don't wear a wristwatch. I gotta tell all of y'all while we're here together, this is spooky as hell to me. That business with the letters on the refrigerator door just about did it for me."

"Skip the tequila, Justin," Debbie Sue said.

Sophia looked at each of them quizzically. "Letters on the refrigerator door?"

"Before we get into that," Debbie Sue said, "I think we need to explain to Justin the change in circumstances. Justin, Sophia's grandmother is Isabella Paredes, the woman I talked to you about. I just found out that she passed away a few weeks ago and Sophia has graciously come in her place."

Justin looked from one to the other. "What's that supposed to mean? I don't understand. This isn't a job I'm putting out for bids."

Debbie caught a silent breath. The edge in his tone was unmistakable. If this fell apart, not only would it be bad for Sophia, it would badly mar the Domestic Equalizers' reputation. "Justin, listen—"

"Debbie Sue, you told me this Isabella person had special abilities." Justin's head began to shake. "And now you're saying she's dead and someone else has taken her place?"

Debbie Sue rapidly explained how her phone call to Isabella had brought Sophia as a representative of her departed family member. She chose to leave out the part about Sophia being destitute and desperate for the money. No point in adding additional tension or suspicion.

When she finished, Justin stared at Sophia. Debbie Sue couldn't read his thoughts. "Have you ever done anything like this before?" he asked her. "Do you even know if you have this . . . this mysterious power? I mean, seriously. I don't want to come across as rude, but I'm not convinced this isn't a bunch of hooey and if you haven't—"

"Let's get that coffee," Edwina said. "Then we can all sit down in a circle and talk about this."

"Yeah," Justin said, seemingly relieved to be doing something normal. "I'll get it."

Debbie Sue grabbed Edwina's arm and dragged her to a seat on Justin's sofa. Sophia took a seat in a wingback chair. Justin soon returned with a tray holding mugs of steaming coffee and set them on the coffee table.

"I don't see the, uh, crystal vase," Debbie Sue said.

"I put it away," Justin said curtly, his eyes on Sophia. He didn't sit down. He crossed his arms over his chest and assumed a wide-legged stance. "I'm waiting."

After a few beats, Sophia scooted to the edge of her seat, her knees and feet tightly together, her palms coming together as if she were praying. Debbie Sue was thinking of praying herself.

"Justin, I understand your concern," Sophia said. "It's a lot of money to spend on someone you know nothing about."

Justin didn't budge. "Oh, don't worry about that. I'm not spending any money until you prove yourself. Didn't Debbie Sue explain that?"

Silence. Sophia's expressive eyes grew wide.

Debbie Sue cleared her throat. "Justin, I told her you had agreed to pay for her trip here and back to El Paso, plus any expenses while she's here. Meals and such. She usually gets her fee up front, but she understands that in this case, the fee is payable only if the results warrant it."

"That's fine," Justin said. "That's what I agreed to. Sorry to come across as a jerk, but I don't intend to be a sucker and allow a stranger with a crystal ball *or* access to the Internet coming into our . . . *my* home trying to make money from the death of my . . . my . . ." Turning away he walked to the back door and looked out, his hands stuffed into his pockets. His jaw muscles flexed. Debbie Sue feared he might break into tears.

She didn't know if Sophia would exit the room in a huff or break into tears herself. She couldn't blame her for doing either. Before she could say anything to try to make everyone feel better, the young visitor from El Paso spoke in a soft, smooth voice.

"Justin, to take advantage of your circumstances and make money from the loss of your loved one, I'd have to be willing to do the same thing to my grandmother. There's no amount of money that could make me do that. She was all I had in the world.

"The one thing I'm unable to do, Justin, is give you a guarantee. A mentalist is merely an open receptacle, a person who can sort of TiVo someone's life. Or not. I have no way of predicting when visions will come to me, or even *if* they will come. If I saw things all the time, continuously, I wouldn't be able to live in this world. I can only promise that I'll share with you what I learn, when I learn it. I wouldn't expect you to pay me if my performance doesn't meet your expectations."

"Yeah," Edwina said, picking up a mug of coffee. "That makes sense."

Justin's shoulders slumped. He ran his fingers through his hair and turned from the door, looking at the floor. "You must think I'm a real jerk."

Sophia smiled. "Oh, no. I would never think that. Your reaction is normal and you're being fiscally responsible. It was earlier this morning, on the road, that I thought you were a jerk."

Justin smiled and looked intently at Sophia. She beamed, looking back into his eyes.

Debbie Sue exchanged glances with Edwina, who was holding her coffee mug suspended as if she were mesmerized. Edwina leaned to Debbie Sue and whispered behind her hand, "What just happened here?"

Debbie Sue shook her head. "I don't know. Maybe that tequila's a good idea."

"I guess you can go ahead and do whatever it is that you do," Justin said to Sophia.

Debbie Sue breathed a sigh of pure relief. The tension in the room had dissipated. With Justin's blessing in place, she shooed him and Sophia out of the house so the Domestic Equalizers could get to work installing surveillance devices.

# thirteen

*D*ebbie Sue and Edwina stood in the living room surrounded by the cameras and audio equipment they had brought inside from the pickup.

"Where do you want to put these?" Edwina asked, holding two cameras.

Debbie Sue tapped her finger against her lower lip, giving the question some thought before answering. "Let's put one over here, near the couch. We can mount it just above this family photo. That angle should be perfect."

"And the other?"

"Well, Ed, I hate to tell you this, but I think it's got to go in the kitchen."

"That's what I figured. You put it in there. I'm not walking in that room again, ever."

Mental sigh. Debbie Sue might as well be pissing in the wind as try to explain to Edwina that if a ghost really was present in this house, it wouldn't be confined to the kitchen. It would have the freedom to be anywhere it wanted to. "No problem. Give it to me."

The minute Justin had escorted Sophia Paredes out of the house he had become uncomfortable. He hadn't been close to such a beautiful woman—or any woman near his age— since Rachel's passing. He hadn't so much as noticed another female, but he had to admit that even his Rachel had not been as striking to look at as Sophia.

They strolled across the yard, with him nervous and searching for something to say. A part of him still felt foolish for agreeing to participate in such an off-the-wall venture. Finally he hit on a subject. "Uh, want to walk out to the corral and take a look at the horses?"

"Sure," Sophia said, and they began to walk toward the corral and barn. "What are Debbie Sue and Edwina doing in the house?"

"Installing hidden surveillance equipment to see if somebody's coming in and messing with things when I'm away from home."

"Oh. I thought they might have ghost-detecting instruments."

"I don't think so." He gave an uneasy laugh. "I'm not sure any of us believe in ghosts."

"I understand," Sophia replied.

They walked in silence a few more steps. "Must be hard on your husband, your being able to read his mind."

"I don't have a husband. But even if I did, I probably couldn't read his mind. I'm not a mind reader, Justin. I know it's hard for people to understand what I have the ability to do. Sometimes I don't understand it myself."

"So if you don't have a husband," Justin said cautiously, "do you live alone?" For some reason he didn't want to hear she might live with some guy or might have a boyfriend. He chastised himself for having those thoughts.

She ducked her chin. "Yes. Until my grandmother passed away a few weeks ago, I lived with her."

Justin heard sadness in her reply. He only hoped she wouldn't cry. He might not be able to handle her tears. "So then, uh, do you make your living, uh . . . fortune-telling?" The question was the best change of subject he could come up with.

She looked at him with wide hazel eyes framed by thick black lashes and he felt his pulse race a little. "I'm not a fortune-teller any more than I'm a mind reader. What I am, Justin, is an elementary schoolteacher. This past school year was my first teaching job. But if you need to attach a label to me, then call me a mentalist. Or even a spiritualist."

"Oh, sorry. I don't know the lingo exactly for people who do . . . what you do."

"I know you're doubtful and I don't blame you. If I hadn't had visions myself for many years and hadn't seen my grandmother perform miracles from the time I was a small child, I'm sure I too would be a doubter."

They had reached the corral. The horses ambled over to the fence and one snorted at Sophia. "Does that mean he likes me?" Her face broke into a smile so bright it threatened the sunshine. "I haven't been around horses much."

"They're naturally curious," Justin said.

"It's funny, yes? I was born in Texas. Most people think Texans live on horseback. But not me."

"These animals belonged to my wife," Justin said. "When she was alive, she treated them like big pets."

"Debbie Sue told me about your wife. Her name was Rachel? She's the one you want to reach out to?"

Justin was stumped for a minute as to what his answer should be to someone like Sophia. "I don't know if I believe that's possible. It's just that some things have happened . . ."

Sophia placed her small hand on his forearm and to his dismay, he found her touch comforting. "Please don't apologize for your doubts," she said. "It's the most natural thing in the world. The fact that you have opened your mind to the extrasensory possibilities reveals much about you. It shows that you loved Rachel very much. And she must have loved you. Did it ever occur to you that she might have turned her back on eternal peace to bring a message to you?"

"No. Well, yes . . . I've wondered. Maybe." God, he was babbling like a fool.

"I'm so very sorry for your loss and I only hope I can help you. I do not want to bring you more grief."

A bloated silence loomed between them. He had faced the awkwardness many times after well-meaning people expressed their condolences, as if they didn't know what to say next. Sophia's words rang more sincerely than any he had heard up to now. With her soft words and gentle touch, like a cozy blanket, an odd sense of warmth enveloped him. He couldn't remember the last time he had felt such tranquility.

Then Sophia broke the silence with a cheery voice. "Tell me what you do know about these beautiful animals. I'm a teacher, but this time I'll be your pupil."

Justin's ego lifted a little. He knew little of horses himself, but he might know more than Sophia. "Well, look," he said and managed a self-deprecating laugh. "This thing on their heads is called a halter." He reached for one of the horses' halters and brought the animal's head around to the fence. The horse snuffled at Sophia and bared its teeth.

"Oh, my goodness. I thought he liked me. Does he want to bite me?"

"No, he's, er, these are mares, so he's a she. She's just being friendly. Saying hello. Pet her nose."

Sophia delicately touched the mare's nose. "I'd forgotten their noses feel like velvet. What's her name?"

Justin scoured his memory for the names he had heard Rachel call these horses. "Uh, Maxie, I think." He was sure he had heard Rachel say Maxie, though he wasn't sure which horse it applied to. "They're registered, so they've got official names as long as my arm, but yeah, I heard Rachel call her Maxie." Justin felt a half smile tip one side of his mouth. He was enjoying himself. Now, not only did he feel like a fool; he also felt guilty.

"Oh, it would be so wonderful to know how to ride a horse. You must have been riding before you were walking."

"Well, actually, Rachel was the horsewoman."

Sophia continued to rub the mare's nose and the mare responded by nibbling at her hand.

"She'll eat out of your hand," Justin said, eager to keep this encounter and his good feeling going. "Let me get you something to feed her." He hurried into the tack room, where bags of oats were stored and scooped some into a bucket. When he returned to the fence where Sophia waited, he told her, "Just put some on your palm and hold it out for her. But keep your hand flat so she doesn't grab your fingers. She wouldn't bite you on purpose, but if she caught one of your fingers accidentally, it would hurt."

Sophia laughed and covered her mouth with her hand. "I can see that. She has such big teeth."

Justin gave her a silly grin. "All the better to bite you with."

God, what was wrong with him? He was acting like a teenager. And he felt as if he had stepped into a vortex.

With equipment tested, calibrated and set in place, Debbie Sue dusted her palms and announced, "Our work is done. Time for Sophia."

"Let's give them a few more minutes alone," Edwina said, plopping down on the sofa.

"Ed, we've talked about this already. No matchmaking."

"What matchmaking? I just need one minute to rest my tired old bones. I'm no kid, you know."

"Your bones aren't tired, Ed. You constantly use your age to your advantage. Depending on the situation, you're either too young or too old."

"Guilty," Edwina admitted. "I'll bend anything to my advantage. It's called a survival instinct."

"No, it's called bullshit," Debbie Sue said. She reached for Edwina's hand and tugged her to her feet. "C'mon, let's go."

"Can't we just wait for them to come back?"

"No, Ed. They probably went to the barn. I want to go to the barn myself. I want to take a look at those horses."

"How do you know they went to the barn?"

"Where else would they go? They're not sitting on the porch in the rocking chairs." She dragged Edwina through the front doorway and toward the barn, platform shoes and all. She spotted Justin and Sophia coming from the shed with a lead rope hooked to the halter of one of the mares.

Despite what she had told Edwina about matchmaking, Debbie Sue had to admit that Justin and Sophia were a truly beautiful couple. Justin was tall enough to cause a woman no bigger than Sophia to have to stand on tiptoe to kiss him on the nose. And Sophia, with her luxurious black hair, her big eyes and her flawless skin, looked like something right off the pages of a magazine.

Debbie Sue was sorely tempted to turn around and return to the house and leave them alone, but her own words to Edwina about matchmaking came back to haunt her.

As if reading her very thoughts, Edwina said, "They look perfect together, don't they?"

"Anyone would look perfect matched up with either one of them," Debbie Sue replied. "They're so damned pretty."

Edwina smirked. "Told you so."

"Looking good together doesn't make a perfect union. They're not even looking at each other. Hell, Ed, Quint Matthews and I *looked* good together. We even had a lot in common. But that didn't mean we were made for each other."

"I have to disagree. Other than Buddy, I can't think of a better match for you than Quint, even if he's a little prone to stray from the herd. He just needs a good woman to tug on his reins every now and then."

"A *little* prone?" Debbie Sue said, incredulous. "You're blind as you are crazy, Ed."

At the corral, Debbie said to Sophia. "Okay, kiddo, the house is all yours."

Justin gave Sophia a wary look. "Exactly what are you going to do?"

"I'm just going to feel for vibes inside the house," she said. "I'm hoping someone from the other side will speak to me."

"Yeah?"

"Hey, Justin," Debbie Sue said before he could say more to Sophia, "would you mind if I ride one of your horses?"

He opened the gate and allowed Sophia to pass through before closing it behind him. He looped the end of the lead rope over the fence rail. "No, of course not. That would be great. These are supposed to be pleasure horses, so they should be giving somebody pleasure."

Debbie Sue wanted to keep him away from the house so Sophia could do whatever she wanted in privacy. "I'll make a deal with you. Let's saddle both of them and you can ride with me while Sophia's inside the house. These sweethearts don't look too rank to me. I'll teach you the basics of riding safely."

Justin hesitated. He hadn't quite gotten around to revealing to Sophia just how little he knew about horseback riding. Finally, he agreed to accompany Debbie Sue. What choice did he have?

"Okay, then," Sophia said. "I'm going back into the house."

Justin couldn't hide the scowl that crossed his face. Now that Sophia was actually down to doing something, he didn't like it. But he had agreed to it. "That's probably a good idea," he said to Debbie Sue.

Sophia turned to Edwina. "Do you mind if I go in alone?"

"Oh, Lord, no," Edwina said. "Hon, you'd have a hard time getting me to join you. I've already told all of you that this isn't exactly my kind of fun and games."

"Edwina, I'm sorry I don't have another horse," Justin said. "If you'd rather ride with Debbie Sue, I can—"

Edwina raised both palms in a gesture of protest. "Nope, you go right ahead. I had an adventure on a horse once. After that, I vowed the only horse anybody would ever see me steering is my 'sixty-eight Mustang. Far as I'm concerned,

the fear factor in horseback riding is a close second to communicating with ghosts. I'll just sit right over there in the
yard under the shade of that sycamore tree and have a relaxing moment to myself." She plucked an iPod from her pants
pocket and freed the earphones. "I'll be just fine. Me and ol'
Merle or George will be right here when you get back."

Sophia walked back toward the house and Justin stared
after her. He suspected his doubt and even his fear was
obvious.

"Ready?" Debbie Sue asked.

"I guess so," he grumbled. "But if I'm going to learn to
ride a horse, I need to learn how to saddle one."

"Great," Debbie Sue said. "I'll show you."

As Sophia stepped onto the porch, the dog that had been resting in the shade of the eaves got up, stretched and sauntered
to meet her. She wasn't surprised that the animal took to
her. Animals had a keen sense of oneness with second-sight
powers. They, much like humans, could react with calm or
they could bolt. She smoothed her palm over the dog's head
and spoke soothingly to him. "You stay out here, boy." He
dutifully seated himself on his haunches at the doorway. She
rewarded him with another stroke to his head and ears and
walked into the house.

Standing in the small foyer, she scanned the living area.
She liked the décor. She had inherited her home in El Paso
from her grandmother. It was accented with the flavor and
bright colors of Mexico, the country of her grandmother's
origin. Justin's home was filled with ruffled curtains and

pastel floral cushions. The living room was so inviting and had such a strong woman's touch Sophia could understand why the previous occupant would be reluctant to leave it.

Walking up the hallway, she stopped and looked at photos of various sizes and shapes with images peering out from antique frames. The images in the pictures had one thing in common. They were all smiling except for one—a man in various stages of his life stood out from the others, not because of his diminutive height but because, in every picture, he frowned. Sophia traced his face with a finger. A chill raced down her spine. Something about this person was so negative, so malevolent that the glass protecting the picture failed to shield the vibes. She jerked her finger away and dug her hands deep into the pockets of her skirt. She wouldn't touch that picture again.

Moving on, she stopped at a professionally made photo of Justin and Rachel on their wedding day. Justin's wife was so much more than a radiant bride. Her beauty and the obvious affection between her and Justin brought a tear to Sophia's eye. She was about to touch the likeness when she heard something. She froze where she stood and listened intently.

The sound was voices. Definitely. Two distinct female voices. They seemed to be arguing and the sound came from what had to be one of two rooms at the end of the hall. The only other women on the property were outside and there was no way Debbie Sue and Edwina could have come into the house and walked past her in the small, narrow hallway.

Moving slowly toward the sound, she eased a partially closed door open, revealing what was obviously the master bedroom. Everything was neat and tidy. The bed was made; nothing appeared to be out of place. The female voices became louder in Sophia's head and Gran Bella's voice wasn't one of them. Then suddenly, they ceased and the room became quiet except for the barely audible roar from a rotating fan in the corner.

The hair on Sophia's forearms rose, chill bumps formed. No question, spirits were here. "Ladies," Sophia said softly, "don't let me stop you. My name is Sophia, I'm just looking around. Go right on with what you were saying." Sophia moved stealthily through the bedroom.

At first, only one voice resumed, whispering in hushed, urgent tones. Then the second voice spoke with frantic inflection. They were arguing! Sophia would give anything to know the reason for the disagreement, but she could only make out a word or two.

Taking a seat on the edge of the bed, she closed her eyes and placed her palms on her cheeks, concentrating and listening. The intensity of the argument increased. Unexpectedly, the bedroom door slammed with an enormous force, making Sophia jump. A throw pillow bounced off the bed onto the floor. Then the argument stopped and the spirits seemed to be gone. Breathing hard, Sophia clasped her palm to her chest. She had no idea how long she had sat there.

She gathered herself, rose on shaky knees, then moved back through the house, out the doorway to the outside. Looking toward the barn, she realized her timing had been perfect. Debbie Sue and Justin were unsaddling the horses. Edwina was walking toward them, at the same time putting her earphones and iPod back in her pocket. Normal. Everything looked very normal.

Leaving the shade of the porch, she approached them.

Debbie Sue came out of the tack room and met her. "Did anything happen when you were in there?"

Sophia managed a faint smile. "We should get everyone together."

Debbie Sue called out to Justin and Edwina. "Y'all come on over here. Sophia has something to say."

Given the floor, Sophia drew a deep breath and placed her hand on her trembling stomach. "I don't know if this is helpful, but in the master bedroom, I heard two women whispering, but I couldn't *see* them. They were in a heated argument, but I couldn't clearly make out the conversation. Just a word or two every now and then and the words didn't really make sense."

"Whoa," Debbie Sue said and tucked back her chin. "Are you sure?"

Justin's face paled.

"Holy shit." Edwina said. "Oh, my God." She placed a comforting hand on Justin's shoulder. "Bless your heart, you're pale, hon. But that's okay. Hearing something like that could take the wind out anybody's sails."

"You couldn't tell what they were arguing about?" Debbie Sue asked.

"I'm not sure," Sophia answered, her brow knit. She turned to Justin. "Was any of Rachel's jewelry ever stolen or did she ever have a disagreement with someone about her jewelry?"

Justin frowned in thought for several seconds. Finally he said, "No, no, I can't think of anything like that ever happening. Why? What did you hear?"

"The words I heard were 'big pearl' and 'little pearl.'"

A Richter-scale-registering shriek pierced the air. Edwina dashed for Debbie Sue's big pickup, her arms frantically waving. She yanked the passenger door open and tried to climb inside, but the toe of her tall shoe caught on the threshold and she fell forward across the seat. She up-righted herself and scrambled into the pickup. The next sound they heard was the pronounced slam of the door and the click of it locking.

# fourteen

*J*ustin was confused. The report of two women's voices, the discussion of pearls, Edwina's response—what did any of it have to do with him or Rachel?

Debbie Sue had left him and Sophia, gone over to her truck and promised Edwina that she intended to call OnStar if the woman didn't unlock the truck door. Debbie Sue was now counting to ten. At the count of nine, the door opened and Edwina slid out.

Justin excused himself from Sophia and walked over to Debbie Sue's truck just in time to hear Edwina bark, "Don't you try and explain this away, Debbie Sue." Justin had assumed Edwina was in big trouble with her partner, but she was far from being contrite and apologetic for her hysterics. "I don't see any way possible you're going to make me feel better," she said to Debbie Sue. "Those two damn women made my life miserable before and they'll do it again."

"Ed, dammit, lower your voice," Debbie Sue said. Then she smiled and waved at Sophia, who was still standing at the corral.

Edwina sounded as if she knew the people whose voices Sophia claimed to have heard. "You're acquainted with the women Sophia was talking about?" Justin asked her. "How?"

"There is a perfectly logical answer to that question," Debbie Sue said.

"I think I'd like to hear it," Justin said. "After all, it's my house where this so-called argument took place."

Debbie Sue outlined a story of how fifteen years earlier, Edwina had come to know of the Paredes family in the first place—the young granddaughter, Sophia, whom Edwina had played checkers with; Edwina's mother-in-law, Little Pearl and Little Pearl's mother, Pearl. "If you ask me," Debbie Sue concluded confidently, "Sophia's only remembering things from her childhood. Edwina's hysterics probably jarred loose memories the poor kid suppressed long ago."

"Are you saying Sophia's a fake?" Justin asked, his patience shrinking.

"I wouldn't go that far. I think she genuinely wants to help and might even have the gift, but so far, everything I've seen has a logical explanation."

"I am so damn tired of that word *logical*," Edwina said.

"Then what is the lo—What's the explanation?" Justin asked.

Before Debbie Sue could answer, Edwina said, "But how

did she know Little Pearl and Big Pearl were dead, huh? Just tell me that."

"Ed, didn't you say yourself that right up until Little Pearl died she went regularly to see Isabella Paredes?"

"She did. I know because she kept in touch. My youngest daughter, Jimmie Sue, was her only grandkid. Little Pearl wanted to be a good grandma to her. Plus, she liked to give me hell every chance she got. She never believed the stories I told her about Jimmy Wayne. She told me right to my face that it was always the woman's fault when a man strayed. The bitch."

Justin had a distinct feeling of losing control of the situation. Were these women as dingy as they appeared to be? "So at best, you're calling this whole thing questionable?" he asked cautiously.

"That's what I believe," Debbie Sue answered, "but at the same time I sure don't want to think it's something Sophia came up with intentionally."

Striving for damage control and placing himself in a position so as not to spend any more money needlessly, he said, "I have nothing against Sophia personally, but like I told y'all earlier, she has to prove herself. And so far I haven't seen anything to make me a believer in this psychic stuff. Or to make me want to spend three thousand dollars." He glanced at Edwina, whose focus was volleying between the house and Sophia.

"A long time ago, when I was quitting smoking," the brunette said, waggling her hand and clacking a bunch of bracelets on her wrist, "I did some reading on this whole clairvoyance thing. ESP, mediums—"

"This is true about the reading part," Debbie Sue interjected. "When Ed was trying to give up cigarettes, she read everything in front of her, whether it needed it or not. She single-handedly kept a whole bookstore in business."

Justin was certain that had to be an exaggeration. He was rapidly losing confidence in the Domestic Equalizers.

"Did you know that these psychic people don't communicate with only the dead?" Edwina said. "They talk to the living, too, by reading their thoughts, same as with spirits."

"And?" Debbie Sue prompted.

"And there's a good likelihood Sophia knows what we're talking about right this minute. Keeping our voices low isn't keeping anything a secret from her."

Justin turned and looked at Sophia for several seconds. "If she really has the power," he said.

Sophia patiently watched Justin and the Domestic Equalizers. They could only be discussing Edwina's dramatic behavior. Luckily, Gran Bella had taught her to not take disbelief on the part of others as a personal insult. For people to admit to the existence of something of which they had no knowledge or had denied their entire lives meant their thinking had undergone a catastrophic change. Doors had opened into venues that were frightening to them. For any medium to try to argue the point or flaunt his or her abilities accomplished nothing. Time and events, more often than not, established a good mentalist's capabilities and made believers out of the skeptics.

Something about the mention of jewelry and pearls was what had sent Edwina into a frenzy. This unexpected development hadn't been helpful at all. In fact, it might have caused some harm. Sophia would have to go more slowly next time with her revelations.

Her next report, she decided, would be so rock solid, so earth shattering, no one would be able to question her. *I'm learning, Gran Bella, I'm learning.*

The threesome was looking at her now, not speaking or moving, just staring. Then they came in her direction, with Debbie Sue in front. Debbie Sue was obviously the leader and the more aggressive of the two Domestic Equalizers.

"Sophia, do you remember the woman Ed was with the first time she came to your home? She was a regular of your grandmother's."

Ah, so this was the foundation of Edwina's hysterics. Sophia remembered clearly now—Little Pearl Perkins and her mother, Big Pearl. Those two were the women she had heard arguing in the bedroom in Justin's house. "Yes. I think it was . . . " She deliberately paused for effect. "Was it Little Pearl? I remember thinking those were such funny names."

Visibly relieved, Edwina shouted, "Yes! You *do* remember." She pressed the back of a skinny hand to her forehead. Thank God."

"I'm sorry," Sophia said, "I don't understand."

"We think," Debbie Sue said, "that perhaps that knowledge of Edwina's past might have clouded your, uh, you know, your ability to see . . . that is, to think . . . Oh hell, I don't know what I mean. Is it possible that your subconscious memory of them and their connection to Edwina is affecting you and your . . . whatever?" Debbie Sue twirled her fingers at her temple.

In spite of Debbie Sue's faltering explanation, Sophia knew what she was trying to say. "Of course," Sophia lied, "that is a possibility."

"Whew, what a relief," Debbie Sue said and turned to Edwina. "See, Ed? I told you." She turned back to Sophia. "Where do we go from here?"

Sophia studied the faces of the three people in front of her. She had a strong skeptic in Debbie Sue, an anxious, sentimental soul in Justin and a confused, fearful believer in Edwina. None of them had faith in Sophia Paredes. "We need to plan a séance," she told them.

"Oh, no," Edwina said, backing up, shaking her head and raising her palms to emphasize her protest. "No way, no how. I do not need to see any dead people. You are not getting me into a séance."

"A séance," Debbie Sue repeated.

Justin stood stone still. "What's a séance?" he said.

Edwina expelled a great breath and folded to the ground in a cross-legged position.

"Ed, you okay?" Debbie Sue asked.

"Don't mind me. I'm just trying to keep it together. If I fall apart, I want to be sitting down."

"You have to participate in the seance, Ed," Debbie Sue said. "Remember what I said about cowboying up?"

"What's a séance?" Justin asked again.

"It's people getting together with a psychic to communicate with the dead," Edwina said.

"Not a psychic," Sophia corrected. "A mentalist."

"Whatever," Edwina said.

"Oh, you mean like playing with a Ouija board, like we did as kids," Debbie Sue said. "But nothing ever happened."

Laymen had such erroneous theories about the spirit world, Sophia thought. Conversing with those from the other side required much more skill and finesse than sitting on the floor with a board and a plastic triangle. "Ah, but you had no one to guide you."

"Well, I'm game," Debbie Sue said. "Let's do it." But the reply sounded like fabricated enthusiasm. "Do we go back inside the house for that?"

It was too soon. Little Pearl and Big Pearl revealing their presence had caused too much agitation around everyone, including Sophia, and they might still be in the house. "Oh, I'm sorry," she said. "I'm unable to do it now. I need some time to meditate, to clear my thoughts and prepare myself to receive messages from the other side. I wouldn't want, as you say, subconscious memories affecting the results."

"Riiight," Debbie Sue agreed, cutting her a suspicious look. "Well, hey, it's almost lunchtime. Shall we grab something to eat and meet back here this evening?"

The last thing Sophia needed was to spend time with Edwina, whose aura did seem to be attempting to intrude on Justin's. "Thanks, but no thanks," she said. "I'll get some lunch when I get back to Odessa. I'm going to my motel room, where I have quiet and privacy for my meditation. I'll meet all of you back here at seven, if that's all right?"

Debbie Sue looked to the others. Justin scowled, but nodded. "Seven's fine."

Sophia smiled and turned to Justin. "Is there a picture of Rachel I can take with me? It will help me in my meditation."

"Well, uh, I guess so." He reached back, brought forth his wallet and opened it. "I've got one right here." He slipped a photo from its acetate sleeve and handed it to her. "I wouldn't want to lose that."

Sophia studied it a moment and smiled. "Thanks. I'll be sure to give it back." She opened her car door and looked at each of them. "See y'all later."

"Right," Debbie Sue said. "Seven o'clock, here."

"Seven o'clock," Sophia repeated. She started the engine and drove away.

Debbie Sue watched as Sophia motored out of sight. Everyone seemed to be stunned to silence. No one said a word. After a long pause, she said, "I've got this funny feeling she isn't coming back."

"I think you're right." Justin agreed. "I don't think we'll see her tonight. Or any other night. At least all I'm out is the cost of a room."

"But what about the picture you just gave her?" Debbie Sue asked.

Justin kept staring straight ahead in the direction of Sophia's car. "I've got others."

Edwina still sat on the ground. "Oh, she'll be back. I can't explain it, but I'm pretty sure we haven't seen the last of Sophia Paredes."

With Sophia gone, Debbie Sue could see no reason for her and Edwina not to leave also. God knew that with an infrequent free Saturday afternoon, there was plenty to do elsewhere. "Justin, we'll come back this evening at seven. If nothing else we can check our equipment for any activity. If we're going to catch someone red-handed, it's best if you leave the house too. Not much chance our vandal will come around if you're here."

"Guess you're right," Justin said. "I've got some business in Odessa. I'll go ahead and take care of it and see you back here at seven."

Debbie Sue climbed behind the steering wheel of her pickup and Edwina plopped onto the passenger's seat. They had driven only a few yards from the house when Edwina said, "Debbie Sue, do you really think Sophia won't come back? I didn't get that impression at all."

"I don't know, Ed. It's just a feeling. She had the oddest look on her face when we were talking to her. Like her mind was a million miles away, like she was planning her escape or something. Hell, I don't know. I'm just saying I wouldn't be surprised."

"I'm working real hard on not letting anything else surprise me," Edwina said. "I've made an ass of myself twice today. I'm not particularly anxious to go for a third time."

Debbie Sue gave her friend a sideways glance and smiled.

"Don't be too hard on yourself, Ed. I think you had good reason to react the way you did."

"You do?" Edwina asked, incredulous.

"Well, yeah. I mean I was looking at it from a different perspective than you were. You reacted from an emotional level, where my reaction was purely cerebral. You know, intellectual."

"Purely cerebral? Intellectual? Since when did you start thinking purely cerebral? Why, Debbie Sue Overstreet, if they ever perform an autopsy on you they'll find your brain smack-dab in the middle of your heart. Cerebral my ass." With a huff, she crossed her arms over her chest.

"Want to put a purely cerebral bet on whether Sophia comes back?"

"You're on," Edwina said.

# fifteen

Justin watched the Domestic Equalizers leave and then sauntered into his house. He stopped in the living room and looked at the motion-sensitive camera the women had installed. It blended into the decor and he doubted anyone who didn't know what to look for would ever notice it.

He recognized it because he'd seen similar devices before. Arson cases had been solved with the aid of such equipment. His training had taught him to recognize and salvage it if at all possible. He had never considered that he would ever see it in his own home, wouldn't have believed it possible, and especially not for the reason intended now. He slowly shook his head. Lord, he would have to remember to keep his skivvies on while walking around the house.

In the kitchen he noted a monitor above the bar, set for a perfect view of the refrigerator door. The Domestic Equalizers appeared not to have missed much, but he still wondered if they knew what they were doing. This business of hiring a fortune-teller had him off balance.

On the bar lay a business card he had casually tossed aside days back after finding it stuck in the frame of his front screen door. He read it again for about the dozenth time: LONE STAR OIL & GAS EXPLORATION, MIKE BOOKMAN, VICE PRESIDENT. A note had been written on the back of it:

> *Mr. Sadler, please contact me at your earliest convenience.*
> *MB*

Justin recognized the address as the Texas Bank and Trust Building in Odessa. He couldn't imagine Lone Star's interest in him. His land had been tested and passed over as a potential drilling site years back. But with time to kill until seven o'clock, he would drop in and see what Mr. Bookman's note meant. Exiting his house via the back door, he double-checked the lock and left his home to whatever or whoever might choose to enter.

Halfway to Odessa he was hit by a pang of hunger. He had been too wired to eat all day. He knew just where he wanted to go, too. Mama Hayes' Family Dining, hands down, had the best food in the Permian Basin. He seldom ate in restaurants. He had become an accomplished cook from taking his turn in the kitchen rotation at the fire station, and once his shift ended, he usually went home and prepared something for himself. With the necessity to eat out, Mama Hayes' was his best choice.

A short time later, he parked in back of the restaurant and inside found a foyer full of customers waiting their turn for a seat. While waiting himself, he looked around the big dining room and was surprised to see Sophia Paredes sitting at a table, sipping iced tea. He walked past the others and went directly to her.

"Hello, Sophia."

She looked up with a wide smile. Lord, her smile did brighten a room. "Oh, hello, Justin."

"How'd you find the best place in town to eat? Did you ask around or did it come to you in one of those visions you said you see?" He gave a huh-huh-huh at his own joke.

She laughed too. "Actually, I entered the word *restaurants* in the GPS and this was the first one it listed. Is it the best in town?"

"Absolutely. Mama Hayes is famous for her fried chicken, chicken-fried steaks and peach cobbler. I highly recommend all."

"Fried chicken is what I just ordered. Won't you join me?"

Justin glanced over his shoulder toward the crowd waiting for tables and scowling at him. "I hate to cut in front of those folks."

"Nonsense. They're waiting for tables of their own, not to share one with me. Please. Sit down."

The aroma of food was overpowering—hot yeasty rolls, something sweet and delicious. And the idea of killing time with Sophia held an equal appeal. For the past year, he hadn't ventured to think about female company, but even if he had, his conscience would have stepped up and reminded him he was a widower and still in love with his wife. Still, his body and a deep yearning in his soul reminded him that he had once enjoyed the company of a beautiful woman and still did. "I don't know, Sophia. Some of those ol' boys might fight for a seat with you."

She smiled up at him again. "Thank you, Justin."

He sat down directly across from her and waited for the awkward moments he expected from dining with a stranger, but they never came. He and Sophia immediately fell into talking and laughing as if they had known each other for years instead of hours. He felt . . . well, comfortable.

Sophia told him about her life growing up as a ward of her beloved grandmother, how hard she had worked getting her education and how much she adored the children she taught. She confessed her desire to leave El Paso. The legacy of the well-known psychic who had raised her was so overwhelming, Sophia could scarcely go anywhere in the city that she didn't hear whispers and experience peoples' reactions to her grandmother's reputation. "If I ever marry and have children of my own," she said, "I don't want that stigma to follow them."

Justin was surprised. He assumed a celebrity-like status would be appealing to a young woman of Sophia's beauty, but talking to her and watching her, he could see that she wasn't particularly aware of her appearance. She seemed to be focused on the life she wanted for herself and her offspring in the future instead of the one she had now.

"I suppose the good part of having a teaching degree is that you can use it anywhere."

"Yes, it is," she said nodding, but then added, "As long as it's in Texas. I could never live anywhere but Texas."

"Oh, absolutely," Justin agreed.

The waitress came with Sophia's food and took Justin's order without bothering to write it down.

"I don't know how they do that," he said as the woman left. "They must take hundreds of orders a day. I'd never get anything right."

Sophia laughed. "It is a challenge. I know because I've worked in restaurants before." She shook packets of sweetener into her iced tea. "I feel terribly impolite eating in front of you. Would you like some of this?" She slid her plate an inch in his direction.

"No, no, you go right ahead. My food will be here soon." He picked up a puffy roll and scooped a little pile of honey butter from a little crockery bowl on the table. "I'll just chow down on these rolls and butter until I can't stand up without assistance."

They both laughed heartily and before they were aware of it, not only had they finished their meals but everyone else in the café had finished too, and vacated the place. Not once in the entire time had there been mention of why Sophia was in Odessa or the occurrences in Justin's life that had brought her here.

Looking around the room, he said, "Well, it looks like we've run everybody off." Justin stole a peek at his wristwatch. "Would you believe it's almost four o'clock? We've been sitting here over two hours." He reached into his shirt pocket and pulled out the oilman's business card. "I came to Odessa to see a guy. I wonder if his office is still open."

"An appointment you had?" Sophia asked.

Justin handed the card to her. "Not really an appointment. This was left in my door a couple of weeks ago. But I guess I don't need to go to their offices. If they really wanted to reach me, they'd have tried again by now."

Sophia studied the card, then looked up at him. He couldn't read her expression, but her demeanor was somehow different. "My goodness," she said all at once. "I've kept you too long. I apologize. You should have told me to hush. I've been prattling on and on."

"Heck, no. I've been having a good time. Doing just what I wanted to do."

"So have I," Sophia replied, her eyes homing in on his.

For the first time in more than two hours an uncomfortable silence grew between them. Justin picked up the green meal ticket and rose. "I'll take care of this. It's part of our agreement."

"Oh. Oh, yes, the agreement." Sophia rose too, and followed him to the register.

Justin wasn't sure if the reminder of his financial commitment to her or the innocent remarks about how much they had enjoyed each other's company had formed a wall between them, but it was there and he couldn't deny it. Looking down at her, he said, "I'll walk you out to your car."

"Oh, uh, no," she stammered. "I'm, uh, going to the ladies' room."

Odd. Why was she suddenly so nervous? He locked his eyes on hers. "Tell me the truth, Sophia. Will you really be coming back to my house this evening?"

She stiffened and lifted her chin. "Of course. I said I would."

"Yes, of course." He mustered a smile. "Well, then. I'll see you at seven."

"Yes, I'll see you then."

Justin walked outside, leaving Sophia inside the restaurant. He drew a deep breath. The last time he had felt that much at ease with a woman had been when he first met Rachel many years before. And the most uncomfortable he had ever felt was just now at the reminder of Rachel and the reason Sophia had come here.

Sophia stood in the restaurant's vestibule and waited until she thought Justin had enough time to get out of the parking lot. She hoped that by doing so she could avoid further encounters and the tension that had developed between them in the last few minutes.

A vision had come to her while touching the business card he had shown her and it was still vivid in her imagination. A dark figure meant Justin harm. Perhaps it was a good thing he missed his meeting with Lone Star Oil and Gas. She considered how she would discuss that bit of news with him. Perhaps this evening she would have the opportunity to talk to him in private. Then, she could disclose what she had seen.

She felt bad for him. The aura she had sensed earlier when

she had touched the photograph in his house had been strong and not particularly friendly. The women named Pearl had been a distraction, but it hadn't overridden the aura. She didn't yet know whether the dark vision she had seen was of Rachel, but if it was, it wouldn't be easy convincing her to abandon the house she had shared with Justin and move on.

Sophia needed to preserve all of her strength. No mentalist with any background or foreknowledge would attempt a full-fledged séance without preparation and meditation. Dealing with spiritual entities could be as demanding on the body as hard outdoor labor. It zapped everything she had in reserve, both physically and mentally.

She pulled a list of items from her pocket. She had just enough time to pick these few things up, rest and meditate and be back at Justin's by seven.

*At Justin's by seven.* That sounded good. She liked Justin. *Really* liked him. Leave it to her bad luck to finally meet someone she would like to know better, only to have her competition be his dead wife.

*Gran Bella, life is so unfair,* she thought woefully.

*I never taught you otherwise,* came the gentle reply. *You really like this young man. Is that why you bought a magazine about sex? Well, no. . .*

Gran Bella's voice came again. *Best to read the Holy Bible.*

"The Bible might teach me how to live my life, Gran Bella," Sophia muttered, "but it won't teach me how to attract a man. I *know* the Bible. I don't know how to appeal to men."

In a barely audible whisper a loving voice replied, *Patience, my sweet Sophia, patience.*

★ ★ ★

Passing Mama Hayes' café, John Patrick Daly had spotted his brother-in-law through a window, sitting at a table with a drop-dead-gorgeous brunette. Had Justin started dating? he wondered. Had he met someone on the Internet?

Normally, John Patrick would have satisfied his curiosity by stopping and going into the café, but he'd had a passenger—a banker with whom he was discussing a business deal. He hadn't exactly relished the idea of asking questions of Justin where the banker could hear him. He had solved the dilemma by stomping the accelerator and depositing the banker in record time at Texas Bank and Trust.

Now back at the café, he was disappointed to see that Justin's truck was no longer in the parking lot. Damn, he had missed him. Then, as he sat there cussing himself, the restaurant door opened and the brunette came out. God almighty, she was a beauty, built like a brick shithouse. Where had a weenie like Justin met somebody as fine as her? She wasn't from around here or John Patrick Daly would have known her.

He eased the Cayenne into a parking slot and watched as she made her way to a small car. He recognized the logo on the bumper of a local car-rental agency. So he had been right. She was from out of town. So why was she here?

The little Chevy started up and she pulled into a lane of traffic headed back into town. This was far too interesting to abandon at this point. He positioned himself behind her.

Within a mile her right blinker came on and she turned

into the parking lot of a SuperTarget. John Patrick parked several cars away from hers, hopped out of the Cayenne and followed her into the cavernous store. He watched as she latched onto a cart and maneuvered it with purpose. No browsing or looking around. Apparently she knew just what she wanted.

In the home décor department, she picked up a handful of candles of various shapes and sizes. In the music department, she chose a CD. After she had moved on, John Patrick picked up the same disc and mumbled the title. "Mood Music for Lovers." *Crap.* He didn't like the looks of this.

Walking briskly and searching for her, he caught up with her in the grocery department, where she added a box of crackers to her cart. She chose some cheese, a container of fresh strawberries, a box of chocolate candy and a bottle of wine. The last item she put in her cart was a bouquet of roses—*white* roses from the floral department.

A tailor-made romantic evening with all the trimmings came to John Patrick's mind.

And he had thought *he* was the one with secrets. He had always believed Justin to be an open book. Apparently he had been wrong.

His worse fears were confirmed when he followed the brunette to the Blue Mesa Inn and watched her carry her purchases inside.

A notion powerful enough to make his head swim hit him and beads of sweat formed across his upper lip. What if she worked for Lone Star Oil and Gas? What if their rep had tired of leaving calling cards on Justin's door and the company had decided instead to send in their heavy artillery?

Was Justin set to spend Saturday night with a total babe who had an ulterior motive? He would see what he could do to alter that situation. An unexpected visit from the dead wife's brother should throw cold water on anything hot.

# sixteen

And I told him we'd pick them up at six. Is that okay?"

John Patrick didn't know what made him look up—the sudden silence in his wife's constant yakking or the pregnant pause heavy with anticipation. "What?" he asked her. "What did you say?"

"I said, silly, that I told Mama and Daddy we'd pick them up at six."

"Tonight?"

"Well, yes, pumpkin." John Patrick heard exasperation creeping into Felicia's tone. "The Cattlemen's Auction has been the third Saturday in June for the past twenty-five years, J. P., and that's tonight."

She came to his side and stroked what was left of his hair,

her touch making him cringe. He supposed she was indebted to him for marrying her. God knew no one else would have stepped up for that torture. Anyone who thought looks didn't matter when the lights were out hadn't been in John Patrick Daly's shoes.

"You know Mama and Daddy don't drive anymore," she said. "Besides, your SUV will have room for the painting."

"What painting?"

"John Patrick." She planted her fists on her hips and stamped her foot, "you didn't hear a word I said. Daddy is donating one of his G. Harvey paintings to the auction. 'Rawhide and Thunder.' He wants you to show it."

John Patrick knew the artwork well. Since it was large, when he carried it out and held it up in front of the well-heeled bidders, only his boots would be visible, if that. He would look comical, which is exactly what his father-in-law, Boots Carlisle, was counting on. Another opportunity for the man to poke fun at the small stature of his son-in-law.

John Patrick bit down on his lower lip. He had been married into the Carlisle family long enough to know how to play this game. He wouldn't put up an obvious fight. The best defense was to appear dumb.

"Me? Can't he get someone else to do that?"

"Daddy's counting on you doing it," Felicia whined.

"Yes," John Patrick answered dully, "I'm sure he is."

As early evening came, Debbie Sue pulled herself away from assisting Buddy with the construction of the deck. "We should call it a day so I can go inside and shower. I need to be at Justin's house by seven."

All afternoon, Debbie Sue had allowed Buddy to delegate menial chores to her, such as handing items to him, holding the end of a tape measure and plugging in various electric tools.

Buddy began arranging his tools neatly on one side of the deck. "Thanks for your help today, Flash. It's nice having you here helping me. Anything I can help you with in the shower? Hand you the soap or wash something you can't reach?" He gave her a devilish grin.

She freed her long hair from the scrunchie holding it in a ponytail out of her way. "Hmm. Now that's a great idea. You could bring the measuring tape with you. I think I could find a use for that."

Buddy chuckled. "You think you're kidding, but I'm right behind you."

She returned his devilish grin. "Oh, yeah?"

He put both hands on her shoulders and pushed her along, following her into the house. They were already stripping as they crossed the bedroom on the way to the bathroom. Her cell phone blasted "The Eyes of Texas" from her purse, which sat on the bed. She grabbed for the purse and pawed inside it for the phone.

"Let it go to message," Buddy said, dropping to the edge of the mattress and prying off his boots.

"I'd better get it in case it's not a telemarketer. It could be Justin. Or Sophia. " She flipped open the phone and answered brusquely, hoping to send the caller a message that she was in the middle of something.

"Debbie Sue?"

*Oops.* Not a telemarketer. "Justin. Hey, what's up?" His tone sounded different. She felt her brow tug into a frown.

"It's John Patrick, my brother-in-law. His wife called me. She thinks he's having a heart attack. She's called for an ambulance."

"Holy cow, Justin. I didn't realize your brother-in-law had heart disease."

"Neither did I. I thought he was healthy as a horse. Hell, he's young."

"Well you get on over there. I'll call everyone who's supposed to show up for the séance and tell them what's happened. We'll just re-schedule. Hope everything turns out all right. You'll let me know, won't you?"

"Sure thing, and uh . . . uh, you know, Debbie Sue, I really think I should be the one to call Sophia and postpone. I'll do it as soon as everything settles down."

That stopped Debbie Sue for a few seconds before she realized Justin *wanted* to call Sophia and needed an excuse. She smiled into the receiver. "Oh, you're right. You should be the one to call her. Good luck, Justin, Hope all goes well. Drive careful, you hear?"

She hung up and turned to a naked Buddy, stopping to admire his masculine glory. "How'd you get undressed so fast?"

"What's happened?" he asked.

Debbie Sue plopped onto the bed and tugged her own boots off.

"The séance is off. Justin's brother-in-law's had a heart attack."

"That's too bad." Buddy pulled her to her feet and pushed her tank top up. She yanked it off and shook her hair free. It fell over her shoulders and past the middle of her back. "God, I love your hair," he said huskily. He buried his hands in it and his mouth covered hers in a tongue-dueling kiss. He stopped for a breath. "I love more than your hair. I love all of you."

"Me too," she squeaked. She loved every inch of Buddy's body and every minute she spent in his arms.

He reached behind her and unhooked her bra, letting it fall to the floor as he nuzzled her neck. "Who's his brother-in-law?" he mumbled.

"Brother-in-law?"

"Hm." His mouth moved down to her breast and he caught her nipple between his lips.

"Damn, Buddy. You are so evil. You know what that does to me. John Patrick Somebody. Hmmm. That feels soo good."

"John Patrick Daly?" Buddy stopped and straightened, surprise registering in his expression.

Debbie Sue had momentarily forgotten that her husband seemed to know, or know of, absolutely every living person, and a few dead ones, in West Texas. She recognized the scowl of aversion on his face. Since he rarely spoke a harsh word against another person, she had to rely on his body language if she wanted to know his negative opinion of someone. Either that or nag him or seduce him until he let something slip. "Do you know him?" She unzipped her tight jeans, wriggled out of them and kicked them away.

"Wow," Buddy said, his gaze raking over her appreciatively. She was wearing red bikini panties today. His hands slid beneath the waistband, he pulled her against him and kissed her as he pushed the panties past her bottom. They fell down around her ankles. "Step out," he said, bending and freeing her foot from the panties. "I wrote a couple of tickets on him when I was a trooper."

Debbie Sue could scarcely think. All she could do was anticipate. "Who?"

"John Patrick Daly." Buddy led her into the bathroom, reached into the tub enclosure and turned on the water.

*Uh-oh.* There was more. A couple of traffic tickets wouldn't elicit a scowl from a seasoned cop like Buddy Overstreet, especially during a heated session of lovemaking. "Aww, come on," she purred. She walked her fingers up his broad chest. "You must know something else. This could be important to my case."

He urged her into the shower and stepped in behind her. "I don't see how. It's only my opinion. Nothing factual or source driven."

"Factual or source driven," she mimicked, as warm water sluiced over their bodies. She picked up the soap bar and began to lather his chest and shoulders. The fragrance of clean lavender filled the small space. "Buddy, you can read people better than anyone I know. Even your Ranger buddies have said so. You've got the instinct of a bloodhound, is what Cal Jensen said."

Buddy chuckled, took the soap from her and began to lather her back and bottom. He gave up on the soap, clutched her bottom, pulled her pelvis against his, lowered his head and kissed her madly. When he lifted his mouth from hers, he said, "In that case, maybe I should be the one conducting a séance."

"You devil," she said softly, looking into his beautiful chocolate-colored eyes and wriggling against his erection. "We really don't have to discuss it right now."

He picked up her hand, turned it palm up and spoke in a sexy, soft voice while he traced a line with his finger. "Ahh, I see much happiness in your future, in about twenty minutes, to be exact."

"Twenty? That long?"

He dropped her hand and began to stroke all of her secret places.

She sighed, letting her questions go away. But only for the moment. She had to know what Buddy wasn't telling her about Justin's brother-in-law all right. But she could wait twenty minutes, until his prophesy for her had come true.

Justin was within half a mile of John Patrick's mini-mansion when he saw the ambulance running cold and it appeared to be moving slower than he was. No need for lights or speed if the patient was dead. His pulse quickened and a sick feeling washed through him.

He stopped, scooted out of his truck and stood on the running board to draw attention. He knew most of the EMS crew personally and he was relieved to see two familiar faces through the windshield.

The driver, Mark Aiken, brought the ambulance to a stop and lowered his window. "He's okay, Justin. He's up at the house. You might want to go on up and see if you can help the wife. She's in worse shape than J. P."

Justin didn't doubt that. Felicia worshipped the ground John Patrick walked on. "Thanks, I will. Was it his heart?"

"Not that we could tell. We followed routine procedure, checking everything out and he appears to be fine. He decided it had to be heartburn. We tried to take him to the ER, but he wouldn't go. He signed a release, so that's it for us."

The second EMT, Vanessa Singletary, leaned across from her seat and joined the conversation. "He can't be too bad off. He felt well enough to make a pass at me."

Justin shook his head. "In front of Felicia?"

Mark gave a halfhearted laugh. "Like I said, she's in worse shape than he is. I doubt she even noticed."

"Listen, thanks to both of you," Justin said sincerely. "You know how much I appreciate all you do,"

"We know *you* do," Mark said. "See you later, guy."

Justin watched the ambulance move away. He didn't have to ponder the emphasis Mark had put on the word *you*. No doubt John Patrick had been an ass. Justin had seen him in that role many times. Now he wished he hadn't called Sophia and canceled the evening. She had been kind and concerned, but he had detected disappointment in her voice.

Undoubtedly a séance was her big moment. But it was more than that—it was her chance to earn three thousand dollars.

In a way, Justin understood. Even preparing to fight something as simple as a grass fire brought on a heightened awareness. If you were somebody who talked to ghosts, he supposed the same adrenaline high accompanied a prospective encounter. Then, if it didn't happen, just like with a fire, a physical and emotional letdown followed.

As he parked in front of the Daly home, John Patrick came out and stood on the front steps, grinning ear to ear as if he hadn't a care in the world.

Justin scooted out of his truck. "Hey man, what's up? You okay?" He looked carefully at the shorter man for any telltale signs of distress.

"I'm fine. Guess I overreacted. I promised those EMT guys I'd see my doctor Monday. Come on in. Had supper yet?"

"Where's Felicia?"

"She's in the bedroom lying down. The maid's with her. C'mon, let's see what's in the fridge."

"Mind if I check on Felicia first?"

"Sure, go ahead. I'll see what I can scrounge up in the kitchen.

Justin crossed the tiled foyer to the hallway. His feet sank into plush carpet as he walked the wide hallway that was lined with western art, highlighted by recessed lighting. He didn't even want to think about the amount of money hanging within arm's reach.

The French doors that led in to the master suite were partially open and he saw the figure of a woman lying supine on top of the bed cover, covered by a throw. A Mexican woman sat in a nearby chair.

"Felicia?" Justin said softly. "It's me, Justin. You okay?"

His sister-in-law lifted her head from the pillow and looked at him with eyes swollen from crying. "Justin. Thank you so much for coming. J. P. insisted I call you. Did you see him? Did he look all right to you?"

Justin walked closer and took her hand, making soothing sounds, but his thoughts were churning. "Yes, yes. He seems to be fine."

"The way he was gasping for air, then falling to one knee—" She burst into tears, but regained control. "I thought I was losing him for sure."

Something wasn't right. John Patrick had dismissed his problem as a simple case of heartburn. Justin wasn't a man given to high drama or hysteria, but what Felicia had described sounded serious. The EMTs who answered the 911 call were two of the best, yet they had showed no concern. Justin wasn't comfortable dismissing the incident without looking into it further.

The only way to know answers was to ask questions. And that was just what he intended to do.

Patting her hand, he told her to rest well and left to find his brother-in-law. He was just where he had said he would be: the kitchen. He had laid four slices of bread on the counter and was heaping layers of cold cuts and cheese and blobs of mayonnaise onto each. Not exactly what someone with a possible heart attack or even heartburn should be eating.

"J. P., what's going on? Felicia's half out of her mind with worry and you're building a hero sandwich?"

J. P. gestured with a flip of his hand. "She tries to make a big deal out of everything. I'm fine." He sliced the sandwiches into halves with a big knife.

"She said you were gasping for air, even falling to one knee. Is that true?" Justin watched his brother-in-law closely. The guy had a guilty look on his face and he didn't answer immediately. "Well? Is it?"

"Okay, I played it up a little," John Patrick admitted. "She had volunteered me for some damned function with her mommy and daddy and I just didn't want to go."

Justin looked at him in amazement. To fake something as serious as cardiac arrest, to deliberately waste the time of emergency personnel who could be missing a legitimate cry for help was unthinkable in Justin's world. "But J. P.—"

"Did I drag you away from something important? A hot date maybe?"

The question caught Justin off guard. "A hot date? Are you kidding?"

"Oh, you can't fool me, buddy. I saw you this afternoon at Mama Hayes'. Lunching with a total babe. Yessiree. If I dragged you away from her, I will never forgive myself."

"Well, no. I mean, yes, I was, but no, it wasn't a date. We had a business arrangement tonight—" Justin stopped abruptly, not wanting to give John Patrick too much information just yet.

"Business? Don't tell me you hired a pro. Hell, Justin, you

don't have to pay for it. I can introduce you to some chicks who'll give it away,"

"It's not like that," Justin said crossly. Now he was losing his patience again. "Tell you what. You seem fine. I think I'll just run along."

"No, not yet. Have a sandwich with me. See? Already got it made."

Justin had had enough of his brother-in-law. He tore a sheet of paper towel from a holder that sat on the counter. "I'll just take it with me. Tell Felicia to get some rest and I'll see her later." He wrapped the sandwich in the paper towel and left through the front door.

John Patrick walked outside behind Justin and watched as he climbed into his truck and drove away. Shit, he had hoped to keep him here a little longer. He shouldn't have given up on his heart-attack farce so soon. Still, he had to grin. He had perhaps disrupted Justin's evening. He had learned his meeting with the hot babe was business and not a date and he had escaped an evening with his in-laws. Not bad results for a plan thrown together hastily.

## seventeen

*J*ustin's call re-scheduling their appointment had left Sophia feeling a letdown. With no séance to conduct, she had no need to rest and meditate, so it was lucky she had bought a magazine to read. She understood Justin's explanation, though, and hoped his brother-in-law was doing well.

All at once, a light supper of cheese and crackers and even the chocolate-covered cherries she had bought for dessert held much less appeal. Sitting in a club chair at the small round table in her hotel room, she sipped wine from one of the hotel's tumblers. She picked another chocolate-covered cherry from its paper cup, popped it into her mouth and washed it down with a sip of wine.

The white roses, sitting in the ice bucket filled with water, gave a false ambience of gaiety to the room. She had bought them for the séance because spirits were strongly drawn to white roses, along with soothing music and a candle's flickering flame.

Leaning over, she reached for another slice of cheese and a cracker, and in doing so slid out of her chair in one smooth move, depositing her bottom on the floor. Oh, goodness, was she tipsy?

She hadn't intended to be. She had wanted only to have a couple of glasses of wine with the cheese and crackers she had bought at Target. But being a nondrinker, she had underestimated her alcohol tolerance, and now, sitting on the floor, she announced to the room in a carefully measured voice, "I'm a towel blowing in the breeze."

Moving back to the chair, she picked up the bottle and poured herself another inch of the delicious beverage, "Or is it *two* towels floating in the breeze? No, that doesn't sound right either." Why couldn't she think of that simple saying? She decided to call Debbie Sue and ask her the correct expression.

She picked up the room phone and pressed for an outside line but instead of a dial tone, there was a hint of background noise.

"Hello?" she said. "Is someone there?"

Just as she started to hang up, a male voice said, "Sophia?"

"Justin?"

"You must have been calling out as I was calling in. Do I need to hang up and let you make your call?"

"No, please don't hang up." She hoped he couldn't tell

from her speech that she had been drinking. She squared her shoulders and assumed an erect posture. "How is your brother-in-law?" she asked carefully.

"He's fine. It was a false alarm." A small laugh followed.

"Oh, thank goodness. I know you're relieved. Why are you laughing?"

"You sound a little like you're three sheets to the wind."

"That's it," she said triumphantly. "Three sheets to the wind. I was just trying to think of that old saying."

Justin laughed again and she smiled. His laughter was warm, sweet and sexy. She wished she could see him laughing.

"When did you start drinking?" he asked, amusement still sounding in his voice.

"Only about a year ago," she answered, "but just on special occasions."

He laughed louder this time. "No, I mean tonight. When did you start drinking tonight?"

His laughter sent waves of warmth through her and she sat on the edge of the bed, envisioning his clear blue eyes lighting up with merriment. She tittered. "Oh. Sorry. After you called I decided to buy a nice bottle of wine, which isn't like me at all. For some reason wine sounded good to go with the cheese and crackers I bought for supper."

"Cheese and crackers is your supper?"

"Well, not yet it isn't."

"So you haven't eaten?"

"Just a few cradders and sheez." Good lord, she had slurred

her words again. "Pardon me, Justin, I meant *crackers* and *cheese*. I'll probably go out and get something in a while."

"Don't you dare," he said, his tone now laced with concern. "You shouldn't be driving. Look, I haven't eaten either. How 'bout I come by and take you to dinner?"

"Oooh, that would be so nice. Could I have a steak? I would really like a big juicy steak."

"You can have anything you want," he said.

"Super. How much time do I have before you get here? I need to put on a new face."

"About ten minutes," he said, "but don't do that. There's nothing wrong with the face you've got."

Justin disconnected. Shit, he had done it again—made a comment about the way she looked. He couldn't seem to talk to her without doing that. She must think he was just one more of the typical horny bastards that were bound to hit on her all the time.

That thought didn't set well with him. He didn't want her to see him in that light. She was a nice person. Hell, *he* was a nice person, so why did he keep acting like an acne-faced teenager failing with lame attempts to win the heart of the popular cheerleader?

Thinking of Sophia made him think of the séance. The subject of re-scheduling would surely surface over dinner. The sooner the mysterious occurrences in his home were explained, the sooner Sophia would return to El Paso. That thought didn't set well with him either. How quickly she would be gone from his life was a sobering reality.

He arrived at the hotel, pulled under the covered curbside parking, and called her again. "I'm here," he said when she answered. "I'll be waiting in the lobby. Don't hurry, I'm a firefighter. We're accustomed to sitting around waiting."

He went into the lobby and took a seat on a sofa near the elevator. He had barely opened a magazine before she appeared. He didn't know if the wine or the quick trip to the lobby had given her complexion a flush, but she was radiant. She had changed into jeans and a white cotton blouse, the same thing half the women in the county wore, but on her it looked far better.

Rising from the sofa, he awkwardly extended his right hand in greeting. His intention was to mention how quickly she had gotten from her room to the lobby, but what came out of his mouth was, "Wow, you look awesome."

Dammit, he had done it again.

"Thank you," she said, blushing a deep crimson and looking down.

He offered her the crook of his arm. "Come on. A couple of good steaks are waiting for us."

She took his arm. "Thank goodness. I don't think I need any more wine and cheese."

The drive to Kincaid's Steakhouse was relaxed and comfortable. Justin teased her about being slightly tipsy and she laughed right along. He liked her self-deprecating nature. He viewed one's ability to laugh at oneself as a sign of good character.

"I probably shouldn't have anything else to drink tonight," she said. "I'd hate looking foolish in front of someone who doesn't know me well enough to overlook it."

"I'm driving, so I won't be drinking. But let's make a deal all the same. No matter what happens tonight, I won't think badly of you if you won't think badly of me."

"You've got a deal," she replied.

The supper, much as lunch had been, went by in a rush. Justin was barely conscious of the food servers who came and went. He was sure of only two things, really—the steaks were outstanding and so was the company.

Eventually, the talk of Sophia's reason for being in town surfaced. With the topic open for discussion, Justin now felt comfortable enough to ask the questions that had been bothering him, and he was learning much from Sophia.

She told him how she'd had these unexplained feelings and visions thrust upon her since her early teens. She might have had "seeing powers" before that, but if so, she hadn't recognized them for what they were. For some reason there had been a connection between puberty and her gift of clairvoyance. The passage into womanhood had awakened her abilities from their dormant state.

She also explained that just because the visions had come to her in other situations didn't mean they would surface for him. Spirits, she told him, were like anyone or anything else—if they *wanted* to communicate, they would. If not, well, it just wouldn't happen.

Justin studied her carefully as she talked. He had no doubt *she* believed she had powers, but he still didn't know if *he* believed it. What wasn't evident was whether her belief had only been pressed into her young mind by her grandmother. If the world of her caretaker and mentor reading people's pasts and presents had been a part of her daily life growing up, how could anyone expect her to not to believe that she too had some kind of supernatural power? He couldn't dismiss the fact that even "non-gifted" people experienced an occasional foretelling of an event. He could easily see how she could construe that normal occurrence as "the gift."

She had made vague references to the cost of caring for her sick grandmother. He knew schoolteachers' pay in many instances was paltry. She had to be in financial straits. His heart went out to her. How could he not pay her even if she failed? After all, hadn't she come here in good faith?

But he had already made the declaration, and made it in front of everybody, that no results meant no money. Period.

"Justin, may I ask you something? And please, if you don't want to answer, don't feel you have to."

He hated questions that started this way. They usually resulted in him being cornered in some way. Despite feeling the tentacles of trepidation, he said, "Sure."

"Today at lunch you handed me that business card from the representative of an oil company."

"Yeah?" he said tentatively, wondering where this could possibly be going.

"I felt something dark and powerful when I held that card. I've thought about it several times since. Could someone from that company mean you harm?"

Justin felt his brow tug into a frown. "I don't know why they would. I don't even know anyone from that company."

"All I know is, I had a very menacing vibe and it's tied somehow to the business card."

A shiver passed over Justin. He had been so absorbed by suspecting the worst, followed by trying to figure out some way to help her, he had failed to give credence to the possibility that she might be able to actually *do* what she claimed. "I don't understand."

"I'm sorry. I don't understand it either, really." She reached across the table and placed her hand over his. "I wish I could tell you more, but I don't know more. Just be very careful in dealing with that company."

"By harm, you don't mean physically . . ."

"I don't know," she said. "I just know they don't have your best interest at heart. Someone is sneaking around behind your back."

Now the hair on the back of Justin's neck was standing up. "And you can't tell me who it is?"

"I'm sorry. I only saw a shadow, a dark male shadow. But whoever it is, he is very small. Not small like a child, but a very small adult. You know, short. Almost as short as I am."

Justin sat back heavily in his chair. Yes, he knew one small adult male very well. He pushed the image that had come to him from his mind and let his common sense take over. He knew lots of short men. Maybe not as short as John Patrick, but all the same, they were short.

But what if John Patrick was who she was imagining? Indeed, Justin had never understood a part of John Patrick. Rachel had tried to forge a bond with her brother, but he had shown little interest in being even so much as friends. Since Rachel's passing, John Patrick had been extremely nice, but Justin had thought it was out of guilt for holding his only sister at arm's length. Could the guy have a grudge against Justin for some reason?

"One other thing that I don't understand has come to me," Sophia continued.

She now had his full attention and he leaned toward her. "Yes?"

She let out a small, self-conscious laugh, "I don't know why, but something my Gran Bella always said keeps playing in my head like a song."

"What's that?"

"Never trust a man who goes by two first names."

# eighteen

Sophia was herself again. Several glasses of iced tea, a huge meal, a scrumptious dessert and coffee had overcome her previous state of being tipsy. In the darkened cab of Justin's pickup, she stole a glance at him as he drove.

The entire evening had been wonderful. She couldn't have asked for a more congenial dinner companion than Justin, but he had been preoccupied. Her mentioning the business card and the short man had hit a nerve. The information that had come to her was so vague, perhaps she should have kept it to herself, but the need to warn him had been strong enough to compel her to say something.

"How do you like Odessa?" he asked, breaking into her deep thoughts.

"I like what I've seen, but I miss the mountains."

"I bet you don't miss the haze of pollution drifting over from the border."

It was true. Mexico didn't have the same air-quality standards as the U.S., and a gray haze made its way from Juarez into El Paso when the wind blew from the south. Sophia laughed. "It sounds like you've spent some time in El Paso."

"Rachel and I went there a few times. She liked bargain shopping in those little shops in Juarez. I used to tease her and say if we lived closer, she'd have to file for dual citizenship."

Much too soon, the Blue Mesa Inn came into sight. "Thank you, for rescuing me from more cheese and crackers and maybe more wine," she said. "My head thanks you too, for the ache it won't have tomorrow."

Expecting him to let her out at the hotel's door, she picked up her purse and reached inside for the diamond-shaped key fob. Instead of driving into the porte-cochere, he chose a parking spot near the entrance.

"It was my pleasure," he said. "Let me walk you to your room." He popped the latch on his door.

She dreaded the awkwardness that always seemed to come at the end of a date. "That isn't necessary," she said quickly and scooted out the passenger door. "I'll be fine, but thanks for the offer." She slid to the ground. Standing beside the open door, she looked back into the cab. "I'll see you tomorrow night at seven."

He gave her a sweet smile. "Okay, then. Seven it is."

She walked into the hotel, knowing Justin hadn't left and was sitting, as any gentleman would, watching and waiting for her to be safely inside. She stopped at the front door, turned and gave him a little wave. He waved too, then backed out and drove away.

Her room was at the end of a long hallway on the second floor. When she first checked in, she had liked that because only one neighbor's noise would disturb her, but now, her door seemed to be very far away and she felt isolated in the vacant hallway. Wanting to waste no time, she hurried to the door and slid the key into the lock.

One step into the room and she saw chaos. Her personal items were strewn everywhere. The mattresses had been removed from the two beds and stood on end against the wall. The ice bucket holding the white roses had been dumped on the floor. Her room had been ransacked!

Fear knifed through her. She gasped and dropped her purse. Its contents scattered over the floor. She glanced into the bathroom. The toiletries she had left on the vanity were strewn all over the counter. A tiny cry escaped her throat. Who would do this? What could someone have been looking for? The only items of value she owned were her grandmother's pieces of jewelry. Thank God she hadn't left them in the room.

As she recovered from the shock, new questions rushed at her. How had someone gotten into her room? And was the criminal who did this still present?

Those thoughts propelled her to move. She backed out of the room into the hallway, then turned and dashed toward the EXIT sign and the steel stairs. At the bottom of the stairs, she shoved the steel door open and spotted the receptionist counter. She hustled up to it and was met by a young woman behind the desk who wore a name tag that said MISTI.

"Miss, miss," Sophia said breathlessly. "Someone has broken into my room. They trashed everything. I think I've been robbed."

The clerk's eyes popped wide and her jaw dropped. "Oh, my God! Are you kidding me? Oh, my God!"

Misti rounded the corner of the tall desk and strode to the elevator. When the car didn't arrive immediately, she quick-stepped to the door marked STAIRWAY. She jerked the door open and mounted the steps two at a time. Before Sophia could catch up, Misti stopped on the landing, gasping for air. She jogged back down to where Sophia stood. "What do you think I should do?"

Incredulous, Sophia stared at the young woman. "For starters," she said slowly, "do you have a security guard? Or maybe you should call the police."

"Of course!" Misti bumped her forehead with the palm of hand.

"We've got a security guard. His name's Brad. Let me see if I can locate him."

She scurried back to the reception desk and Sophia followed. Misti yanked open a drawer. It was stuffed almost to the point of overflowing. She rooted around in it until she came up with a two-way radio. Fingers shaking, she pressed a button. "Brad? . . . Brad, can you hear me? . . . Over?" No response. She pressed the button again. "Brad, answer me, forgodsake. We got an emergency here. Brad? Are you around? Over?"

A unkempt man with a scruffy beard sauntered into the doorway behind the reception desk and leaned a shoulder against the jamb. He filled the doorway. Dressed in blue-and-white-striped overalls and a T-shirt, he looked nothing like a security guard, but he did have a black gunbelt strapped around his hips and some kind of weapon in an attached holster. "Yep, I'm here. What's up?"

Misti pressed the "talk" button again and spoke frantically into the receiver. "There's a lady here. She says somebody broke into her room." Misti moved the device away from her mouth, seemed to remember something and returned it again. "Over?"

Was this a joke? Sophia couldn't be certain, but she thought the man the clerk was talking to was none other than the security guard in the doorway. Standing in front of the clerk, Sophia had a full view of him.

"What's the room number?" he asked, appearing to be totally unperturbed.

Sophia could stand this no longer. Speaking over the receptionist's head, she said to the man in the doorway, "I'm in two-ten."

Misti thrust the radio toward her. "Here. You have to say 'over.'"

The man pushed his shoulder off the door frame and came forward, his hand extended. "Hello, miss. I'm Brad Pitt."

Sophia looked from the security guard to Misti and back again. "You're Brad Pitt?"

"Yes, ma'am. Have we met before?"

Sophia caught her dropped jaw and forced her mouth

closed. "No, it's just that, well, your name . . . Do you get teased about it?"

Looking at her quizzically, the security guard scratched his head. "No, ma'am, I never have. They's lots of Pitts in these parts. Maybe you're thinkin' of my cousin Harry. His life's a livin' hell, lemme tell you."

"No, I don't know him," Sophia said quickly. "Uh, could we go to my room now? I'd like to see if anything is missing."

"You didn't look around?"

"Well, no, I was afraid someone might still be in the room. So I rushed downstairs as quickly as I could."

"Ahhh . . ." he said, brow raised, head nodding. "That was real smart of you. Okay, let's go see what's goin' on."

Sophia trailed behind him to the elevator. They rode to the second floor and she followed him up the long hallway. Two doors from her room he threw his arm out and across her path and nearly clotheslined her. "Oh, sorry," he said.

She grasped her neck and cleared her throat. ' "S'okay," she croaked.

He pulled his gun and crouched, looking left and right.

Sophia made no further physical attempt to stop him, musing that a man who was named Brad Pitt, was seven feet tall and wore overalls that looked like mattress ticking didn't need any advice from her, but she whispered, "Do you really think you need a gun? I'd hate for someone to get hurt."

"I'm a professional, ma'am. Please let me work." Still in a crouch, he crept toward her room. In less than a minute, he returned. "Ain't nobody in there, ma'am, but boy-howdy, they left a mess." He fished a cell phone from his pocket and flipped open the cover.

"Who're you calling?" Sophia asked, now suspicious of anything Misti or the security guard did.

"Callin' the cops. Risk management, you know."

From the appearance of the Blue Mesa Inn, Sophia was surprised that anyone associated with it was concerned with risk management. "Oh. Well, I wanted to go inside and see if any of my things have been stolen."

Plastering the phone against his ear, the security guard nodded his head. "But don't touch anything." He spoke into the phone. "Art? This here's Brad. Got a little robbery attempt down here at the Blue Mesa."

Sophia's shoulders sagged. Nothing like this had ever happened to her. She was torn between fear and anger. Suddenly the soothing voice of Gran Bella came to her. *Everything is fine, querida. You are in no danger. You must keep silent and watch. What goes around comes around.*

Before Sophia could have more conversation with Brad, two uniformed cops came trotting up the hallway and entered the room, their hands on their pistol grips. Another man arrived in street clothes. He introduced himself as a detective and showed his badge. A man with a large black suitcase accompanied him. All disappeared into her room. She backed out of the way and paced the hallway.

Soon the detective came out, a pen and a small spiral notebook in his hand. "Anything missing?"

Sophia crossed her arms, cradling her elbows, trying to hold her composure. "I looked only briefly, but everything appears to be there. I don't have anything worth stealing but my jewelry and my purse. They were both with me."

He jotted notes. "You can't think of anybody who'd do this or what they might be looking for?

"No. I live in El Paso. I don't know a living soul in Odessa."

"Mind telling me what you're doing here?"

Did he suspect *her* of something? Sophia bit down on her bottom lip, debating if she should tell the truth. Should she mention Debbie Sue and Edwina? Or Justin? This detective might be acquainted with all three of them. And if she revealed she had come here to communicate with spirits, he might lock her up. But if she didn't, he might lock her up anyway. "I'm, uh, a teacher. I'm, uh, thinking of relocating," she lied. "I just came up to look around the area."

He gave her a raised-brow look. *Phooey!* He didn't believe her.

"So if you don't know anyone in town, nobody knows you were coming up here?"

"Uh, no one. I have no family."

"Not married?"

"No."

"No friends you might have mentioned your trip or your plans to?"

"No, no friends. I have no friends." And sadly enough, that was almost true.

"Hmm," the detective said. He jotted more notes. The man with the big black suitcase came out of the room. The detective turned to him. "All done? Get anything?"

"Got a few prints. Don't know how useful they'll be. This is a hotel room, you know."

"You dusted for fingerprints?" Sophia asked, surprised. At first she had believed they weren't taking her situation seriously. "Will you need mine?"

"Probably not a bad idea." The detective handed Sophia a business card. "Just show up downtown and hand the clerk at the front desk my card. Tomorrow's fine. You think of any new info you want to tell me, give me a call."

"Yes, I will," Sophia answered, eager to be rid of the detective. Once in the room, she might very well call up a vision and the vandal. "Can I go inside now?"

"We're all finished." The detective gave some kind of signal with his eyes to the security guard.

"I'll go in there with you, miss," Brad Pitt said.

They walked back into the room and Sophia perused the wreckage. Now everything was dusted with black fingerprint powder. When she had satisfied herself that nothing was missing, she told Brad Pitt, "I'm going to repack my things. I need another room. Preferably one close to the lobby. I'll be down in a few minutes."

With the security guard gone, Sophia scraped her toiletries off the bathroom vanity into her makeup bag with a one-armed sweep. In a matter of minutes, she repacked her suitcase, glad she had brought very little with her.

She emptied the wine bottle down the bathroom sink, then returned to the room to put the remaining food in a sack. The open box of chocolate-covered cherries caught her attention. A piece sat there in its little paper cup and a half-moon bite had been taken out of it. The gooey white fondant center had spread over the bottom of the paper cup and the cherry sat there only half covered by a chocolate shell. She *never* bit into a chocolate-covered cherry for only half a bite. Doing so was too messy. She preferred putting the whole candy into her mouth and chewing and savoring the delicious mix of chocolate and rich fondant and maraschino cherry.

Someone besides her had bitten into that candy. Her breath caught, her pulse quickened. "Oh, my gosh," she whispered.

With trembling fingers, she gingerly picked up the tiny white cup and placed it in the center of her palm. She carefully closed her fingers around the candy and closed her eyes, willing an image to come to her. Soon a sensation began to course through her and a filmy vision emerged.

She was sitting at home in her living room, cozy and comfortable, with a bowl of popcorn, watching a movie. On the screen, a man was tossing her things around her hotel room, looking in earnest for something, but the vision didn't reveal what. He was small, but he was not a juvenile. Nor was he a vagrant. He was well-dressed. Something was familiar about him, but she didn't know what. If she knew a man that small, surely she would remember him.

The image that had been conjured up from the oil company business card reappeared. She had assumed that man meant Justin harm, but perhaps she herself was who he wanted to harm. Perhaps the image wanted to harm them both. An unexpected shudder passed over her. With a gasp she opened her hand and the candy fell to the floor.

Gran Bella had been right. She would keep quiet about this and watch and wait. Perhaps the image in her vision would make himself known.

Sitting now in the safety of his SUV, John Patrick was bathed in sweat, giddy from an adrenaline rush. Yet, he chuckled. He knew he wasn't living right, so how could he explain that things were falling into place for him?

That Justin's lady friend was staying at the Blue Mesa Inn, a hotel that still had keyed locks, was purely good fortune for John Patrick. The Blue Mesa was a nice enough place, impeccably clean inside and out, American owned and operated, but still a little behind times in the way of security. John Patrick had learned at an early age how to break in to locked doors. The knowledge had come in handy when his old man had locked the liquor cabinet or the desk drawer where he kept cash for emergencies.

John Patrick reviewed the events. As soon as Felicia had dropped off to sleep, he had left the house and driven to Odessa and the Blue Mesa Inn. Even earlier than that, after discreetly following Justin's lady friend to the hotel, he had pried her room number out of the nitwit at the reservation desk. His plan had been to pretend he had the wrong room and use his charm to work his way into a conversation with the woman and find out who she was. Justin had been so evasive about her identity, John Patrick felt he had no other choice. But when he found that she wasn't in, he had taken advantage of the opportunity for a little breaking and entering, and had sneaked into her room to see what he could learn.

Hearing the key in the door's lock, he had quickly ducked into the bathroom, stepped into the tub and drawn the shower curtain closed. He stood there like a statue, holding his breath while the woman came into the bathroom twice. He had no idea what he would have done if he had been discovered. Mercifully, she finally left the room entirely, allowing him time to step out, grab a towel and wipe debris and footprints from the bottom of the tub and take the fire-exit stairs to the outside. And he believed not one damn soul had seen him.

The break-in hadn't given him all of the details he wanted, such as a portfolio or an interoffice memo might, or something else that would tell why Justin's lady friend was here. The only information he gleaned was that she was a size eight and wore a 34C bra. And from a luggage tag, he learned that her name was Sophia Paredes of El Paso.

That was enough to work on.

Justin sat in his truck parked in his driveway for a long time, the upbeat emotion resulting from the pleasant dinner he had just had with Sophia overridden by dread of entering the house again. Guilt assailed him. He still loved Rachel, missed her more than he could ever express, but he was drawn in an inexplicable way to Sophia Paredes. At the same time, common sense told him nothing was wrong with that. He needed to move on. He was lonely. And he was too young to become a celibate hermit. All of his friends told him he could find someone—*should* find someone—and maybe have a couple of kids.

He was more confused than ever.

He pumped up his courage and stepped out of the truck. Entering the front door, he saw nothing different. The afghan was still folded on the end of the sofa. No magazine out of place, no roses on the coffee table. He walked into the kitchen for a glass of water and automatically glanced at the refrigerator door.

*Whoa!*

A new message was spelled out on the slick surface:

*BLEV IN SP*

"Oh, my God," he whispered and began to shake all over. He quickly set down his water glass and gripped the edge of the counter. After a few seconds, the trembling passed. He looked around the room, "Rachel?" he asked softly. He stood in the center of the kitchen and made a circle, looking around the room. A shiver crept up his spine, but he was met with nothing but silence. "Are you here, Rachel? What are you trying to tell me, Rachel?"

# nineteen

Sunday morning. Debbie Sue loved Sunday mornings. She had risen early and was dressed and had coffee on to drip when she looked across the kitchen and saw Buddy, his shoulder braced against the doorjamb. With his thick black hair sleep disheveled, his shadowed unshaved jaws and his body-builder physique, he looked bad-boy sexier than any grown man who was a serious-minded Texas Ranger should.

"Hey, Flash, whatcha doing?" he said.

She sailed over, planted a kiss on his lips and handed him a mug of freshly made eye-opening brew. "I tried not to wake you, honey-bunch. I intended to sneak out and give Rocket Man a sudsy bath and a massage. Lord, he's cantankerous when he doesn't get his rubdowns."

"Poor old horse. He's probably got arthritis." Buddy lifted his mug and sipped. "I've got a touch of it myself. When you finish with Rocket Man, wanna give me a massage?"

Debbie Sue grinned, returned to the counter and dropped slices of bread into the toaster. "Not on your life, cowboy. The last time I agreed to give *you* a massage, I lost almost a full day."

He gave her his best Elvis snarl. "Can't help it if I'm a hunk of burnin' love."

Debbie Sue laughed with sheer delight. Last year, Elvis's famous blue suede shoes disappeared in the middle of Salt Lick's first-ever Elvis birthday celebration and Debbie Sue and Edwina had found the thief. Ever since, Buddy had been doing his imitation of Elvis's trademark routines. If his tough-as-leather peers saw him this morning, they wouldn't believe this was the starched shirt, don't-baffle-me-with-bullshit James Russell Overstreet Jr. they knew.

This was her personal, private Buddy, sharing the side only she ever saw, which made the moment all the sweeter. To Debbie Sue, his letting another woman see this part of him would be the worst kind of betrayal.

In seconds, the toast popped up. She covered the slices with mounds of butter, then grabbed a paper towel and her mug and headed for the back door. "I'll be at the barn if you need me, King."

"TCB, Little Mama." Buddy pointed a finger at her and curled his lip, though, admittedly, seeing his lip curl wasn't that easy, hidden as it was under his thick black mustache.

When she approached the corral, Rocket Man nickered

and pranced and displayed youthfulness that was no longer his. He had been her best friend and companion for more than twenty years, and properly cared for, he could last many more. She knew of people who had thirty-year-old horses. That's what she wanted for her Rocket Man—more years filled with warm, sudsy baths and massages.

A foot from the corral her cell phone blared "The Eyes of Texas." She dropped the remainder of her toast on the ground for the birds and dug the phone from her back pocket. Checking the face plate, she saw the caller was Justin. She hadn't heard from him since he had called about his brother-in-law last night. "Hey Justin, how's your brother-in-law?"

"Oh, he's fine. It was a false alarm. Sorry I didn't call you last night and let you know. I got tied up."

Debbie Sue could only hope he didn't mean that literally. "Well that's good, I guess. Has anything else happened at your house?'

"Not a thing. Maybe y'all scared off whoever, or whatever, it was."

"Hmm, I wonder. Did you get a chance to speak to Sophia?"

"Yeah, we, uh . . . well . . . uh, we had dinner last night. It seemed the reasonable thing to do."

Good Lord, the guy was stammering. Well, well, well. Wouldn't Edwina Perkins-Martin, matchmaker extraordinaire, like to know *this* development? Debbie Sue straightened from assembling brushes and grinned. "Reasonable. Right."

"I mean, I did agree to pay for her meals while she's here.

I figured taking her to dinner was the smartest thing to do. That way, I can keep an eye on the expense."

Debbie Sue grinned all the more. "Oh, absolutely. Smart thinking. You're right. Food was part of the deal all right, and you don't want to let the cost of it get out of hand. Did y'all decide a time to reschedule the séance?"

"Tonight. Seven o'clock. I hope that's okay with you and Edwina."

Debbie Sue bit down on her lower lip. Man, this was a predicament she hadn't counted on. Sunday was always and would forever be the one day of the week that was hers and Buddy's alone. Edwina and Vic felt the same about their Sundays. Between Buddy's job taking him all over half a dozen West Texas counties, sometimes with no more than a minute's notice, and Vic's long-haul schedule, a free Sunday was a prized day. Vic might even be leaving on a haul tomorrow.

"Well, I don't know . . ."

"Oh, gosh, I'll bet you don't work on Sundays," Justin said. "Doing the séance would cut into the time you and Edwina have with your husbands, wouldn't it? You'll have to excuse me. I've taken off work for the next couple of weeks and when I'm not following my routine schedule, I completely lose track of time."

"I know what you mean," Debbie Sue said. "It's just that—"

"Please don't apologize. It's me who should apologize. I didn't think."

"But it's your money we're talking about," Debbie Sue

said. "If we don't do it tonight, Sophia could be here another day or more. And you'd have to pay for it."

"Yeah, I see what you mean," Justin said slowly. But then in a much brighter tone, he said, "I guess I'll just have to deal with it."

*Oh, yeah,* Debbie Sue thought. *Edwina would definitely like to know about this new development.*

Debbie Sue agreed to tomorrow night and snapped her phone case shut. "Rocket Man," she said, scratching the horse's ears, "something's haunting Justin Sadler and I don't think it's his ex-wife."

Sophia awoke to the sound of air brakes outside her shrouded ground-level hotel-room window. Her new room at the Blue Mesa Inn was exactly the same as the one she had vacated, except for a ground-level view of the front parking lot instead of a weedy vacant lot. And that was the worrisome part of her move.

Before going to bed, she had engaged the chain and the deadbolt and wedged a chair back under the doorknob—in case someone broke through the other hardware without waking her while she slept ten feet away. She half expected visions of the mystery man to haunt her slumber, but she had slept undisturbed until the big rig jockeys started their engines. Unfortunately, the light-blocking curtain did nothing to block out noise. She rolled over and glanced at the bedside clock radio. Ten o'clock? Surely it wasn't really ten o'clock. She often told her friends that if she slept past seven in the morning they should call an ambulance for her.

She plodded to the bathroom, stopping briefly to pick up the small carafe that was a part of the courtesy coffeemaker the hotel furnished. Assembling it took more dexterity and patience than she owned this morning. She overfilled the coffeemaker and the excess water spread across the vanity. *Crap.* She grabbed a bath towel and soaked up the water.

Reaching back, she turned on the shower and allowed it to run while she gathered her toiletries from the suitcase she had thrown together the night before. In the bottom was the box of chocolate-covered cherries. She lifted it out, removed the lid and stared at the half-eaten piece.

How could something as innocuous at a piece of chocolate missing its gooey center bring her such dread? In a sudden show of moxie she grabbed the paper container with her fingertips, carried it back to the bathroom and flushed it down the toilet. "Take that, you short, mysterious man."

Fifteen minutes later, the hotel's ringing phone brought her out of the shower. She didn't know how many rings she had missed, but given that no one except Justin and the Domestic Equalizers knew she was here, she rushed to answer and stubbed her toe on the corner of the bed box. *Ow-ow-ow.* She grabbed the receiver and blurted a hello.

"Hi, Sophia. This is Justin. How are you this morning?"

Immediately, tension from the morning's trivial events disappeared. His voice had a soothing effect that was wonderful, yet troubling at the same time. She was supposed to be here helping him and all she had done thus far was share meals with him, enjoy his company and elicit a reaction from an outside party by mentioning pearls. None of that was what she had expected on her first official spirit hunt. "I'm good, thanks. I'm a little embarrassed to admit I've been up less than an hour."

Justin's laugh was so warm and sincere it surrounded her like a warm blanket. She smiled too, and tucking her foot and throbbing toe beneath her, took a seat on a nearby chair.

"Uh, listen," he said and she heard uncertainty in his tone. "Tonight isn't going to work for Debbie Sue and Edwina. It was presumptuous of me to assume they'd be available. I feel terrible. So far you've come all the way up here for nothing."

Sophia suppressed her impulse to tell him he was wrong, that the time she'd been here, notwithstanding the break-in, had been wonderful. "I hope nothing's wrong."

"No, not at all. It's just that they want to be with their husbands, it being Sunday and all."

"Oh, that's understandable," she said, but she was already trying to figure out what she would do the rest of her day. She knew no women friends in the area other than Debbie Sue and Edwina. She had no spare money to shop. She didn't even have the money to browse, with gasoline being so high. Her expenses might be covered, but she hadn't been reimbursed for them yet. The only other person she knew was Justin.

Would she be too forward to suggest they do something together?

After a couple of seconds, he said, "I'm going to ride the

horses again today. Would you like to come along? Debbie Sue says those two horses are kind of buddied up. It'll help me if someone else rides the other one."

"Buddied up?"

"That's a horse term Debbie Sue used. When horses spend all of their time together, they don't want to be separated. The one that gets left behind gets upset. It's kind of like being barn-sour."

"Oh, I see. Gosh, Justin, I haven't ridden a horse since I was a young girl. My best friend back home had horses, but like I said, it's been years."

"Debbie Sue says it's a skill like anything else. The more you do it, the better you get. Maybe it's like riding a bicycle. Once you know how, it comes back to you, even if you haven't been on a bicycle in a while."

"And the calmer the horse, the less you get bucked off," Sophia added with a laugh.

"Yeah," Justin agreed, laughing also. "You've certainly got that right. These horses should be calm. They've been brushed and petted to the max in the last few days. So do you want to give it a try?"

"I'd love to. I can be there in an hour. Should I bring something for our lunch?"

"Thanks, but don't bother. My fridge is full of food. We'll throw something together here and take it with us. We'll just turn this horse ride into a picnic."

"That sounds terrific, Justin. See you soon."

# twenty

*J*ustin tossed the phone on his bed, plopped a Dallas
Cowboy insignia cap on his head and walked outside.
He had spring in his step and even whistled a tune as
he marched to the horse corral. He felt great.

The mares stood at attention, ears tipped forward and stiff,
watching his every step. Perhaps their mood matched his.
"Hey, girls," he said as he slid the bar on the corral gate to
the left and squeezed through the opening. "Ready to do it
again?"

The horses nickered and milled around. He took that as
a yes.

He dragged a blanket and saddle from its tree in the tack
room and began to saddle the most cooperative horse, being
careful to duplicate the steps Debbie Sue had shown him yes-

terday. When he had both horses saddled, he filled a bucket with oats and emptied it into the two feeders. Strangely contented, he watched the horses eat until an approaching vehicle caught his ear.

He wiped his hands against his jeans, opened the gate and stepped out of the corral, smiling like a nut as he anticipated seeing Sophia. Then his mood plummeted when John Patrick's Porsche came into view. *Damn.*

Not only did he not want to explain to his womanizing brother-in-law who Sophia was and how he, Justin, had come to know her, he didn't want John Patrick to even meet her. Besides an urge to protect Sophia from an unabashed wolf, there was her warning about a short man. If that had any validity, Justin didn't know, but ever since he had heard it, he hadn't been able to avoid feeling guarded about his brother-in-law.

He walked over to the SUV's driver's door. The power window slid down. John Patrick was holding a beer bottle by the neck. A bouquet of yellow roses tied with a green ribbon lay on the passenger seat. What was *that,* a good-will gift for Felicia? Justin surmised that some things were better left unknown and didn't even ask about the roses.

John Patrick raised the beer bottle in greeting. "What's up, bro? Thought you'd be at work."

*Then why did you come here?* Justin wondered, but he managed a wan smile. "Normally I would be, but I took a few days off. I've got too much vacation time on the books. You know how it is."

"Thankfully, I *don't* know how it is. I've never had a job, you know? At least not one where I worked for wages." He chortled as if he thought that fact was funny. "But you know me. I'm always out here somehow making money, spending money and trying to figure out how to get everyone else's money." After he finished enjoying his own joke, he gestured to the barn. "You've got both horses saddled. Plan on doing some trick riding?"

"I've been doing some riding. And enjoying it. The horses like it, too. I invited a friend out and we're going for a ride and a picnic."

John Patrick's brow arched. "A friend? Would this be a female friend, I'm guessing?"

"Matter of fact, it is," Justin said, looking his brother-in-law in the eye, hoping the direct look and the abrupt answer would discourage more questions.

John Patrick laughed again. "Why, you ol' dog. It's about time you got out and about. Anybody I know?"

"No. She's not from here."

"Ah. An out-of-town squeeze. Cool. Where'd you meet her?"

Justin deliberately didn't answer the question. "You coming in?"

He started toward his front porch. When he didn't hear the Cayenne's door open, he stopped and looked back. John Patrick sat there, his expression grim.

Even from a few feet away, Justin could see a sheen of sweat showing on his brother-in-law's forehead. Was he sick again? Or was he shaken by the prospect of entering his deceased sister's former home? In the years Justin had known

John Patrick he had seen little that fazed him—not a fed-up wife, not pissed-off in-laws, not the irate husband of a married lover. "You feel all right? You're not getting sick again, are you? Hell, you look like you just saw a ghost."

John Patrick gave a jittery heh-heh-heh. "No, I'm fine. Listen, I'm gonna run on—"

His sentence was stopped by the sound of another approaching vehicle. Justin's stomach dropped as he saw Sophia's little white Aero coming up his driveway. John Patrick looked back and saw it, too. *Shit.* Now, forward was the only direction to go.

"Well, whadda you know?" John Patrick said, appearing to have fully recovered. "Looks like I stayed around just long enough."

Sophia's car came to a stop behind John Patrick's SUV. A beaming Sophia emerged. Though wearing jeans and clearly dressed for comfort, she looked like something out of a hot Trace Adkins video. If she could somehow move in slow motion the look would have been complete.

Her long black hair was pulled back in a ponytail that swung when she moved. A plain white T-shirt was stuffed into the beltless waistband of her jeans, which were well-worn and hugged her legs, displaying definition in her thighs and butt not visible earlier when she had been wearing a skirt. God, she was a knockout.

"Hi Justin," she said. "I'm so glad you invited me to go riding. I hope I don't embarrass myself."

Justin laughed. "You can't embarrass yourself in front of

me on a horse. If you'll remember, I just started this horse-riding business yesterday myself."

Sophia grinned. "Uh-oh. If I'm the more experienced between the two of us, then we've got a problem."

Justin was set to reluctantly introduce her to his brother-in-law when, grinning like a monkey, John Patrick introduced himself. "But my friends call me J. P.," the guy added with a lascivious grin.

Sophia bent forward and looked into car, returning his smile. "Nice to meet you. I'm Sophia." She extended her right hand.

John Patrick took her hand and held it longer than a mere introduction warranted. She quickly lifted her hand from his and placed it behind her. Justin was certain he saw a change in her demeanor.

"Justin tells me you're not from around here," John Patrick said, undeterred.

She stepped backward a couple of steps. "Yes, I'm from El Paso."

"Ah, El Paso." John Patrick looked her up and down. The guy was practically drooling. Justin felt an unfamiliar anxiety. His philandering in-law was enjoying the moment too much and a weird urge to drag Sophia away from the Porche's door coursed through Justin.

"I've always had a good time in El Paso," John Patrick said. "Too bad I never ran into you there."

Sophia shot a glance at Justin that he couldn't read. Something was going on, but Justin didn't know what. He desperately wanted John Patrick to just leave. "Uh, Sophia, I've got the horses saddled. Why don't you check them out and decide which one you want to ride."

She moved back from the car door and gave Justin her attention. "You mean I should try to figure out which one I'm the least likely to fall off of?" She followed that statement with a small tinkling laugh that filled Justin with pure joy and he felt that silly grin form on his mouth again. "Yep," he answered.

Sophia turned and walked toward the corral, but stopped once and glanced back at John Patrick, who assessed her with another leer. Justin sensed Sophia wanted to say something, but instead she gave him a quick look, turned and continued toward the corral.

They watched her open the gate into the corral. Finally John Patrick said, "Damn, Justin, my man. I thought she was a show stopper from a distance, but she's better-looking up close than—"

"Excuse me?" A cold anger inched up Justin's spine and he glared at his brother-in-law.

John Patrick looked as if someone had planted a fist in his gut, but he recovered quickly with a self-conscious snicker. "Hey, don't get pissed off. I'm just saying . . . "

"Yeah, well, listen, J. P., I hate to leave good company, but I . . ."

"Oh, yeah. No problem. I need to run too. Have a good time riding horses." He sneered, placing unnecessary emphasis on the last two words. "I'll be seeing you, buddy." His dark-tinted window glided upward.

John Patrick's visit as well as his odd reaction to the invitation into the house earlier still puzzled Justin, but for now, he was more interested in Sophia. He stood a few extra moments and watched the Cayenne's departure, then stuffed his hands in his pockets and walked toward the corral.

Sophia apparently didn't hear him approach. She was preoccupied whispering to one of the horses. He could hear the tone of her voice, low and soothing. "Is that the one you've chosen?" he asked.

Her head jerked up and she looked at Justin in surprise, as if she had been completely unaware of him before now. He was close enough to see her facial features and sadness in her eyes. He had no doubt she was near tears. He quickened his steps to the gate. "What happened?" Was she trying to show a brave front to a pain-inflicting injury? "Did you get kicked?

He had barely entered the corral and closed the gate when Sophia came toward him, the look in her eye somehow different. He could swear he had seen it before. "These horses wouldn't kick me," she said. "They know me. They love me."

*Whoa!* What the hell did *that* mean? "Uh, they do?"

Sophia came closer, placed her palm on his chest and slid it up to his neck. The next thing he knew, her mouth had found his in a crushing, tongue-thrusting kiss and the weight of her body had pressed him back and against the fence.

Justin wanted to push her away, but the only thought in his mind was how good she felt and tasted and how long it had been since he enjoyed this basic human need. He returned her kiss with the same unbridled heat. He trailed his mouth down her neck, nibbling at her fragrant golden skin. Pressing her lips to his ear, she made a small moan and whispered, "I've missed you so much, my marathon man."

"*What?*"

Justin shoved her away with such force she landed on her back in a bed of fresh hay. "Marathon man" was the name Rachel had tagged him with on their honeymoon, after they had made love four times in one night. The name had returned at times during other private moments. No one—no one living, that is—knew that intimate, private joke except Rachel and him.

He looked with disbelief at the body of Sophia sprawled in front of him. *Rachel?* Was he looking at Rachel? Then it dawned on him that whoever she was, she was still female and he had knocked her flat. He moved to her and offered her his hand. "Rach? Babe?" he asked softly. "Are you okay? Let me help you up."

Sophia levered to one elbow, looking around as if in a daze. "What—what happened? What just happened?"

He heard fear in her voice and his heart sank. *Sophia.* He had lost Rachel again. He was so confused and shaken he wanted to turn and run, but then, Sophia sounded as if she too was confused and shaken. And she was an innocent party in all of this.

Bending to one knee he took her in his arms and rocked to and fro murmuring soothingly, "It's okay. It's okay. Are you all right?"

"I think so," she said.

He held her at arm's length and looked into her face searchingly. Though Sophia and Rachel shared no physical resemblance, he still wasn't one hundred percent sure just who he was facing.

"How did I get down here?" Sophia asked. "Did one of the horses throw me? I don't remember even—"

"You don't remember what just happened? You don't remember kissing me?"

Sophia gasped and drew back. "I did what? Why would I do that?" Her hand flew to her mouth and her eyes grew wide.

"It was Rachel. Rachel was here, wasn't she?"

Tears rimmed Sophia's eyes and she grabbed Justin's arm. "I'm so sorry. How painful that must have been for you. Please forgive me, I'm so—"

"Don't say that," he whispered.

Her sincerity touched his heart and he covered her words and mouth with a single kiss.

Turning onto the county road, John Patrick struck the steering wheel with the palm of his hand. *Fuck.* He had been given the perfect opportunity to get more information on the mysterious out-of-town visitor, but here he was leaving, and he still didn't know any more now than he had known before. She was Sophia, she was from El Paso and she was a total hottie. Had Justin taken time off work to spend with this lovely Sophia?

John Patrick glanced at the bouquet of yellow roses lying on the passenger seat. His plan had been to leave it on the seat of one of the rocking chairs on the front porch. The very idea of Justin seeing the roses there the second he came to a stop in front of his house had been tantalizing. Well, that idea has just gone down the toilet. *JP U R Ashole.* After seeing that message on the refrigerator door, He doubted he would ever enter Justin's house again.

He reached over and grabbed the bouquet, pressed it against his nose. They smelled as sweet as Sophia had looked. He supposed he could take them home to his wife. She was still pissed about missing the charity event with her parents.

*Fuck that!*

He buzzed down the window and tossed the roses out to die on the dirt road.

# twenty-one

Debbie Sue moved her cell phone to her opposite ear as she walked through her house and out the back door. "You do? . . . Justin, are you sure?" She waved at Buddy, trying to draw his attention. "It's kind of odd you'd want to do this, because my husband was bugging me about it earlier."

Buddy killed the power to the drill and came toward her, wiping his hands against a towel he had stuffed into the back pocket of his jeans. He lifted his chin inquiringly. "What's up?"

Debbie Sue held up her index finger and continued, "Let me talk to him and I'll call you right back." Snapping the phone shut, she turned her full attention to her husband.

"What's going on, Flash? Who was that?"

"Justin. He's suddenly anxious to do the séance tonight. I think he'd do it this very minute if I agreed." Debbie Sue pulled the towel from Buddy's pocket and wiped a smear of dirt from his cheek.

"But I thought you told him—"

"I did. I told him Sunday was our time together."

"That's right."

"He wants to know if you'd like to come too." She stepped away from him and began busying herself with gathering nails and returning them to their box.

Buddy slapped his thigh and let out a whoop. "Are you kidding me? Man, this is great! Did he include Vic in the invitation?"

"Yes. He wants Ed to bring Vic, too. That is, if he wants to come."

Buddy chuckled wickedly. "Oh, he'll want to be there. I can almost guarantee it."

Debbie Sue looked at him, unable to believe what she had heard. "You can't mean you *want* to go? I didn't think you were serious. You *really* want to participate in a seance?"

"Why wouldn't I? I've spent the better part of my adult life solving crimes shrouded in mystery for the most part. This is another method I've never been exposed to or explored."

Debbie Sue felt her scalp tingle. Buddy had never been present when she was in command . . . or as he would put it, "taking the lead in an investigation." She didn't want to be scrutinized or judged or criticized by him, no matter how well-meaning he might be. For some reason criticism from a loved one just didn't set well. She supposed it was the fervent desire to please, only to feel that on some level you had failed or fallen short. "Buddy, I don't know if it would be such a good idea for you and Vic to be present."

"Why?"

"This is a serious matter and if you only want to be there so you can make fun . . ."

Grasping her upper arm, he turned her to him and spoke in earnest. "Flash, I would never go just to poke fun or make light of another person's grief. You know me better than that."

"I know. I know you'd never do that."

"Then why don't you want me there?"

"I'll be self-conscious, Buddy. I'll feel like a little kid when his parents visit the classroom."

Clasping her shoulders, Buddy bent his knees until his eyes were level with hers. "I'm not going so that I can judge you, darlin'. I'm going purely as a spectator. Besides, I'd think the lady from El Paso would be directing the whole thing. I mean, what the hell do the rest of us know? Right?"

"Yeah, you're right." She mustered a smile. "Sorry I misjudged you, sugarfoot."

"Don't worry about it." He straightened and kissed the top of her head. "Now, help me finish up here. Do I wear my own turban or will the psychic be handing out some of hers?"

"*Aarrgh!*" Debbie Sue reached to grab his fleeing behind. "Buddy Overstreet, you're an asshole!"

From a safe distance he called back, chuckling. "No, I'm not. I just know how to yank your chain."

Muttering cuss words under her breath, Debbie Sue dug her cell phone from her pocket, flipped it open and speed-dialed Edwina's number.

After four burrs, Edwina picked up. "Hey, Dippity-Do. What's happening?"

In less than a minute Debbie Sue delivered the message that Justin wanted the séance tonight and if it meant bringing significant others, then bring them.

"Oh, crap," Edwina said. "Vic will be all over this. When I told him earlier he couldn't go, I thought I was gonna have to give him a time out for pouting. Is Buddy going?"

" 'Fraid so. I can't remember the last time I saw him this eager to do something. He considers it an opportunity to learn a new investigative technique."

"Vic just thinks it sounds like a good time," Edwina said.

"I guess it couldn't do any harm having them there. If they don't start laughing, that is. I'm gonna threaten Buddy within an inch of his life if he does."

"I wish that was all I had to worry about," Edwina said in a near whisper. "You know, um, I've already told Vic all he needs to know about my past. He hasn't asked me many questions, but I've tried to answer truthfully to every one of them."

"Then what's the problem? I don't get it."

"Um, well, uh . . . you know, it might come out that I, uh . . . oh, never mind."

Debbie Sue had never heard Edwina stutter and stammer so. "That you what, Ed?"

"Nothing. But what if something should happen—"

"Ed, forgodsake," Debbie Sue said, now lowering her voice to match Edwina's, "what could be so terrible that Vic doesn't know? Or that I don't know?"

"Dammit, Debbie Sue, I was arrested once. For prostitution. It was over twenty years ago, but . . . Just get to Justin's a little early. I'll tell you all about it."

Edwina disconnected and Debbie Sue stood there, staring at her cell phone. Good God almighty, what in the hell were they stepping into?

Justin dropped his cell phone back into his shirt pocket and turned to Sophia, who sat demurely on the sofa. After the occurrence in the horse pen he had no intention of letting another day go by without tackling the situation head-on. Enough pussyfooting around. Time for action. Without her agreement, he couldn't proceed with the séance. He sat down on the ottoman opposite her and told her everything.

To his great relief she was eager to go ahead. She said she already knew about the roses and the misplaced items, but her interest was piqued by the story of the letters on the refrigerator.

"Okay," he said, "Debbie Sue's going to call me back after she talks to her husband and to Edwina. But I want to make one thing clear."

Sophia's eyes widened. "Okay."

"It's going to just be us six. If anyone, especially my brother-in-law, shows up, we stop everything. Agreed?"

"Whatever you want, Justin."

"Good. Sorry to be so dramatic, but I had to make that understood about my wife's brother. What's next?"

"I need some things. I bought them earlier, but they're in my hotel room in Odessa. However, you might have some of them here already."

"Like what?"

"Earthbound spirits respond to"—she began counting off on her fingers—"candles of any shape or size. They like soothing music and fresh flowers, preferably roses."

"I've got the music and a rosebush out back, but the only kind of candles I have is a box of birthday candles. You know, the small kind you stick on a cake."

Sophia shook her head. "I know I said any kind, but I'm afraid those won't do. I can drive back to the hotel and get the ones I bought. It won't take long."

"It's not necessary for you to make the trip alone." Justin plucked his truck keys from the hook on the wall. "Come on. I'll drive you." Stealing a glance at his wristwatch he noted with surprise that it was already after two o'clock. "We've got a few hours to kill. We'll get the candles and grab something to eat. Suddenly I'm starving."

"It's the adrenaline," she said softly.

"Yeah," he replied, "I recognize it. I gotta tell you, mine is running at a maximum level right now. What do you say we chow down on something greasy and deep-fried? You know, push it back to normal?"

"Great," she said, smiling.

Justin walked with Sophia to the passenger's side of his

truck, opened the door and helped her in. He rounded the front end and climbed behind the steering wheel. As he snapped his seat belt in place, she said, "There's something I need to tell you, Justin."

He drove slowly, listening intently as she recounted the story of the break-in at the hotel. She ended by saying, "Nothing was missing and Brad Pitt saw to it that I was moved to another room on the ground floor, near the registration desk."

"Did you say Brad *Pitt*?"

"Trust me, it isn't the one you think."

"Why didn't you tell me about this sooner? Or at the very least you should've called me last night."

"That's sweet of you to be concerned, but involving you wouldn't have changed anything. And I wasn't hurt." Sophia reached out and touched his arm. "There's more."

In the next mile she gave an account of the half-eaten piece of candy and her visions of the small man. "Your brother-in-law is that person, Justin."

Justin's heart leaped. His head jerked toward her involuntarily. He'd had an intuitive moment of his own after she first mentioned a small person back in the diner. But suspecting it and knowing it and having a psychic see it were entirely different things.

"I saw it first when you introduced us and he held my hand," she added.

Justin's heart pounded. He braked hard and came to a stop on the shoulder of the road, staring straight ahead, trying to filter information.

It was then he noticed something lying on the road just ahead. His mind still numb, he lifted his foot from the brake and inched forward until he was even with the object. He moved the gear shift to park, opened the door and slid out of his truck. He walked over to the object and saw a small, bedraggled bundle of yellow roses. They appeared to have been run over, and not much was left of the yellow petals, but a green ribbon was still in place around the stems—the same green ribbon he had seen on the roses lying on John Patrick's car seat.

Suddenly, like a crossword puzzle where the one consequential word could provide a dozen solutions, everything began to fall into place. The disruptions in Justin's home when he was away at work; John Patrick's preoccupation with what Justin was doing and when, where he was going and why; the constant companionship John Patrick had offered. Justin had naively misunderstood it all, but now he clearly saw that it wasn't Justin's welfare John Patrick had been consumed with. Justin's ruination was what his brother-in-law sought.

But why? What reason could compel the brother of a deceased sister to use her memory to torment the man who had loved her more than life itself? Jealousy? Revenge?

More than those two emotions, two others would more likely spur motivation in a man like John Patrick. Money and power. To John Patrick, those two were like addictive drugs.

Justin shook his head. None of this made sense. There were still too many questions to which he had no answers.

But if Sophia couldn't supply them, Justin would damn well see to it that John Patrick did.

"Justin?" Sophia's soft voice came from inside the truck. "Are you all right?"

He turned and looked at her, saw concern in her eyes. "I'm fine. Probably better than I have been in a really long time."

Returning to the driver's seat, he explained the roses to Sophia. Before he finished, his cell warbled. He fished it from his shirt pocket and checked the face plate. The caller was Debbie Sue. He fervently hoped she and Edwina could be present tonight, but whether they came or not, he was more determined than ever to move forward. He pressed into the call and said, "Hello."

"Okay," Debbie Sue said flatly, without returning his greeting, "we're all in for tonight, including my husband and Edwina's. What time do you want us there?"

## twenty-two

During the remainder of the drive to Odessa, Sophia stared out the passenger window, pretending to take in the view, though there was little to see. Self-doubt and sweaty-palmed fear consumed her. She had never undertaken a séance alone and now her first had grown to five participants.

She knew from her grandmother that the more parties involved, the greater the likelihood that an uninvited visitor from the other side might drop in. She had seen her grandmother, a seasoned mentalist, handle this congestion of souls many times. Working like a traffic cop at rush hour, Gran Bella had been capable of moving spirits around to avoid conflict. Sophia was only too aware that she was anything but seasoned, too aware that she was as much a virgin in this situation as a sixteen-year-old whose first date was the prom.

She was disturbed that a spirit had already used her as a vessel earlier today in Justin's barn and she hadn't even seen or felt it coming. The normal forewarnings—facial numbness, eye twitching, a drop in temperature—hadn't assailed her. The last thing she had remembered was taking the reins of the horse and stroking its neck. The next thing she knew she was sprawled on the ground at Justin's feet, with him glaring down at her with an expression of horror, stammering, *You kissed . . . who kissed. . .*

Sophia didn't even remember kissing him. His deceased wife's spirit must have taken over her body. What pain experiencing a manifestation of Rachel in a stranger's body must have inflicted on Justin. Fortunately, he had snapped back to reality. To cause that, she, Sophia, must have said something she didn't remember saying. Squeezing her eyes tightly shut, she pled, *Gran Bella, I need your help tonight. Be strong when I am not. Help me maintain control.*

The pickup's slowing caused her to open her eyes again and she saw they were entering the parking lot of her hotel. Justin parked nose-in across the lot from the entrance.

"I'll walk in with you," he said, "in case you have someone waiting for you in your room again."

Having him beside her was comforting and made her feel secure. She nodded. "Thank you, Justin."

They walked through the lobby and rounded the corner

into the hallway. She stopped at her door and dug the key from her purse. Justin stepped forward and held out his hand. "Let me go first, okay?"

Sophia placed the key on his open palm. He unlocked the door, eased it open and tentatively stepped into the room. She followed closely on his heels. No more than two steps into the room he threw out his arm, and she ran into it. "Call the police," he ordered. "It's happened again."

Sophia peeked around his outstretched arm and felt her face heat. "Uh, actually, nothing's been disturbed, Justin. This is the way I left everything this morning."

Justin snickered. Then they both began laughing, releasing the pent-up tension the morning had pressed upon them. Sophia wiped a tear of mirth from her eye. "I'm so embarrassed. I promise I'm not normally such a slob."

Justin shook his head. "This time, I'm glad you were. I needed the laugh."

The moment over, she excused herself and went further into the room and grabbed the plastic Target bag of candles. Then she rummaged in her suitcase and pulled out a small black box. She had brought it just in case, not really anticipating using it, but after this morning it was unquestionably needed. "Okay," she said looking around. "I think I have everything I need except the roses."

"I've still got a few roses in my backyard," Justin said. "We could just cut some."

"Are they white?"

"No. No white ones."

"Perhaps we can stop at Target. I know they have white ones."

"No problem," Justin said.

They left the hotel and Justin drove to the nearby Target. After she purchased a dozen white roses, he drove them to Mama Hayes' to eat. There, they sat in relative silence enjoying their meal. Some of Sophia's nervousness about the coming séance had dissipated and her feeling of isolation had lessened too. She was even able to look up occasionally and smile at Justin.

In an odd way, she felt as if Gran Bella had taken her hand. She was a warrior mentally preparing for a battle. She had the tools of her trade at the ready and her grandmother was poised to help. *Whoever is out there harassing Justin*, she thought with a sly but inward grin, *bring it on*.

Debbie Sue and Buddy arrived at Justin's house early. Debbie Sue desperately hoped Vic and Edwina would show up early enough for Edwina to fill her in on the bit of news she had mentioned over the phone. Prostitution? Edwina? No way. Sex for money? Not Edwina. Charging for it would make it a job and Edwina liked sex too much to turn it into a chore. Debbie Sue just wasn't buying it.

After introducing Buddy to Justin and Sophia, Debbie Sue said, "Excuse me, y'all. I'm gonna check the surveillance cameras." She looked at Justin. "Any new activity? Anything strange going on in your house?"

"Nope," Justin answered.

"I'll just take the cameras into the kitchen while y'all talk."

She plucked the camera from behind the family photo, then pulled the book on plumbing, which was really a spy camera, from the book shelf, then carried them into the dining room. Sitting at the table, she watched as Justin's everyday life unfolded before her. Seeing nothing telling, she pressed FAST FORWARD. Images sped past until something caught her eye. She reversed and pressed PLAY again. The book seemed to be moving, capturing dizzying images ceiling to floor and back again. Debbie Sue's breath caught. She sat there mesmerized, couldn't take her eyes off the screen.

The movement on the screen came to a halt and Debbie Sue found herself looking at a framed photograph of Rachel. The camera's focus stayed on the picture for almost a full minute. Debbie Sue's eyes bugged. Who was holding the damn camera? Had Justin taken it from the bookshelf where she and Edwina had placed it and walked around the house with it?

Then the camera was on the move again, stopping finally at the refrigerator door in the kitchen. The letters on the refrigerator door began moving on their own. The picture suddenly became blurry and unfocused. Then, just as quickly as the picture had gone haywire, it cleared up again, showing a new message on the refrigerator door:

BOO
RS

Blood began to swish in Debbie Sue's ears. She could hear air entering and leaving her lungs. She squeaked and slapped her hand against her mouth. What the fuck was going on?

Debbie Sue left her chair and walked into the kitchen. The letters on the refrigerator door were scattered all over the door, spelling no particular words.

Well, this was just crazy. She walked back into the living room. "Hey, Justin, have you seen any new messages on the fridge's door?"

"Not a one," Justin said. "Why do you ask?"

"Oh, nothing. Nothing. Just checking." Debbie Sue walked back to the camera on the dining-room table and sped back to the shots of the refrigerator door, checking the date. The message had been filmed earlier that day. But who did it target? The Domestic Equalizers? This was a frivolous message. Who *else* could it have been directed to? Was Rachel's ghost showing a playful side?

A shiver slithered up Debbie Sue's spine. "This is ridiculous," she mumbled. "I don't even believe in ghosts."

Just then a loud roaring, clattering noise came from outside. It made her think of a road grader crossed with a tank. She walked back into the living room and followed Justin, Sophia and Buddy out to the front porch. An enormous set of shiny chrome handlebars with a motorcycle attached came into view, and even from a distance, she recognized Vic Martin riding it. This must be the bike Vic had been working on around the clock, the one he wanted to be proud of when he met his navy buddies again in Terlingua.

Vic Martin just naturally looked as if he was born to be wild. He could be riding a tricycle and people would address him as "sir." His head was as bald as an egg and a Fu Manchu mustache framed his mouth. Today he had on a sweatshirt with the sleeves torn out, showing bare biceps thick as most men's thighs. His denim-clad legs were stuffed into black, thick-soled, mid-calf boots. Mirrored wraparound sunglasses covered his eyes. Debbie Sue was glad she knew Vic as well as she did or she would've been scared to death.

As she waved, she assumed Edwina was following him in the Mustang . . . until she saw skinny arms wrapped so tightly around Vic's middle they seemed to be part of the folds in his sweatshirt.

"My God," Buddy said, "is that Edwina on the back of that bike?"

It had to be, Debbie Sue thought, but she had seen Edwina refuse to ride in a vehicle with the windows open for fear of destroying her hairdo. How in the world had Vic persuaded her to crawl on the back of a motorcycle? Before the idea left her head completely, Debbie Sue knew the answer. Edwina would do anything for and with Vic. If he truly wanted her on the back of his "hog," Edwina would bite the bullet, toss back a couple of tequila shots and throw caution to the wind—along with her hair, makeup and most assuredly, her talonlike acrylic nails.

Vic made a circle in the driveway, revving the motorcycle's motor to a deafening pitch, his laughter barely audible above the din. Debbie Sue covered her ears with her palms until Vic killed the engine.

It was then that she got a full view of Edwina. While a protective motorcycle helmet didn't fit Vic's ultra-macho image of himself, that didn't mean he wouldn't want his beloved spouse to wear one. A Salt Lick High School Steers gold football helmet encased Edwina's head. Number fifty-seven was stenciled on both sides in black. Debbie Sue couldn't bear to think of what it had done to the carefully molded and sculpted beehive hairdo Edwina always wore.

At this moment, she also wore a fixed smile, as if her face were paralyzed. She had that frozen, painted-on expression of one who had accepted her fate, like one of those passengers left on the deck of the Titanic as water began creeping up her thighs. Staring at her old friend, Debbie Sue bit her lip.

"Sorry," Vic called to her. "I'm like a kid with his first two-wheeler." He pushed the kickstand down with his heel, turned his head and spoke to Edwina over his shoulder. "We've been having a helluva good time, haven't we, Mama Doll?" He patted Edwina's hands. "You can turn me loose now, Mama Doll. We've stopped moving."

Edwina's arms slowly unlocked from around Vic's waist and she carefully lifted her skinny self from behind her husband. She was finally on her feet, but she stood perfectly still, listing slightly to the left. She appeared to be in a daze. A flashback zoomed through Debbie Sue's brain of the moonlit night several years ago when she and Edwina, along with

Paige McBride, had rescued Rocket Man and two other horses from a horse thief and Edwina, who had never ridden a horse, had found herself astride a runaway.

Vic, too, dismounted from the bike and caught her elbow. "You okay, Mama Doll?"

"Mmmph," Edwina said, taking a cautious step, her arms extended from her sides. She was wearing a bright yellow oversize sweatshirt and orange leggings and Debbie Sue thought immediately of Big Bird.

"Do I have bugs on my teeth?" Edwina tilted her head back, looked up at Vic and bared her teeth.

"I don't see a thing, sweetheart," Vic replied, studying her teeth.

"Thank God," Edwina mumbled and hobbled toward Debbie Sue.

Vic, too, came over and brushed Debbie Sue's cheek with a peck. "Hi, darlin'. This was my baby's first ride on my hog." He grinned at Edwina pridefully.

"I would've never guessed," Debbie Sue said.

Buddy stepped off the porch. "Hey, Vic." He extended his right hand to Vic.

"Hey, Vic, let me introduce you to everyone," Debbie Sue said, and proceeded to do just that.

"Let's go inside." Justin urged the group back onto porch and toward the front door.

Following Justin, Sophia and Buddy, Vic took the porch stair in a single step, but Debbie Sue caught Edwina's arm and held her back. As soon as everyone was out of sight, Debbie Sue said, "Ed, are you sure you're all right?"

Edwina gave a shaky thumbs-up. "Be honest, Debbie Sue. Do I really have bugs on my teeth? " She bared her teeth again.

"I don't see a thing. Honest. Your teeth look fine."

"That's what I was afraid of."

"What do you mean?"

"We hit a big bug about three miles back while I was screaming. If he's not on my teeth, that's means I swallowed him."

"Oh, no, Ed—"

"Shit! I think I'm gonna puke."

Debbie Sue had intended to tell her partner about the message on the refrigerator door, but this didn't seem to be the time. She squarely faced Edwina and began to undo the helmet's chin strap. "Take off this, this . . . whatever this is. The strap is so tight you probably can't breathe. Where'd you get it anyway?"

"My neighbor's boy. He's not on the football team anymore."

Edwina carefully removed the helmet. Debbie Sue's hand flew to her mouth. "Oh, my God, Ed. You look like a Mickey Mouse topiary at Disney World."

Edwina touched her hair gingerly. "Well, hell. Why not? Y'all can relax now. If you were thinking something scary might show up tonight, it just did."

Something scary had already shown up on the refrigerator door. "You're not scary, Ed." Debbie Sue gave her a one-armed hug, then dug her pickup keys out of her pocket. "Here, let me see what I can do." For the next few minutes she tried to work some magic on Edwina's hairdo, but with only a truck key for a tool, the results weren't spectacular. She stepped back to get a better look at her handiwork.

"How's it look?" Edwina asked.

"Not so great, but better. If I only had a brush and some hair spray." Debbie Sue could no longer keep from laughing. "Also a tube of concealer, some foundation and blush. Then everything would be fine."

"Hell, I'm going home."

"You don't have a way to go home. What did you expect when you put on that helmet and got on the back of that motorcycle?"

"Hell, Debbie Sue, I didn't expect to get here alive. I figured it wouldn't matter how I looked. I figured they'd mess me up at the autopsy anyway."

Debbie Sue took her shaky friend by the arm. "Well, you've shown Vic you're a good sport. And you've stayed with your pledge to try anything once before you die. You don't have to ride it again. Buddy and I'll give you a ride home tonight."

"To hell with that," Edwina said, lifting her arm away from Debbie Sue's grip. "Vic's planning on me riding to Terlingua with him this fall. And if that sweet man wants me there, then pick out your crayons and color me in."

"Bad hair, bugs on your teeth and all?"

"Hell, yes. I don't care if I look like a tractor's windshield and the bride of Dracula combined." She stared off into the distance. "Maybe I'll cut my hair real short. That would work. You'll pray for me won't you, Dippity-Do?"

Debbie Sue laughed again. "You might not know it, Ed, but I already do. All the time."

They had already opened the front door and walked into the foyer of Justin's house before Debbie Sue remembered she hadn't asked Edwina about the arrest for prostitution. *Fuck,* this evening wasn't starting out all that great and she had no reason to believe it would improve.

# twenty-three

Sophia looked toward the front door as Debbie Sue and Edwina came in. Vic was in the middle of telling Buddy an animated story of how much time he had invested in bringing a dilapidated Harley back to life. He was even more excited that his better half was going to travel with him to Terlingua.

Startled when Vic bounded into the room, Sophia had been torn between hiding behind the sofa and fleeing through the back door. From the comments Debbie Sue and Edwina had made about him, Sophia could see he was everything she had expected and nothing she could have imagined. He looked like a hard-core survivor of *The Ultimate Fighter*—rough hewn, scarred, muscled and worn. But his boylike excitement over his new toy was genuine and somehow sweet.

While he might be ecstatic, one look at Edwina's disheveled state told a different story.

"Hi, Debbie Sue, Edwina," Sophia said. "Vic was just telling us about the work he's done on his motorcycle. I've never ridden one. I'm afraid I'm a chicken."

"Oh, you shouldn't be afraid," Edwina said. "It's safe as a . . . uh . . . what was that again, hon?" she said to Vic.

"Safe as a baby in its mama's arms," Vic answered with a broad grin.

"Yeah," Edwina said, unsmiling. "Safe as a baby. Now that I've ridden with you, maybe being a baby is the right approach. No makeup, no hair, no teeth working double duty as a bug screen. And the notion of me wearing a diaper probably isn't a bad idea."

Vic's bellowing laugh filled the room. "Isn't she great?" His huge arms engulfed her thin body in a hug. "This woman's what every man wants and most will never have." He planted a kiss on her cheek and smiled down at her affectionately.

Edwina visibly melted. Her shoulders sagged and she blushed a deep hue. Sophia was moved, but she couldn't let herself be distracted.

*It's time,* she told herself. She cleared her throat. "We should get started. Let me tell you some basic rules. We'll sit in a circle, holding hands at first until contact is made. No matter what happens don't disturb me or anyone else that a spirit might have inhabited—"

"Inhabited? Anyone else?" Edwina's eyes bugged. She gasped. "I thought that could only happen to a medium!"

Surprised and troubled by Edwina's vehemence, Sophia worked to speak in an even tone. "Normally, yes. But sometimes spirits will take control of an easy receptor."

"Mama Doll," Vic said, rubbing her arm. "This doesn't mean a spirit will inhabit you."

"Yeah, Ed," Debbie Sue added. "I wouldn't call you an easy receptor."

"Didn't you hear what she said?" Edwina snapped. "God, I've practically got 'Look at me. I'm an easy receptor' tattooed on my forehead."

"Whatever happens, Edwina," Sophia continued, "you're in a safe environment. A spirit cannot make you do anything your own free will wouldn't."

"If that was meant to make me feel better you don't know me very well," Edwina grumbled.

"Go ahead with the list, Sophia," Debbie Sue said, giving Edwina an evil eye. "We're listening."

Holding two fingers up, Sophia went on. "No laughing and no breaking the bond of the circle on your own. If a spirit moves you from the circle, that's fine. And lastly, no hysteria, okay?"

"Hysteria," Edwina repeated.

"Is that all?" Justin asked nervously. "Are we ready to start?"

Sophia produced the white roses she had bought at Target and reached into her plastic sack and pulled out the white candles. She handed them around the room like party favors.

"If each of you would please distribute these throughout the room and light them." She turned to Justin. "Do you have a vase for the roses?"

"Sure do." Justin picked up the paper flute of roses and walked toward the kitchen, stopping briefly to sort through some CDs and make a selection. The soothing sounds of Kenny G's soprano saxophone filled the room.

Sophia motioned everyone into the dining area, which was just off the kitchen. Let's all sit," she said, gesturing a circle around the oval dining table with her hand. "Boy, girl, boy, girl."

The five participants pulled out chairs and took seats around the table, leaving one of the end positions for her.

Justin came from the kitchen with a wonderful cut crystal vase holding the roses. "Where do you want them?"

"Just place them in the center of the table."

He did and the subtle scent of the roses floated all around them in the small room.

"This looks more like a romantic dinner party," Buddy said, eyeing the vase of flowers.

Sophia smiled. His comment seemed real, no sarcasm intended. He was heart-stoppingly handsome, she thought, and the ultimate gentleman. He was serious and solemn in his demeanor, exactly how she had always imagined a Texas Ranger would be. "Spirits respond to a flickering light. The music and flowers conjure up pleasant earthly memories."

"Are you sure they're not remembering their own funerals?" Vic asked.

"That's an interesting question, Vic," Sophia said. "I suppose it's possible." She went to the light switches on the wall and turned off all the lighting, leaving only the candles' golden glow as illumination.

Taking her seat at the head of the table, she placed the black box in front of her. She had kept it in the sack with the other accessories until now. She feared it might be too theatrical for the séance first timers, but she had seen Gran Bella use its contents with success many times.

"What's in the box?" Edwina asked.

"These are items that help the spirits connect with us. With a group this large, any number of entities could emerge. We might need a little help."

"I don't understand," Justin said. "I thought we were trying to make contact with Rachel."

"We are hoping to," Sophia said in a soothing, sweet voice, "but the comings and goings of others cannot be predicted. These items give the spirits identities."

"You've got my curiosity up," Debbie Sue said, rising a little in her seat to see the contents of the box. "Let's see the stuff."

Sophia removed the lid and lifted out a pack of cigarettes, a lighter, a cigar, a small ashtray, a pair of glasses, a package of gum, a shot glass and a half pint of Wild Turkey whiskey.

"Damn," Edwina said. "This looks like a party to me."

"If it's not, it's sure a good start," Vic added.

Sophia smiled. "We might not need any of these things. We'll just have to wait and see. Now, would everyone please take the hands of the people next to you and remember, do not break the circle until contact is made."

"God, hold everything," Edwina said. "I gotta pee." She rose and trekked from the room.

"Oh, I forgot to mention that. Does anyone else need to leave?"

"I'm good," Debbie Sue replied and all three men mumbled agreement.

After what seemed an eternity, Edwina returned, "Sorry, y'all. I figured it was better to go now than deal with a catastrophe later."

"Now," Sophia said regaining everyone's attention, "please join hands."

Sophia led a brief prayer asking for guidance, and after a chorus of amens, she closed her eyes and began. "We are here to communicate with the spirit in this home," she intoned, followed by silence. Outside, crickets chirped, a coyote howled, but no noises pervaded the house. Sophia willed her mind to remain centered on making contact.

It wasn't unheard of that a mentalist would have to try several sessions to reach an earthbound spirit and sometimes it never happened at all. She suspected this group of realists—a professional cop, a retired soldier, a professional firefighter and two amateur detectives—wouldn't accept that explanation. They would see the failure of a spirit to appear as an excuse or possibly even a con game. The worst possible thing she could do now was to let herself be distracted and anxious, but at this particular moment she was becoming very distracted and miserably anxious.

After an extended silence, her senses told her someone was present, waiting and watching. Something was happening—

not to the group, but to Sophia. A spirit or spirits were close at hand. Still, part of her insecure subconscious feared nothing would happen. She spoke again. "We are here to communicate with the spirit in this home."

At that moment, she felt a slight brush against her arm. Opening one eye, she saw that Debbie Sue was reaching over her and pulling a cigarette from its pack. She had broken her link with her husband and with Vic and was now disencumbered. Buddy's eyes were open and he was watching her suspiciously. Sophia lifted her hand, signaling him to remain silent.

Sophia had not seen Debbie Sue smoke any of the times she had been in her presence, but if a nicotine craving increased with tension, the present circumstances would certainly play on a smoker's nerves.

Debbie Sue tapped the end of the cigarette on the table, then with the practiced habit of one who had smoked a long time, placed the cigarette into the corner of her mouth. She picked up the lighter, clicked on a bright yellow flame, lit the cigarette's end and drew in deeply. She sighed and expelled a plume of smoke. She combed her fingers through her long reddish hair, pushed away from the table and propped her ankle on her knee. She stared intently at Edwina.

By now the breaking of the chain and the odor of cigarette smoke had prompted all eyes to open and everyone's attention was glued to the smoker. Buddy, Vic and Edwina's faces showed jaw-dropping astonishment, while Justin looked on with what Sophia determined was curiosity.

Edwina's eyes bugged. "Debbie Sue, what do you think

you're doing? You've never smoked a cigarette in your life."

Sophia felt a deep trembling within. This bit of news was all she needed to recognize that a spirit had indeed come forward and entered Debbie Sue's body. She had become a receptor. And Sophia doubted the guilty spirit was the soul of Justin's sweet departed Rachel. Why Debbie Sue had been chosen Sophia might never know, but clearly the spirit was a strong entity and had seized the opportunity to come forward.

Sophia knew she had to take control of the situation quickly. The spirit was the least of her worries now. She was more concerned with the living and their reaction to the unexpected visitor.

"Welcome," she finally said. "You behave as if you haven't smoked in a while."

Debbie Sue cut her eyes from Edwina to Sophia. "You're the medium, aren't you? You're a pretty little thing. Part Mexican, huh?"

Before Sophia could answer, Buddy grabbed her forearm in a viselike grip. "Is Debbie Sue all right? What's going on here? I don't like this."

The smoker turned her gaze on Buddy and looked him up and down lasciviously. "I'm only borrowing her, handsome. She's just fine. You know, I kinda like the cut of your jib, if you get my drift."

"Would you like to share your name with us?" Sophia asked in an even voice. "Do you have a message for someone or is there someone you'd like to speak to directly?"

The smoker drew a long, deep pull on the cigarette.

"Yeah." She looked across the table at Edwina. "Christ-on-a-crutch, Edwina. What in the hell did you do to your hair? It looks like you combed it with a hand mixer. In plain words, you look like shit."

Sophia darted a look at Edwina, who sat as if in a trance, eyes bigger than saucers and unblinking. Finally, a mouse-like squeak came from Edwina. She went from a state of unblinking to blinking rapidly. "Lit-Little—"

"Lit-Little . . . Lit-Little . . ." Debbie Sue said, mocking Edwina. "I see time hasn't made you any smarter. I'll never understand what my sweet baby boy saw in you. He could have had a dozen other women, but for some godforsaken reason he married you."

She took another drag off the cigarette and tamped the butt into the ashtray. She gestured to Vic, who had placed a protective arm about Edwina's chair and was leaning into her. "Who's this dude you've picked up? He looks like a dildo with a face."

Buddy leaned forward. "That's enough. I don't—"

Sophia stopped him by raising her palm. She watched Edwina cautiously, looking for a signal her expertise was needed, but apparently the last remark by the visitor had been a trigger.

Edwina no longer appeared frightened or dumbstruck. Squinting and propping one elbow on the table, she leaned forward. "Little Pearl, you've never been anything but an old bitch. You can say what you want about me, but don't you dare say anything against Vic Martin. This man is the best thing that was ever born. He treats me better than anybody ever has, including my own kin. And by God, he liberated Kuwait! And another thing, your precious *baby boy did* have a dozen other women, all within a month after marrying me!"

Debbie Sue's shoulders sagged, her chin dropped and rested on her chest. As quickly as the soul had appeared it seemed to have departed its living receptor.

Sophia sensed everyone was poised to speak, but she held up her palm, gesturing them to silence. She would be the only one to speak. "Debbie Sue, are you with us? Are you all right? . . . Debbie Sue? Can you hear me?"

Debbie Sue raised her head and looked around the table with a bewildered expression. Turning to Buddy she asked, "My mouth tastes like a bird pooped on my tongue. And I'm feeling kind of sick to my stomach." She sprang to her feet and rushed toward the hall bathroom, from where retching sounds emanated seconds later.

Buddy rose, walked back into the living room and returned carrying his hat. "Sorry, folks, but this is enough. We're calling it a night."

Before he could march toward the bathroom, Debbie Sue returned. "Not on your life, Buddy Overstreet. We're really close to something happening here. I say let's keep going."

"You don't remember anything?" Sophia asked.

Debbie Sue looked at each person. "What am I supposed to remember? Did I crow like a rooster?"

"Are you still feeling ill?" Sophia asked.

"I'm better now. Must have been something I ate." Rubbing her stomach she looked at the group, "Well, how 'bout it? Aren't we gonna keep going?"

Buddy firmly plopped his Stetson on his head. "The only place we're going, Flash, is home. Sophia, Justin, sorry, but I really think I need to get her home."

Vic pushed his chair back and took Edwina by the upper arm, easily lifting her to her feet.

"Same here," he said, looking at Edwina with pure adoration. "After all that, there's someone I know who deserves a good back rub."

"God, I hope that's me," Edwina said.

"You bet it is, Mama Doll."

Sophia could see everyone was shaken. She felt helpless and drained herself. The group's departure would leave only her and Justin. A séance with only two was frowned upon. Leaving a living participant unprotected in case the medium was overtaken by an unfriendly source was too dangerous.

Debbie Sue hung back. "Y'all go on out," she said, patting Buddy and Vic on their backs. "Me and Ed need to talk to Justin for a minute. Shoptalk, you know?"

"I want to go with Vic," Edwina said.

"Ed, shh," Debbie Sue said. She walked with her husband and Vic to the front door and stood watching until they were outside. As soon as she closed the door, she said, "Listen, y'all, I know those two guys. There's no use arguing with them about us staying. But they're both going out of town tomorrow afternoon and we're gonna finish this thing. Ed and I'll be back here tomorrow night."

"We will?" Edwina said, wide-eyed.

"Yes, Ed, we will. I know something happened. And I

can hardly wait to hear the details from Buddy on our way home."

By now, Edwina had her purse in hand and was standing by the front door.

"Don't forget to call me when you can, Ed," Debbie Sue said to her. "There's a story you haven't finished telling me."

"There is?" Edwina said.

"Oh, yeah, Ed. There is."

"The story is me getting home in one piece on the back of that motorcycle."

# twenty-four

*S*tanding in his front doorway, Justin watched the Domestic Equalizers and their spouses drive away into the darkness. God, his head was whirling. He'd had Rachel, then lost her and now he had an opportunity to have her again—not physically, but he would have her again spiritually. He was no longer in denial. He no longer questioned his own sanity or Sophia's claims. She *did* have the ability to conjure up souls departed from this world and if one had chosen to communicate with Edwina, perhaps tomorrow night the communicating spirit would be Rachel.

"Justin?"

Sophia's soft voice interrupted his musing and he turned

to her. "Sorry, I was lost in thought. Are you all right? I mean, these sessions must be hard on you. Is there anything I can do for you?"

A hint of moisture glistened in her eyes. "Then, then you believe me? You believe *in* me?"

"I believe in you, Sophia. You've been fair and upfront from the beginning. You have a special gift and I'll be forever indebted to you. Beyond what I've agreed to pay you, I mean. Without even knowing the outcome, I'll always be thankful. You're going to bring my Rachel back to me."

"Back to you?"

Sophia echoing his questions only added to the confusion that continued to boil in Justin's brain. He seemed to be saying the wrong things, but then he didn't have a clue what the right things were either. He decided on a more direct approach. He cleared his throat. "I'm sorry, but I'm a little baffled. Did I say something wrong? Have I *done* something wrong?"

Sophia moved to an armchair in the living room and picked up her purse. Hooking the strap on her shoulder she looked at him again, her eyes filled with an emotion he couldn't interpret. All he knew was that a man could get lost in those hazel eyes.

"Justin," she said firmly. "I need to be sure you understand that I can't, as you say, bring Rachel back to you. Our duty, or rather, *my* duty, is to help her cross over. She was crying at the barn because she's a soul in anguish, Justin. One that needs to be guided to the light. Unlike Little Pearl, Rachel isn't a spirit who enjoys making an earthly visit to harrass. Her soul is supposed to be at rest, but something has been holding her earthbound. I fear that something is *you* and the way you continue to hang on to her. She left the message on the refrigerator door for someone to help *you* let her go. You must send her away, Justin."

How could he send Rachel away? Wasn't she already gone? Aside from that, he didn't know if he had the will to send her away. Flesh-and-blood woman or spirit, wasn't she still his wife? He didn't want to lose her a second time. He swallowed hard, suppressing a sob. "But on our wedding day, we swore . . . *I* swore to love her until death do us part.

Sophia came to him and took his hand. "And you did that, Justin. I have no doubt that you did that. I also have no doubt that nothing in your vows said you owed her life-altering fidelity after death. You can't be faithful to a spirit and still live a normal life on earth."

Justin knew that, but hearing Sophia verbalize it had a profound impact on him. What was wrong with him? Typically, he had too much common sense to get caught up with spirits and seers.

Sophia led him through the open doorway and pulled the door shut behind them. Standing on the porch, illumination supplied only by stars and the lamp shine through the window, she said softly, "Why don't you stay with me tonight at the hotel? You shouldn't be alone. Fear of the unknown is just part of this business and I'm largely unfazed by it. I've been present many times when my grandmother had to help the living while guiding a loved one's spirit into the light. I don't want you to be afraid, Justin."

*What was she suggesting now?* Justin yanked his hand from hers and stared at her. "I am *not* afraid of Rachel." But even as he said it so firmly and emphatically, he wondered. Maybe he *was* afraid and didn't know it.

"Of course you aren't. I didn't mean to imply you were frightened. But you must understand that the spirits do not have the same personalities as their mortal hosts. I feel you need to be away from this house for tonight. You need a distraction. Won't you please come with me?"

He shook his head. "No. Sex with someone I barely know would cause more problems than it would solve."

She drew a quick breath. Her eyes grew wide and her lips parted. After a few beats, she said, "I'm sorry, Justin. I didn't mean to suggest . . . There are two beds in my room. All I'm offering you is company."

At that, Justin felt his self-righteous bluster collapse and he felt stupid. He found himself helpless to offer a reason not to go with her. The fact was that her invitation wasn't even remotely seductive, but rather, an expression of genuine kindness and humanity. And not since the day he buried Rachel had he needed both of those things as much as he needed them tonight. "I guess I could do that. Let me grab a few things from inside."

He re-entered his home, threw some things in a small duffel and returned to the front porch.

"Wow, that was fast," Sophia said.

"I don't require much. Besides, if I need makeup I'll just borrow yours." He followed up that remark with a chuckle, a feeble attempt to lighten the moment.

Sophia smiled. "That's okay. But I'm a little darker than you are."

As the car drove away, a noiseless shuffling of letters on the refrigerator door occurred:

*C U AGIN.*

At home, even after brushing her teeth several times, Debbie Sue still had a nasty taste in her mouth. A million thoughts and questions raced through her mind. On the drive home, Buddy had told her about her body having been taken over. She deliberately hadn't told him about the "Boo" message on the refrigerator door. Mostly because she didn't know what to think. Her common sense and her innate skepticism were being dismantled. Not only did she not know what to think, she didn't know what to do. She felt uprooted.

And now she wondered if she should tell Edwina about the "Boo" message. Edwina had seemed traumatized by the evening's events from beginning to end. After riding to Justin's house on the back of Vic's Harley, hearing that a ghost had sent another message to the Domestic Equalizers just might push her over the edge. Hell, Debbie Sue was on the edge herself.

She checked her own refrigerator door and was relieved to see no message. She didn't really believe Rachel Sadler's ghost had made its way from Justin's house to hers, but the way things were going, who knew what might happen next.

She opened the refrigerator door and stared at its contents. She didn't know what she was looking for, but adrenaline was pumping through her veins. She was on a mission to consume something sugar laden and carb loaded. Buddy had stepped outside or he would be giving her a lecture on the merits of eating healthy. Health issues be damned, she intended to pig out.

Her cell phone blasted "The Eyes of Texas" and she knew without looking that at this time of night, the caller was Edwina. She grabbed her purse, dug out the phone and flipped it open. "Is that you, Ed?"

"Debbie Sue," Edwina gushed, "are you all right? This is Debbie Sue, isn't it? Or is it Little Pearl?"

Debbie Sue returned to the refrigerator. She was more focused on a round plastic container that had been pushed to the back of a shelf than on answering Edwina. She bent down and pulled out the container.

"Girl, if you don't answer me I'm gonna blow a gasket," Edwina declared.

"It's the real me, Ed. Cool your jets. And your gaskets."

"How do I know it's you? I need a signal."

"Oh, forgodsake, ask me a question only Debbie Sue Overstreet would know the answer to."

"Oookaaay. Let me see . . . Who's the only other person you've slept with besides Buddy?"

"Quint Matthews," Debbie Sue answered with finality.

"Who's got the biggest package?"

"Dammit, Ed, I'm not discussing packages with you."

"I know. But I figured I'd give it a shot all the same. Inquiring minds want to know."

Debbie Sue propped the phone between her ear and her shoulder as she peeled the top from a bowl and sniffed the contents, which appeared to be pudding. But she couldn't recall a time she and Buddy had ever had pudding. Taking that as a sign the stuff should be gotten rid of, she dumped whatever it was down the garbage disposal.

"When y'all were driving home, I suppose Buddy told you everything that happened at Justin's," Edwina said.

"Yeah, he yakked non-stop all the way home. When we went out to Justin's, I think he really believed *nothing* would happen. Seeing it with his own eyes really got his attention."

"Was he scared?"

"I don't know. Sometimes you can't tell what Overstreet the Stoic is thinking. He was awestruck, for sure. But being a total realist with both feet on the ground, he wasn't yet ready to surrender to the ghost idea. You know Buddy. If something happened he couldn't explain, he probably didn't believe his own eyes."

"Hm. Vic was impressed. Not blown away, but impressed."

"He wasn't scared?"

"Nah. Vic's been eyeball to eyeball with machine-gun-toting terrorists. To him, a little ghost is child's play. But I'll tell you this much, Debbie Sue, I was scared shitless. I thought I was gonna have a heart attack."

At that moment, Debbie Sue decided to postpone telling Edwina about the "Boo" message, at least not until this whole thing had reached a conclusion. In fact, Debbie Sue thought, she might never tell her. "I know. But why, Ed?"

"My God, Debbie Sue. A dead person took over your body and I saw it with my own eyes. If I hadn't already gone to the bathroom, I would've peed my pants. Don't you remember? Didn't it affect you in some way?"

Debbie Sue gave up on the contents of the refrigerator and began to rummage in the cupboard, found half a tube of Pringles. "You know, Ed, I don't remember a thing. Not one thing. But I sure as hell can still taste cigarettes. I swear, I don't know why anyone smokes. I know the nicotine is addictive, but I can't figure out why. *Blech!*"

"There's not a day goes by that I don't miss it," Edwina said wistfully.

Debbie Sue didn't doubt it. She still remembered the ordeal of Edwina kicking the smoking habit years back. In some ways, the pain hadn't ended yet. Edwina still constantly quoted from the many books she had read to distract her from smoking.

"Buddy told me this Little Pearl person said some pretty lousy things to you, Ed. I feel bad those words came out of my mouth."

"You couldn't help it. I know that. But it made me remember what a black-hearted bitch she was. Made me appreciate Vic more than ever."

"That isn't possible."

Edwina sighed. "Yeah, I know."

"I wish we hadn't had to leave," Debbie Sue said. "I wish we could've seen what might have happened next."

"Humph. There's not a doubt in my mind the next person to make an appearance would have been Rachel Sadler. But Buddy obviously wasn't willing to take the chance. And Vic wasn't gonna disagree with him."

"Oh, hell, no. Buddy Overstreet was jaw-clenched set on us leaving. And you know how tight his jaw can get." Debbie Sue finished off the tube of Pringles. "So, Ed, quit stalling and let's hear it before Buddy comes back into the house. Why were you arrested for prostitution?"

"Where did Buddy go?"

"He went outside to pee off his new deck."

"But it's only a foot off the ground."

"It's a man thing, Ed. If he's got a deck, he's got to pee off it. So tell me why you were arrested."

"It's a dumb story," Edwina said. "When I was married to Jimmy Wayne and lived in El Paso, he got fired from his job almost the day after we got married. Not just any ol' job suited Jimmy Wayne's, uh, sensibilities, so he had a hard time getting hired somewhere. We had bill collectors hounding us, so I found a job as a seamstress in a strip joint."

As far as Debbie Sue knew, Edwina had never sewn a stitch. Her brow tugged into a frown and she stared into space, trying to envision Edwina hunched over a sewing machine sewing thongs and pasties. "Strip joints need seamstresses? I'd come closer to believing you were a hooker."

"Thanks a lot."

"Hell, Ed, you can't sew. You told me yourself you thought a stitch was something you got in your side if you ran too hard."

"Trust me, there wasn't a whole lot to sew. It was more like gluing and taping. I went through cases of Super Glue. Anyway, I didn't know it then, but apparently, the owner was running an after-hours nooky concession in the back room. The cops raided it and took everybody to the station, including me."

Though the arrest had occurred years ago, Debbie Sue felt compelled to defend her longtime friend. "But you weren't selling . . . er, nooky . . . Were you?"

"Oh, hell, no," Edwina said. "But it took a while for them to sort out that little bit of information. Meantime, my little girls were staying at home with—"

"Oh, no, not Little Pearl," Debbie Sue finished.

"That's right. She couldn't find Jimmy Wayne to tell him to come and get me, naturally, so she had to come down to the courthouse and post my bail. She never let me live it down."

"Have you told Vic about that?"

"Yep, on the way home tonight."

"If I know Vic, he wasn't mad."

"Nah. He kind of likes that I'm a woman with a record. He even wants me to sew up another one of those costumes for myself."

Debbie Sue grinned, knowing that Vic was serious and

that Edwina would do it. She only hoped the crazy woman didn't show up in the Styling Station wearing the costume.

"So what about tomorrow night?" Edwina asked, lowering her voice. "Are we really going back again?"

"You bet your ass we are."

"Oh, hell, Debbie Sue. Do we have to?"

"Of course we have to, Ed. We're too deep into this to give up on it now. Buddy hasn't even told me not to. I think he knows he'd be wasting his breath. What did Vic say about another session?"

"I think he'd love to be there, but since he can't, he just said make sure I don't hurt anybody."

"So there you have it. Approval. What more do you need?"

"Extra underwear?"

"Listen, Ed, if Little Pearl shows up this next time, you'll be ready. You just tell her to take a hike. I mean cut her from the fuckin' herd, Ed. You don't have to take abuse from a dead woman. From what Buddy said and what you've told me, she sounds like a big-ass bully. Stand up to her and she'll hightail it."

"That almost sounds like you knew her," Edwina said.

"Well after all," Debbie Sue said on a chuckle, "we've sort of shared the same skin."

"And she and I've shared the same kin," Edwina said.

"It's like in *The Lion King*, Ed. The circle of life. *Hakuna matata*."

"Yeah, yeah," Edwina replied. "Tuna and tomata."

# twenty-five

T hough Sophia chatted casually about nothing all the way to Odessa, and Justin dutifully chatted along with her, in the back of his mind, he couldn't stop thinking about seeing Debbie Sue become a different person right before his eyes. If Edwina hadn't said Debbie Sue had never smoked in her whole life, he wouldn't have believed what he had seen.

They reached Sophia's hotel after nine o'clock. She excused herself and left the room immediately. Now that a few miles and a little time had passed since the bizarre and disturbing incident had occurred in his home, Justin wondered if she regretted inviting him to her room.

He should have followed her in his own truck instead of riding with her in the rental car. Why hadn't he? As it was now, the only transportation between them was the Aero and he couldn't take it and return to his home and leave her stranded.

He picked up the remote control, powered on the TV and stretched across one of the beds, surfing through TV channels, glad to have the preoccupation and noise. Besides everything else that was going on, he was doing his best to understand the knotty position he had put himself in—alone in a hotel room with a beautiful woman he hardly knew. The decision to accept her invitation now seemed questionable at best. He knew from experience that people in crisis often make poor decisions, and he felt that was certainly what he had done. Crap, he didn't typically act out of foggy emotions.

He could well imagine what his co-workers at the fire station would say to him—*Damn man, when did you become such a wuss?* A sardonic grin curled Justin's mouth. He would like to see his fellow firefighters go through what he had over the past few days. Being seen as a wuss was the least of his concerns.

The sound of the key in the lock catapulted him from the bed to one of the armchairs. Having Sophia see him lying on the bed seemed too intimate, too presumptuous. The door opened and she came in with four canned soft drinks and packages of snacks, balanced on a long, flat box.

He got to his feet and walked to her to lighten her load. "What in the world have you got there?"

She gave him a self-conscious smile. "When I checked in the other day I noticed a bunch of games behind the reservation desk. I asked if I could borrow one for the evening and, well, how about a game of Monopoly?"

Overcome with relief and appreciation, he threw one arm around her and pulled her against him in half a bear hug. "I'll be damned. You know, I don't think I could go to sleep if I had to. A board game is just what we need. Thank you, Sophia."

"Careful," she said, laughing. "We'll have drinks, Fritos and fake money everywhere."

Justin laughed too, the earlier tension eased. "I haven't played Monopoly in years. I have to warn you though, I'm an absolutely ruthless real-estate tycoon. I might come across as a nice guy, but when it comes to Monopoly, I make Donald Trump look small time."

Sophia raised one eyebrow. "Oh, really? Okay, I've been warned." She opened the box and placed the Monopoly board on the table. "You be the banker. I don't need to be around that much money, even fake. It makes me do wild things."

While she set out the accessories, Justin took a seat opposite her and removed the rubber bands from stacks of funny money. "In that case, I'd better relieve you of those funds quickly."

The ensuing hours passed quickly, the only thing occupying Justin's thoughts being the quest to buy Boardwalk or acquire another railroad. He hadn't felt so unencumbered in so long. Laughing out of sheer pleasure instead of behaving like a grieving widower, the way people seemed to want him to do, had almost become an alien activity.

One thing he had learned about being a grieving wid-ower—if he laughed, some thought he was laughing too soon and he must not have loved his wife. Conversely, if he didn't show a lighter side now and then, they said he was trapped in his grief and refusing to face reality.

As Sophia reached across the board to move the top hat token, Justin took her hand in his and spoke as sincerely as he knew how. "I just want to say thanks again, Sophia. I was feeling a little embarrassed earlier and you managed to not only make this night fun, you helped me forget about every-thing but winning this game."

"You don't have to thank me," Sophia said. "I enjoyed it too. I was a little uncomfortable myself once we first got back to the room. I had even begun to think I shouldn't have invited you here. But now . . . well, I've had so much fun and we've laughed a lot. I haven't had much to laugh about in the past year, or anyone to laugh with."

Justin felt like a clod. He had been so absorbed in his own despair he had completely overlooked something Debbie Sue had told him. Sophia had taken care of her dying grand-mother for months and finally lost her just weeks ago. Debbie Sue had explained that the grandmother was Sophia's only family and that Sophia had been raised by her alone. So, in essence, Sophia had lost her mother. And he hadn't offered a single word of condolence. "I should have told you before, Sophia, but I just didn't think of it. I'm sorry for your loss."

She smiled and he felt as if the heavens had opened. "That's okay, Justin. We've both lost someone. I've found that when

I'm so hurt, it's hard to take myself to someone else's pain and sympathize. I assume all people are that way. So I understand how you feel. Empathy is a better word than sympathy."

"Yeah, I guess you're right." After a few seconds of silence, he rubbed his palms together and said, "I don't know about you, but all this wheeling and dealing has worn me out." He began to put away the Monopoly game. "We probably should hit the sack. Which bed do I get?"

"You take the one on the left. I've already slept in the one on the right."

"Left it is. I'm going to the lobby and give you some time to get ready for bed. Is half an hour enough?"

"Half an hour is perfect. Thank you for being a gentleman, Justin."

"That's the only way to be with a lady," he said and picked up the room key.

He stepped into the hallway, locking the door behind him, and pushed the room key into his jeans pocket. He was demonstrating chivalry, though he wasn't sure that was his first choice. Sophia was beautiful and sweet and he hadn't been with a woman since before Rachel passed. Maybe he would have preferred to crawl in bed with Sophia and smother her with kisses. The situation and opportunity seemed right, but the timing couldn't be worse. Sleeping with the person who would facilitate a conversation on your behalf with your departed wife was . . . He fumbled in his mind for the right word. Hell. There was no way around it; it was shitty.

He strolled through the small lounge off the lobby and was

surprised to see it was filled with a group of young people sitting, standing, milling around and laughing loudly. They were clearly in their cups.

Looking for other options, he noticed a darkened doorway with a sign displaying drink specials in Club Hideaway. He hadn't known this hotel had a bar, but the sight was welcome. A cold beer sounded good.

He crossed the lobby and stopped at the club's doorway, allowing his eyes to adjust to a dimly lit interior. A computer screen at the bar offered video poker and a jukebox in the corner played music. He could make out a few couples sitting at tables, their faces softly spotlighted by candle glow from inside red lanterns in the center of each of the tables. Otherwise, the room was mostly empty.

A waitress breezed past carrying a tray of empty glasses. "Just sit anywhere, honey. I'll be with you in just a minute."

Selecting the closest unoccupied table, Justin sank to a seat and looked around. A couple sat at a table beside him. He had seen the woman before. He wasn't sure where, but she looked familiar, and the man . . . *oops.* He knew the man and he also knew that the woman sitting close to him was not his wife. Club Hide*away* was more of a hide*out.* Flustered, he nodded a greeting and quickly diverted his attention.

He spied a small man alone at the bar. An empty glass sat in front of him, but he had a full one in his hand. He was so short his feet dangled above the floor as if he were a kid occupying an adult-size chair. The figure was someone Justin recognized instantly and knew all too well. His brother-in-law, John Patrick Daly.

Justin's first inclination was to make a quiet, unobserved exit, but on second glance, his brother-in-law looked so forlorn, Justin was reluctant to abandon him. He was, after all, family. What John Patrick might be working on or how he might be scheming against Justin personally was unknown, but clearly the guy needed a friend at the moment.

Justin rose, walked over to the bar and seated himself on the stool beside his brother-in-law. John Patrick turned his head slowly and looked at him with a bleary-eyed expression that was quickly replaced by one of shock. He leaned far away, holding his glass suspended and assessing Justin head to toe. "What in the hell are you doing here?" he slurred.

"I was seeing a friend to her room and decided to come in for a beer," Justin lied. The last thing he wanted was to go into some drawn-out story of how he ended up here, playing Monopoly and spending the night with a woman he hardly knew. John Patrick wouldn't believe him anyway.

"The hot babe you introduced me to at your place?"

Annoyance pricked Justin, inciting the same call to protect Sophia that he had felt in his driveway when John Patrick first met her. But before he could reply, the bartender came up, picked up the empty glass with one hand and swiped the bar with a damp towel with the other. "What can I bring you, buddy?"

"Coors Light, please," Justin answered, tamping down his aggravation. After all, John Patrick's crassness didn't apply to just Sophia; he had the same obnoxious attitude about *all* women. He hadn't even respected his own sister.

"I'll take another," John Patrick said, pointing to his half-empty glass.

"Sorry, man," the bartender said. "I gotta cut you off. You're past your limit."

"I don't have a limit, you asshole. Now bring me a damn drink or I'll have your fuckin' minimum-wage job. I know people."

And Justin knew the law was on the side of the man serving the drinks. He didn't want the situation to get out of hand. "Sir, I'm a friend of his. Don't worry. I'll take care of him." He turned his attention to John Patrick, "Come on, J. P. Let's not make a scene."

To Justin's amazement John Patrick agreed, offering a silly one-sided grin. "You're right. Sorry, man," he said to the bartender. "Didn't mean any harm."

The bartender gave John Patrick a long hard look as he set the ice cold bottle of beer in front of Justin. Justin paid and, apparently satisfied trouble had been averted, the barman backed away and turned his attention to a television at the far end of the bar.

Justin was about to tell his brother-in-law he had showed real maturity when John Patrick reached inside his jacket and pulled out an expensive-looking silver flask. Twisting his body away from the bartender's view, he unscrewed the top, filled the near empty glass with amber liquid and lifted it to his lips. After a long swallow, he said, "Fuck that butt wipe. *I'll* decide when I've had enough."

Alarms went off in Justin's head. He was certain John Patrick was well past the legal alcohol limit for driving. The guy posed a threat not only to himself, but also to everyone else on the road. A stark memory exploded in Justin's brain. The drunk driver who had taken Rachel replaced John Patrick in Justin's mind's eye and a deep pain almost made him cry out. Even after a year, he couldn't bear to think of a drunk driver without feeling a mixture of revulsion, horror and grief. No way could he let his brother-in-law drive. A plan came to him. If he could lure John Patrick into a state of congeniality, he could then persuade him to let himself be driven home. "How come you're drinking alone, J. P.?"

"You wanna sell me your place?" John Patrick suddenly blurted, ignoring Justin's question.

Justin hesitated a few seconds before responding to the question that had come from out of the blue. Of course it wasn't a new question. Justin had lost track of how many times John Patrick had asked it. He shook his head. "We've been all over this. Rachel picked out the place. I've told you, I'll never sell."

"How about if I made it really worth your while?"

Confused, Justin looked at him through narrowed eyelids. "Why are you so intent on buying my place? You live in a mansion on some of the best rangeland around. My place is too small to run cattle and it isn't suitable for farming. I don't get it."

John Patrick attempted to put his elbow on the bar but missed the edge and almost fell from his perch. Steadying himself, he sat straighter than normal and looked at Justin.

"You really don't know, do you? Your head is actually stuck so far up your ass that you don't know."

Justin decided to keep the conversation going. As long as John Patrick was talking, he wasn't drinking and driving. "I don't guess I do. I thought you were willing to take it off my hands because you felt I'd be happier being away from the memories."

"Bullshit. I couldn't care less about your damn memories. So you're telling me that your half-Mex girlfriend hasn't made her company's pitch about the gas deposits?"

"My girlfriend? You mean Sophia? She's not my girlfriend and she hasn't said a word about gas deposits, bank deposits or any other kind of deposits. She's a schoolteacher."

John Patrick appeared to be studying him intently. "You really don't know. I can't believe you really don't know."

Justin was running out of patience. This conversation was like riding a carousel. It kept going in a circle, never reaching a destination. And now he wanted off the ride. But while his patience had worn thin, his curiosity hadn't. "Look, J. P. We're friends, family even. We go back a long way. Why don't you just cut out the bullshit and tell me the truth? It's obvious now that concern for my well-being isn't what's had you hanging around me and my place the past year."

But even as he asked the question, a glimmer of understanding of John Patrick's behavior began to glow deeply within Justin. He knew several rural property owners who had become rich overnight from gas producers drilling on their land.

"You dumb shit," John Patrick said. "You're sitting on top of one of the richest gas pockets they've found since the Barnett Shale around Fort Worth. Your mineral rights are worth millions."

Justin could only blink while his brain tried to absorb what he had just heard. The business card left on his screen door suddenly made sense. Unfortunately, now, the friendship and concern his brother-in-law had shown him in the past few months also made sickening sense. Had Rachel's spirit come because she was trying to tell him this news?

"You want the truth?" John Patrick went on. "The truth is I've got plans. Big plans. And big plans need big money. You think I'm gonna live where I'm living, do what I'm doing, to my dying day? Because if you do, you'd better think again."

"You aren't planning on leaving Felicia. Her dad would kill you."

"Let him try. That tightwad ol' sonofabitch has never done a thing for me, but if I tell him I'm at the front of the line to get a piece of real estate with gas and oil rights, ol' Boots will co-sign for me. Then, when the money starts rolling in from the royalties, I can pay off the loan and get free of Boots and his daughter both."

"But there must be other pieces of real estate you can buy. Why my place?"

" 'Cause I know for damn sure the gas is there. I know a woman who's a geologist. She showed me the seismology reports months ago. Hell, man, I can't fuck around forever. I want to get going on my plans."

"Don't you know I would've helped you? If you had just asked me."

"That's the whole fuckin' point," John Patrick said, his voice rising. "I don't want anybody's help. I can do it myself." His shoulders sagged and he crumpled against the chair. "My whole damn life I've been telling people I could do it myself."

Justin looked at the diminutive man and his heart went out to him. He'd never before considered how difficult life might have been for him. Living in a part of the world where everything was supposed to be bigger, he had surely been the brunt of jokes his entire life.

"What are these big plans you're talking about?"

"Brother, I intend to build the biggest honky-tonk in West Texas. On a par with Billy Bob's in Fort Worth. West Texas needs something like that. I know you're pure as the driven snow, Justin, but surely to God you've been to Billy Bob's."

Justin felt his jaw drop. Indeed he had been in the Fort Worth honky-tonk once or twice. And every time he had gotten lost. Jesus, it covered three acres. It had thirty-two different bars. And John Patrick intended to re-create it in Odessa, Texas? "Uh, are you sure about this, J. P.?"

"Hell, yes, I'm sure," John Patrick answered. "I'm gonna get celebrities in. I figure people will come all the way from El Paso. New Mexico, even. I'm gonna introduce myself to Tag Freeman. You know Tag Freeman's place in Midland, don't you? I'm gonna see if ol' Tag can get some of his rodeo celebrity friends to make appearances."

Tag Freeman was a world-famous rodeo bullfighter who had founded the family-oriented restaurant, Tag Freeman's Double-Kicker Barbecue and Beer, in Midland. It was a rip-roaring success. Justin had eaten there many times. The man was a celebrity, for sure. "Well, yes, but—"

"I might even get ol' Tag to go in with me on a little barbecue joint inside the place," John Patrick said.

Just recalled his last visit to Billy Bob's, where he had indeed eaten barbecue brought in from one of Fort Worth's best barbecue establishments. He supposed John Patrick could have a similar arrangement if Tag Freemen agreed to go along.

"I hear ol' Tag's best buds with Quint Matthews. You know who Quint Matthews is, don't you?"

The more John Patrick talked, the brighter a light glowed in his eyes. Justin could see his brother-in-law was dead serious. "You mean the guy who's been world champion bull rider three times? Everyone knows who Quint Matthews is. At least, everyone in Texas."

"Exactly," John Patrick exclaimed. "Between him and Tag, they're bound to know the whole rodeo industry. Not to mention country western music stars."

Justin studied John Patrick for a few seconds. Who was Justin Sadler to throw cold water on any man's dreams? "Tell you what," he said. "Give me your keys. I'll drive you home tonight and after you sober up, we can sit down and discuss all of this. You can give me more details of your plans. You've got a better business head than I do. If I'm about to become a millionaire I can't think of anyone who could give me better business advice."

John Patrick studied him for a long time, then suddenly reached into his pocket and produced a key fob. He handed it to Justin. "Thanks, buddy. I owe you one."

"I'll be back in five minutes. Wait for me here."

# twenty-six

As soon as Justin disappeared from the barroom, John Patrick hopped off the barstool, leveled a glare at the couple, who had snickered at him, and threw a wad of bills on the bar. He reached into his pocket and pulled out his second set of keys. He had never needed anyone to drive him home before and tonight wasn't going to be the first time.

Weaving as he went, he walked outside and made his way to the parked Cayenne, cursing himself for the stupid error he had made telling Justin his plans and disclosing the natural gas find. He might have had too much to drink, but he wasn't so drunk he couldn't comprehend the consequences of what he had done and said.

But there was no point in beating himself up over it.

Justin would have found out about the windfall eventually, no matter what happened. If not from the woman from El Paso, then any day now, from a representative of the drilling company who would make contact.

Reaching his SUV, he stopped, leaned on the fender and drew a deep breath of unpolluted air. The cool crispness was revitalizing. And as the air filled his lungs, a new plan began formulating in his brain.

Justin was known as a good guy. In fact, John Patrick wished he had a dollar for every time he had heard someone say, "Justin Sadler is such a good guy." Bullshit. As far as John Patrick was concerned, Justin Sadler was a hick and a naive redneck. Why, if he, John Patrick, had been born with Justin's height and only half his hair and good looks, he would rule the fuckin' world.

But if Justin wanted to sit down and talk business, John Patrick would do it. And if Justin wanted to help him out, John Patrick would allow him to do that, too. His well-meaning brother-in-law had been right about one thing— he did have a better business head on his shoulders. And cooking the books would be a snap. He would soon have the money he needed and no one would be the wiser.

He left the hotel parking lot, tires squealing. Pulling onto the highway he laughed at the turn of events. Yep, just when you thought life had handed you a bad dose of medicine, a cure came along.

Justin spent his whole trip back to Sophia's room digesting the news about the natural gas find. His steps carried a distinct buoyancy. Everything around him seemed even more surreal and out of focus than it had during and after the séance. But beneath it all a thrill lurked. If John Patrick could be believed, Justin Evan Sadler was a millionaire.

He rapped lightly on Sophia's door to warn her he was back, then inserted the key and went inside. Sophia was under the covers, lying on her side, watching TV.

"Hi," she said, smiling. "You look like you just scratched off the winning lottery ticket."

Justin looked at her for a few seconds then burst into laughter. "In a way, I did. Listen, I need you to do me a favor."

"Sure."

"Throw some clothes on, would you? I ran into John Patrick in the bar. He's had too much to drink and I need to drive him home. As you might guess, someone driving drunk has a bigger effect on me than it might on other people. If you'd follow me in the rental, I'd appreciate it."

"Of course," she said, sitting up.

Justin started for the door. "I'll wait outside while you dress."

"I'll be right out."

He waited only a few minutes outside the room before Sophia emerged, combing her fingers through her long hair, then pulling it back into a long pony tail. "I've scrubbed my face for bed already. I must look a fright. Don't look at me too closely."

Justin restrained himself from telling her how beautiful he found her. He cleared his throat and said, "Let's go."

Entering the bar, Justin looked around. No John Patrick.

But money had been scattered on the bar in a haphazard manner.

"Excuse me," he said to Sophia and left her side, heading for the door marked DUDES. Entering and exiting before the door had time to close, he returned to Sophia's side. "He's not in the men's room."

"Maybe he needed to get some air."

"Bet you're right. Let's go outside and see."

Quickstepping, Justin led the way to the outside parking lot. Again, no sign of John Patrick or his high-powered SUV. "Damn, I don't know where he parked."

"Do you have the keys?"

"Yes," he said, reaching in his pocket and pulling out the Porsche fob. He dangled it in the air.

"Does it have a button for the lights or the horn?"

"Of course." He smacked his forehead with his palm. "Why didn't I think of that?"

"Women are taught this practically from birth. Obviously you haven't lost you car in a packed mall's parking lot."

Justin raised the key high and pressed the buttons, but heard no horn, saw no flashing lights. He jogged to the side of the building, with Sophia right behind him. He saw no sign of John Patrick or his car anywhere. "You've got the rental's keys with you, right?"

Sophia dug in her purse and pulled out the tagged ring. "Here they are."

"Great. Give them to me. We've got to catch a Porsche."

Sophia scrambled into the passenger seat of the compact rental, Justin scooted behind the wheel, started the car and accelerated in the direction that John Patrick would most likely have taken to reach home. Justin knew the Aero rental would never catch up with the Cayenne. His only hope was John Patrick hadn't opened up the SUV's powerful engine. Unfortunately, he also knew the driver loved nothing more than pushing anything to its limit.

He toyed with the idea of calling the highway patrol, but decided he preferred catching up with John Patrick and getting him to pull over. Lucky for all, the nighttime traffic on the West Texas highways was scarce. He and Sophia had met only one car traveling in the opposite direction.

He unclipped his cell phone and handed it to Sophia. "Locate John Patrick's number and call him for me. If we can get him, maybe I can talk him into stopping."

After a few seconds Sophia said, "Got it. Sorry it took so long. I'm not familiar with this phone."

Taking it from her, Justin listened to the burrs, his hopes diminishing as he heard each one. When John Patrick's outgoing message for voice mail engaged, he snapped the phone shut and returned it to the holder clipped to his belt. "Damn. He's not answering."

"Maybe he's home already," Sophia said.

"I hope not. He lives about five miles farther north than my place and another five or more off the highway. If he's already home, he flew under the radar."

"Is there someplace he'd go besides home?"

Justin laughed sardonically. "Oooh, yeah, but I don't know all of those addresses." A few beats of silence passed, with Justin thinking of the inebriated man who had taken

Rachel's life. He swallowed hard. "I hate to think he's putting someone's life in jeopardy. I'll drive as far as his house. If his vehicle isn't there, I'll call the DPS.

"That's probably best," Sophia said softly.

They rode in silence until they reached the turnoff that led to John Patrick's house. Justin said a silent prayer that the familiar black Porsche would be parked where it usually was when John Patrick was home—on the circular drive in front of the house. Rachel had told him once that she thought her brother did that so that he could make a fast getaway if he needed to. But when the Daly home came into Justin's headlight range, his hopes were dashed. He saw no sign of the Cayenne and drove back to the main highway.

"Let me try his cell one more time." He reached for his phone again and keyed in the stored number. He waited for an answer that didn't come.

"What about calling his house?"

"I don't want to upset his wife needlessly. I'd rather call the troopers. If it turns out he's home and parked in the garage or something, then no harm's done. On the other hand, if he's still out driving around, they'll find him." After a long, guilt-laden pause, he added, "And they'll nail him on a DUI. He could go to jail."

Sophia reached over and touched his forearm. Her touch had a soothing effect, easing the conflict he felt. "I know it's hard for you to call them, but it's the right thing to do."

"Yeah. Lives could be at stake. And don't I know that better than anyone." Keying in 9-1-1, he gave the operator the information and was thanked for his call and his service to the community, but he ended the call feeling more heel than hero.

"I know you feel bad, but you had no choice," Sophia said. "You had to do it."

Justin sent a sideways glance at his passenger. Was she reading his mind and thoughts? Was she capable of that?

"I didn't read your mind," she replied. "I don't have the power to do that. But I do think you're the kind of man who wouldn't take enjoyment from a situation like this."

"I appreciate that," Justin said. "Say, uh, I hope you don't mind, but we're about a mile from the entrance to my place. I'm feeling better now and if you wouldn't mind, I'll just—"

"Don't apologize. It makes perfect sense you want to go home. I've had a wonderful evening. Let's just pretend we had a date and I'm taking you home."

Justin chuckled. "I suppose that would be in keeping with the way things are done these days, wouldn't it?"

"That's what I hear," Sophia said, laughing too.

With his gate in sight, Justin slowed. He crossed the cattle guard and eased up the winding driveway. His headlights spotlighted his home and much to his utter disbelief, there, in front of *his* house, sat the Porsche, driver's door open, lights on. As Justin came to a stop behind the SUV, he could hear the motor purring like a contented cat.

"I'll be damned. I didn't even think to look here."

"At least he's off the road," Sophia said with a sigh.

"That's a plus." He switched off the ignition. "Looks like I'll be babysitting tonight."

"I'll stay just long enough to make sure everything's all right."

Justin dreaded what lay ahead. He had been cordial to John Patrick in the bar, but after the revealing conversation, he didn't know how long he could maintain that façade. He opened the door and slid out.

At the Porsche he stopped, leaned inside, and killed the engine and lights. John Patrick might have no concern for the price of gas, but Justin didn't see the point in the waste. As he closed the door, his eyes landed on his own front porch, bathed in the weak glow of the porch light he had turned on when he and Sophia left earlier. There, lying face down and motionless was a body. Justin recognized the clothing. John Patrick.

*Passed out,* Justin thought. He expelled a breath and left the Cayenne. He walked over and gently nudged his brother-in-law with his toe, "Hey J. P., get up." No response. He nudged again, a little harder. "Get up, J. P. You can't sleep it off out here on my porch. The coyotes will drag you off."

Sophia came alongside him. "Are you sure he's all right?"

Justin looked at her. "I assume he's passed out."

Squatting, Justin made a visual inspection of his brother-in-law, looking for signs of trauma. He picked up his wrist and felt for a pulse.

Taking his shoulder, he gently turned him over until he lay on his back. "Jesus," he mumbled and dragged a nearby chair closer, raised John Patrick's feet and placed them on the chair. Without a word to Sophia, he grabbed his phone and for the second time in the evening, called 9-1-1.

"What's wrong?" Sophia asked after he disconnected.

"I don't know, but he's barely breathing and his pulse is so faint I had trouble finding it. The other night, I thought he was lying about the cardiac problem, but maybe he wasn't."

"Shouldn't he be covered up?"

"Yeah, what was I thinking? I'll be right back." Justin went into the house and grabbed the first thing he found— the afghan from the couch. Rachel's afghan.

Outside, Sophia took the throw from his hands and spread it over John Patrick's still body. She pressed her hand against his forehead for several seconds. Justin couldn't see her face, but her body language told him something was happening. "If it's his heart, I doubt he'd be running a fever," he said. "I think he feels clammy."

Not moving from her place beside the unresponsive body, Sophia looked up at him with sadness in her eyes. "When the paramedics get here, be sure they understand that he's suffering from post-traumatic stress disorder as well."

Justin stared at her in disbelief. "Are you kidding? How? What do you know that I don't?"

"Let's just say that what this man has been through to-night, I wouldn't wish on my worst enemy."

Justin didn't say another word. He sank to the porch floor, his body pressed against John Patrick's to keep him warm while they waited in silence. His imagination was running wild with what might have occurred, but for a reason he couldn't understand, much less explain, he chose to not ask questions.

Every few minutes he picked up his unconscious brother-in-law's wrist and felt for a pulse. It was there, but barely. Still, he was alive. If Sophia hadn't been here, Justin would have assumed it was his heart or that he had passed out from overdrinking. Could a person truly be shocked to the brink of death? He'd heard of it before, but never witnessed it.

In less than twenty minutes the wail of the ambulance's siren pierced the night's quiet. The horizon, black as velvet, displayed a splash of brilliant color. "Here they come," Justin said.

He recognized the ambulance driver as Mike Greenwich, a man Justin had worked with many times. His partner was a young Mexican man Justin had never met. Both were removing paraphernalia from the back of the EMT unit when Justin approached. "Hi, Mike. Glad to see you."

"Hey, man." He gestured toward his partner. "This is Julio. He's new." He peered around Justin's body. "I thought this was your address when the call came in. What's going on?"

"I just got home and found my brother-in-law like this." He tilted his head toward John Patrick's still body.

"Is that a kid?" Julio asked, as the trio moved to the body.

"Naw, he's a full-grown asshole," Mike said. "What'd little Johnny do this time? Fall down and go boom?"

Mike and his companion laughed, but grew silent when Justin stopped them with an icy glare. "This is my wife's brother, guys." After a pause, he continued, "His pulse is faint and breathing is shallow. He's cold and clammy to the touch. He's been drinking heavily but no signs of vomitus, passageway is clear, no obstructions. Reflexes are normal with no response to painful stimuli. Pupils are normal, not fixed and dilated. I don't have a cuff here at my house, so I didn't take his pressure."

"Let's get him on the bus, Julio," Mike said. "You drive. I'll call the stats in." He put out his right hand. "Justin, it's good to see you, man." He turned to Sophia. "You want to ride with our patient?"

"I'll ride," Justin said. He looked at Sophia. "Do you want to follow us or return to the hotel?"

"I'll go back to the hotel."

"Will you be all right?"

"Absolutely. I'm fine."

"Here, take my cell number so you can call me if you need to." He said the numbers and she entered them into her own cell phone.

"Good luck," she said, "and will you call me in the morning and let me know how things are?"

"Of course," Justin said, "thanks for . . . well, thanks for everything."

His eyes lingered on hers.

Sophia smiled. "I'll give you this much, Justin Sadler, you sure know how to show a girl an interesting time."

## twenty-seven

Sophia watched the ambulance pull away into the night. After hastily entering Justin's cell number into her digital address book, in the window that asked for a description of the party, she keyed in "someone special" and snapped the phone shut. Her feeling for Justin wasn't a schoolgirl fantasy. He *was* someone special. In only a few days she had seen traits in him she didn't think existed outside of romance novels. He truly was a knight in shining armor and all any girl could hope for.

Taking a few moments to study his home before leaving, she was tempted to enter. The pull was overpowering, but she resisted. A time and a place existed for all things, and even though this was the place, the time wasn't until tomorrow evening.

She climbed into her car and drove away slowly, suddenly drained of energy. She needed to get back to the hotel. Her body needed rest and her mind needed peace for the coming ordeal.

She was so lost in her own thoughts that before she knew it she was at the hotel. She parked close to the entrance, entered the hotel and walked to her room, all without interruption. Once inside, she sat on the edge of the bed and removed her shoes. Signs of the Monopoly game they had been playing earlier and hadn't put away entirely were scattered over the table. Smiling at the memory, she dug out her phone, flipped the case open, pressed the key and waited until she heard Justin's baritone voice.

"Hi, Sophia. You at the hotel?"

Tucking one foot under her, she grinned foolishly. "Safe and sound. How's your brother-in-law?"

"He's the same. They're going to admit him. I called his wife, Felicia. She's a wreck. Her father's driving her here. They should arrive any minute."

"Have they said what they think is wrong with him?"

"No, they're calling in a neurologist and I suspect the next thing that will happen is a battery of tests. Right now he's stable but unconscious."

"Hm. Well it could be worse."

"Yeah, it could always be worse."

"Uh, this might not be the time to bring it up, but tomorrow night—"

"Please don't tell me you think we should cancel the séance tomorrow night," Justin said.

"No, quite the contrary. I was going to say that absolutely nothing should keep us from moving forward. There's an angry spirit in your home, Justin. All of the signs are there and every time I'm there, I sense it. I think it would be dangerous to delay."

"You don't mean *dangerous* as in *dangerous*? Surely you aren't serious about that."

"I wish I wasn't. I don't think you should go back there tonight."

"I'm not afraid, Sophia. Whatever is in there has been there for months and it hasn't hurt me."

"But it's under new stress now. It's unpredictable. Just trust me, okay?"

"Hey, I trust you, Sophia, okay? I probably won't be able to get away from the hospital tonight anyway. Uh-oh, Felicia just walked in. I need to go. See you tomorrow night. Sleep tight."

Her thoughts miles away, Sophia's body moved mechanically as she laid her phone on the bedside table and rubbed the cold chills that had formed on her arms.

The early-morning preparations for a full day of business had Debbie Sue flipping the sign in the Styling Station door's window from CLOSED to OPEN. Over the years her customers had become her friends, and normally, she was anxious to see most of them. But this morning she was more eager to see Edwina.

The events of the evening before had kept her awake most of the night. Then this morning, after half an hour of tantalizing foreplay followed by mind-numbing sex with Buddy, then bidding him a farewell laced with *I love you*'s and *I'll miss you too*'s, she had rushed to the phone and called her friend and partner.

The idea of connecting with those who had passed on was intoxicating, and if props and accessories were needed in building a bridge to the other side, no one could be better at filling that need than Edwina.

The sound of a car door slamming in the back of the salon sent Debbie Sue scurrying to the back door. Just as she reached it, Edwina appeared, her customary quart-size Dr Pepper in one hand and a brown paper grocery sack in the other. Removing her rhinestone-encrusted sunglasses, Edwina handed the sack to a squealing Debbie Sue. "Here's everything you listed," she groused. "But Halloween is months away. What are you up to?"

"It occurred to me last night, Ed, that if a pack of cigarettes can conjure up an unexpected spirit, the possibilities are limitless with other enticements."

"Enticements? Hell's bells, Debbie Sue, you've gone from a half-assed skeptic to a full-fledged nutcase. We're supposed to be connecting with Justin's sweet little wife, not auditioning for Dancing with the Dearly Departed."

Ignoring Edwina's grumbling, Debbie Sue started removing items from the bag and laying them out on the manicure table. "Oh, wow. This is all perfect, Ed. I knew I could count on you."

"I can see you're dead set on this, no pun intended," Edwina said and released a big sigh. "At least tell me who to expect." Sorting through the assortment of items on the table, she lifted up a short black wig, styled in the bouffant look from the sixties. "Why did you want me to bring this? Who do you expect to claim it?"

"That's the only thing I could think of for Patsy, plus I brought an album of hers mom left at the house."

"You honestly think Patsy Cline will show up in Justin Sadler's dining room?"

"Why not? If the only requirement is that you be dead, she fits that category."

"Uh-huh, and this?" Edwina picked up the T-shirt she had bought as a joke in a store on Sixth Street in Austin. It was plain white, decorated with the bright red proclamation, FUCKIN' CLASSY.

"You really have to ask?" Debbie Sue said.

"I'm thinking Anna Nicole Smith," Edwina answered.

"Right. We can ask her if she took that overdose on her own."

"And these?" Edwina held up a pair of red four-inch-heeled Jimmy Choo shoes, which Debbie Sue knew to be one of her most prized possessions.

"Actually, those go with these," Debbie said, gathering a silk headscarf and a handful of rhinestone bracelets. "It was hard to figure out what Marilyn would be drawn to, but I knew she'd want to look sexy."

"Marilyn? As in Monroe?" Edwina flapped a skinny hand at Debbie Sue. "You're crazy, Debbie Sue. Why are you interested in digging up these particular people?"

"Don't you get it, Ed? These deaths are all mysteries in a

way and there are all of these conspiracy theories out there. No one knows exactly what happened to these people in their last moments."

Edwina frowned. "No one knows what happens to anybody in their last moments, even if there's a crowd watching. Patsy Cline's departure isn't a mystery. Everyone knows her airplane flew into a mountain in a storm."

"Okay, okay. Maybe they're not all real mysteries. But they were celebrities that people loved and they died young. Seriously, Ed, wouldn't you love to ask Marilyn how she really died and settle it once and for all? Can you even imagine learning the answer to that question?"

"What I'm learning, girlfriend, is that you've gone off the deep end of crazy."

"No, I haven't. Think about it, we may never have another chance like this in our lifetime."

"And thank God for that."

"There has to be someone you'd like to talk to, Ed. Someone you've never met but always wanted to. Someone you've got a question for."

Edwina's heavily mascaraed eyes squinted and she appeared to be mulling over that question. Suddenly she grabbed the sack and headed for the rear entrance. "I'll be right back."

Debbie Sue followed her to the back door and saw her scooting into the Mustang. "Wait, where are you going?"

Edwina's head popped out the open driver's window. "To my house. My Elvis jumpsuit is hanging in my closet. I won't be gone but a minute."

As Debbie Sue watched Edwina back out and speed away, she couldn't keep from grinning. "Elvis Presley . . . cool."

By early afternoon Debbie Sue's excitement had infected Edwina and they were both talking in whispers about the coming evening's event.

"You don't dread tonight?" Debbie Sue asked.

"Not after meeting up with Little Pearl again. I figure I've faced my demon and come out the better for it. I mean, when you come right down to it, what could a spirit really do? I'd most likely do more harm to myself than it would."

"That's right," Debbie Sue agreed. "So you're not afraid to attend the séance again tonight?"

"Scared shitless, but ready all the same. If even one of those people really shows up, it'll be fun."

The Christmas bells tied to the front door jangled and Debbie Sue and her friend looked toward the sound. Sophia's head poked through the doorway. "Are y'all still open?"

"Heavens, yes. Get in here," Edwina said. "What have you been up to today?"

"Not much, I slept late, went to the mall and walked around. Just killed time mostly."

"We were just talking about tonight," Debbie Sue said.

"I hope you both plan on being present."

"There's not a ghost of a chance we'd miss it." Edwina cackled at her own joke. "Get it? *Ghost* of a chance?"

"Ed, I think we all got it," Debbie Sue said. "Listen, Sophia, I want to ask you something."

"Sure." Sophia took a seat on one of the manicure stools.

"Edwina and I have some things we'd like to bring tonight."

"What kinds of things?"

"Just a few items to add to what you had on the table last night."

"Oh. Oh, I get it . . . Sure, that's fine, but I want both of you to understand that I can't guarantee whomever you want to see will appear. Inanimate objects are to make a spirit more comfortable and easier to recognize, but nothing is promised."

Debbie Sue looked to Edwina and nodded her head. "I think we both understand, don't we Ed?"

"Abso-fuckin'-lutely."

Sophia laughed. "Good. Well I came in for a specific reason."

Debbie Sue placed her hand on Sophia's shoulder. "Ohmigosh, here we are prattling on about what *we* want. How can we help *you*?"

"I've never had a manicure or a pedicure. Do y'all do that?"

"You're looking at the best there is," Debbie Sue said, waving her thumb between herself and Edwina.

"Is it expensive, I mean, uh . . . how much does each one cost? If both are too much, maybe I can have just one of the two if both are too much." She hesitated, then hastily added, "It's not that I don't have the money. I do. I just don't know if I have enough."

Debbie Sue knew exactly where the younger woman was coming from. It hadn't been that long ago when she had resided in the state of being broke. She gave Edwina an all-knowing wink. "It's funny you'd ask for those two services. We run a Monday special on spa treatments, don't we, Ed?"

"Uh . . . yes, yes we do," Edwina replied, taking the cue perfectly.

"Great. What is it?" Sophia asked.

"It's, uh . . . help me out here, Ed. What is it again?"

"What is what?"

"The Monday. Spa. Treatment. Special," Debbie Sue said, putting emphasis on each word.

"Oh, that . . . it's, uh . . . it's free! Yep, that's it. It's free."

"How in the world can you afford to do that?" Sophia asked.

"You'll have to ask Debbie Sue," Edwina replied. "She has the business head here. I just go along with whatever she says."

Sophia leveled a look at Debbie Sue.

"Well, we don't advertise it," Debbie Sue said. "We give it to the third person on Monday that asks the price of a manicure or pedicure."

"And I'm the third?"

"You sure are," Debbie Sue said brightly.

"Congratulations," Edwina added, patting her thickly padded chair back. "Let's get started.

Sophia moved from the stool to the chair and removed her shoes while Debbie Sue rolled the pedicure stand closer.

Positioning themselves, Debbie Sue and Edwina went

to work on their new client. Before long, the conversation came around to Justin, and Sophia relayed the story of the previous evening's events.

"I spoke to Justin a couple of hours ago," she said. "There's been no change in his brother-in-law's condition. He's still unconscious. The neurologist they called in is stumped. All the testing they've done shows nothing. They're supposed to be getting an opinion from a cardiologist."

"Good Lord," Debbie Sue said. "John Patrick's a young man, close to my age, what in the world do you think happened to him?"

"It has to be his heart," Edwina said smugly, her tone dripping with confidence.

"Why do you say that?" Debbie Sue asked.

"Just look at him. His growth is stunted. It's understandable he would have other health problems too."

"So now anyone that's *short* needs to live in fear of a premature heart attack? Is that what you're saying? And where do you get your medical information, Ed, the *Enquirer*?"

"No, Miss Smarty Pants, I'll have you know I don't read the *National Enquirer*. I saw it on one of my soap operas."

"Now there's a bank of knowledge to rely on," Debbie Sue said.

"From what I've heard of John Patrick, he was probably dead drunk when y'all found him. He *was* drunk, wasn't he, Sophia?"

Sophia nodded. "Justin said he'd been drinking, but it was more than just that."

Edwina's right eyebrow arched into a high peak. "Really?"

"I don't have, I mean I don't know of—I'd . . . I'd rather not say."

Debbie Sue exchanged looks with Edwina. Sophia wasn't telling them everything and Edwina had to have figured that out too.

Debbie Sue was trying to decide the best way to frame her next question when Sophia said, "I can't tell you what happened to John Patrick. I'll just say to you what I said to Justin. Please trust me. Conjuring up the dead is never predictable and shouldn't be taken too lightly. Dealing with the other side is not a parlor game."

Debbie Sue exchanged another look with Edwina. This time, both of Edwina's brows moved up her forehead and she mouthed, "Oops."

Debbie Sue moved to where the bag of paraphernalia sat, the rhinestones on the Elvis jumpsuit glistening enough to catch anyone's eye. She nudged it further under the counter, out of sight. "We'd never ask you to tell us anything you don't want to, Sophia. And as far as taking things seriously, we're totally on board with that. We understand it's not a game."

"Totally," Edwina agreed, nodding.

# twenty-eight

S ophia stayed at the salon longer than she had expected to. The hours with Edwina and Debbie Sue had flown by. The stories of their exploits as Domestic Equalizers had her in stitches. The two women were so uninhibited and entertaining.

Eventually they closed the salon and went to Hogg's Drive-In for a plate of mile-high nachos, an order of French fries heavily sprinkled with garlic salt and some of the best beer-battered onion rings Sophia had ever eaten.

They parted, agreeing to see each other again in a couple of hours at Justin's house. The time with the women had been good for her; she had a better feeling about tonight than before.

Enroute to the hotel, she called Justin. She hadn't spoken to him in hours and was anxious to hear any updates.

"Hi, Sophia," he said, a voice that elicited a smile from her every time she heard it.

"Hi, how are you?"

"Good, thanks. I'm tired, but good."

"Are you home?"

"Yeah, I got here about an hour ago. Dealing with Felicia has worn me out. There was a time I thought I'd like to be a crisis negotiator, but after today I'll never think that again."

"Is there news of John Patrick?"

"He's still unconscious. Sophia, is there anything you can tell me that the doctors should know?"

"Me?"

"You told me he was in a post-traumatic state. Apparently, you were right. All tests have been perfectly normal. What did you see when you touched him?"

Sophia closed her eyes and drew a breath. "I'll tell you when I see you later."

"But if it's something that would help—"

"It wouldn't help, Justin. I believe what I saw is what caused him to go into shock. He's experiencing emotional trauma, but there's nothing the doctors can do about the cause. They can only deal with the effect."

"That's pretty much what they've decided. I told them he experienced a personal tragedy and his condition is just the way we found him."

"You didn't lie."

A beep came through the phone. "Hold on a minute," Justin said. "I've got another call coming in." Several seconds passed before he returned to the line. "Sophia, I gotta go. It's Felicia. She's convinced that John Patrick's condition is the result of an alien abduction. She wants me to get in touch with a group out of Roswell, New Mexico, that specializes in kidnappings by aliens."

"Oh, my goodness. You're kidding, right?"

"I only wish I was. I've got to try and talk some sense into her, but don't hold your breath. I'll see you later."

"Okay, later."

Left with nothing but the road stretching ahead of her, Sophia thought about Felicia's theory for her husband's condition. She supposed it wasn't really any more far-fetched than what had actually happened.

Seeing a ghost, an extremely angry ghost, could throw any unsuspecting human into a catatonic state. Alcohol consumption reduced a person's ability to think logically, to filter sights and sounds, and John Patrick's ill-prepared mind had simply snapped from the overload.

When the time was right she would tell Justin about the kerosene can in the trunk of John Patrick's car and the reason he had gone to Justin's house. Apparently weary of his plots against Justin always producing the less-than-hoped-for result, John Patrick had decided to burn him out, corral and horses included.

At that, Rachel's ghost had presented itself. And when John Patrick bragged of his intent, his sister's ghost had gone into an unearthly rage. No earthbound creature could ever be forewarned sufficiently of a spirit's fury and the justice it was capable of delivering.

Sophia could still see the vision in her mind. Rachel's specter had swept toward John Patrick, no longer in the human form he last remembered his sister, but in her present condition in the grave—rotting skin clinging to bone, black vacant holes where eyes had been, strawlike hair and decaying clothing flying and flapping. An icy wind had accompanied her and the screams of banshees. Teeth bared, she had screamed a sound too horrific for description and swooped down and around and thrust her icy apparition through John Patrick's flesh-and-bone body twice before his mind shut down.

Sophia had concluded from listening to Justin talk that Rachel had been a wonderful human being, capable of great love and humanity, but, as she had pointed out to him, a spirit just wasn't the same personality as the living being. Its frustrations could be many, ranging from not being allowed to cross over, to its own brother abusing the former love of its human life, not to mention its human life being snuffed out fifty years too soon. An unsettled spirit could experience great anger and resort to anything.

Stopping in a parking space at the hotel, she turned off the ignition and reached for her purse in the passenger's seat. "Sweet Justin," she said aloud. "I hope you never have to see that."

And at that moment, her peripheral vision caught movement in the backseat. Her gaze shot to the rearview mirror, now fogged over from a sudden drop in temperature. The rear seat was empty, but she was sure she had seen or sensed someone or something. The hair on her forearms stood at attention and a discernable shiver, not related to the car's chilly interior, ran down her spine.

The thick accent of Gran Bella whispered in her ear. "Come inside, Sophia. We'll have an opportunity to meet Rachel later."

Debbie Sue sat at the gated entrance to Justin's home, listening to a duet between Tim McGraw and his wife, Faith Hill. She never heard Faith Hill these days without thinking of Avery Deaton, whom they had met two years ago while investigating the disappearance of Elvis's blue suede shoes. Avery was almost a dead ringer for the famous singer.

Debbie Sue and Edwina had agreed to meet here at Justin's gate, but neither of them had wanted to arrive at his house first or alone. The bag of accessories sat on the passenger's-side floorboard. Being the chosen body in the previous séance and not having actually witnessed a spiritual visitation with her own eyes, Debbie Sue had mixed emotions about another session. Her hope was that this time someone other than herself would be chosen as the receptor.

Buddy had persuaded her to film this event with a higher grade camera that those used for surveillance or the throwaways she usually bought for photographing crime scenes. If he couldn't be present he wanted to know what to expect and how to deal with the aftermath.

The sound of a roaring engine and the light from a car

old enough to sport only a single headlight on each side of the front grille revealed Edwina's approach. When Edwina's 1968 Mustang came into view, Debbie Sue raised a hand in greeting, shifted into gear and started up Justin's driveway.

The only car parked at the house was the black Porsche Cayenne, just as John Patrick had left it, Debbie Sue assumed. She was surprised they had arrived before Sophia, but the girl couldn't be far behind.

Ironically, Justin greeted them as if they had arrived for a housewarming or a party, with expectations of great gaiety, hardly indicative of the gathering's true intent.

"What's in the sack?" he asked, as Debbie Sue dragged her loot from her pickup's backseat.

"Oh, just some things Ed and I thought might help," she said. "We talked to Sophia about it this afternoon. She said it was all right for us to bring them."

Justin nodded. "I'm sure it is. I was just curious."

Just then the headlights of another vehicle shone against the wall.

"Sophia's here." Justin strode from the room and out of the house.

Debbie Sue would have had to have been blind to miss that his eyes lit up like a kid who had been handed a new toy. She glanced at Edwina, whose brow lifted knowingly. "Don't say it," Debbie Sue told her.

"Humph. Do I look like I'm gonna say I told you so?"

"We've got more important things to think about, Ed. Buddy got me this fancy camera. He wants me to film tonight's session. Whatever happens, do *not* stop the camera."

"Where's the camera?"

"Here." Debbie Sue pointed to a silver ornament on her handbag. "This is the lens. The camera's in my purse."

"As I live and breathe. That's pretty damn cool."

"I've been dying to try it."

"I wish you'd use another expression."

"Listen, Ed, I don't know about you, but I hope this whole thing ends tonight. I can't remember when my nerves have been this jacked up."

"I hear ya, girl. I've been so jumpy I've scared myself a time or two. If someone yelled 'boo' right now I'd pass out cold."

"Kind of makes you wonder what John Patrick saw on that front porch, doesn't it?"

"Oh, shit, you don't think that's what's wrong with him, do you?" The elevation in Edwina's tone couldn't be denied. "This is scaring the bejesus out of me, Debbie Sue. I've changed my mind. Let's go home. We can ease out the back door. Let's leave this to Sophia and Justin to figure out."

"We can't do that, Ed. We're in this up to our tits. We are staying to the bitter end."

"That's another expression I wish you wouldn't use again."

Debbie Sue looked toward the sound of the front door closing and smiled as Sophia and Justin re-entered the room. They looked like a couple well suited for each other—young, good-looking, with a bright future before them. No one would ever guess they were part of a ghost hunt.

After saying hello, Sophia went directly to the business at hand. "I'll light some candles and dim the lights. Justin, can you please put on the same music you had on last night? And Edwina, if you'd please bring that vase of roses off the coffee table."

"What do you want me to do?" Debbie Sue asked.

"Why don't you put the enticements on the table?"

Debbie Sue cleared her throat. "All of them? Ed and I brought some stuff, but—"

"Oh, yes, please do include what you brought."

"Okaaay," Debbie Sue with hesitancy. Remembering Sophia's admonishment back in the salon, Debbie Sue was almost embarrassed to reveal what she and Edwina had brought. She felt as if she were trying to turn the evening into a carnival act. Sophia had been right when she said this was a serious situation.

"Maybe I'll just put your stuff out, Sophia. That's probably all we need." She closed the top of the paper sack and rolled it down, then placed it on the kitchen counter.

"No, please," Sophia insisted, picking up the sack. "There's no way of knowing what might appeal to a spirit." She reached into the sack. "Let's see what we've got."

Debbie Sue looked for but didn't see any particular facial expression from Sophia as she removed the wig, bracelets, head scarf or T-shirt, but she saw her eyes widen when she lifted out the Elvis jumpsuit.

"Is this an Elvis costume? You think we might conjure up Elvis?"

"Not really, but we sure as hell hope so," Edwina said.

Sophia drew a deep breath. "Okay, then. Looks like we're

all set." She looked around the room. "If everyone will please take a seat. Justin, you sit here to my right. Debbie Sue, sit on my left and Edwina, you sit across from me, please."

All moved to their respective chairs and sat down, instinctively joining hands to form a circle.

After Sophia led the prayer and a chorus of amens followed, she continued, "We are here to communicate with the spirit in this home."

Everyone in the group remained silent. The only sound was the soft music in the background. Debbie Sue was sorely tempted to open an eye and peek but fought off the urge.

Seconds passed, Sophia spoke again, her voice soft and even. "We are here to communicate with the spirit in this home."

Nothing. Music played. Seconds and then minutes passed. Edwina squeezed Debbie Sue's left hand and she returned the acknowledgment.

Sophia said again. "We are here—" She stopped suddenly and said nothing else.

Debbie Sue felt as if her blood pressure had plummeted. Something was happening, but she felt that this time, she had not been chosen as the receptor. What blood pressure she had remaining fell even further when the grip Sophia's hand had on hers relaxed and she was suddenly freed from her hold.

Opening one eye she looked at Edwina and then Justin, both of whom were transfixed. Turning to look at Sophia, she saw that she was paying attention to no one, but was intently studying the articles before her. She reached for the obscene T-shirt and laughed when she read the logo. "This is certainly appropriate, isn't it?"

She pulled the garment over her head and continued her search on the tabletop. "Let's see . . . Oohh, I love these!" She slipped the bracelets onto her wrist.

Debbie Sue was finally able to loosen her tongue. "Marilyn? Is that you, Marilyn?"

Sophia looked at her and a sneer crossed her lips. "Who the fuck is Marilyn?"

Okay, so Marilyn Monroe was out. Most likely Patsy Cline too, and definitely Elvis.

Sophia picked up the tube of lipstick and twisted it up. "Nice color." She swiped it across her lips. "How about it, Edwina, does this color look good on me?"

Edwina's eyes flew wide, her mouth dropped open and a guttural sound came from her throat.

*Okay,* Debbie Sue thought. *She knows Edwina by name. That cancels out Rachel.*

Sophia ran a finger along Justin's forearm and gave him a come-hither look. "My, my, who do we have here?"

*Definitely not Rachel. But who in the hell. . .*

"If I'd have known a good-looking man was going to be here, I would've fixed up a little . . . Debbie Sooz, you should have warned me."

*Debbie Sooz? Jesus Christ, Debbie Sooz? Only one person in the entire world had ever called her that.* Her palms flew to her cheeks. "Pearl Ann?"

"Pearl Ann!" Edwina all but shouted.

"Who's Pearl Ann?" Justin asked. "Is that Little Pearl?"

"No. It's Pearl Ann Carruthers," Debbie Sue answered breathlessly. "She was murdered a few years ago. You should remember, Justin. Edwina and I broke the case."

He frowned in puzzlement. "Oh, yeah. I think I do remember that."

"We found your murderer, Pearl Ann," Edwina said smugly.

"So I heard. What? You think we don't get the news on the other side?" Sophia sashayed around the room. "Say, does this body make me look fat? What about this hair?" She picked up a sheaf of long hair and let it fall. "I never thought of myself with dark hair. How come you never gave me dark hair, Debbie Sue? You colored it every other color."

Debbie Sue ignored her questions. She had questions of her own. "Why are you here, Pearl Ann? Why?"

"We're trying to talk to Justin's wife," Edwina said.

"I know Rachel. Sweet little thing. I convinced her to let me go first. You don't think I'd miss a party, do you?"

"Well, you always did love to party," Edwina said, and crossed her arms over her chest.

"Bet your sweet ass, I did, Four-eyes." Sophia raised her arms and stretched. "Damn, it feels good to stretch. That's one of the bad things about having no body and living in a coffin. You can't imagine how much you miss stretching."

"Among other things," Debbie Sue whispered to Edwina.

"Say, do you ever see . . ." Edwina started to say, but suddenly Sophia sat back down and her shoulders sagged. Everyone watched in anticipation.

Sitting straight again, Sophia slipped the bracelets from her wrist and drew a deep breath. "We want to speak to the spirit known as Rachel. Rachel, are you there? It's time for you to appear, Rachel."

Without another word Sophia looked down at the T-shirt she was wearing and pulled it over her head, then patted her hair into place. She folded the T-shirt neatly and returned it to the table. Turning her gaze to Justin, she smiled sweetly, "Hi, Marathon Man."

Justin didn't know whether he should laugh or cry, grab her to his chest or push her away. It was Rachel, then again it wasn't. A tear rolled down her cheek and he fought to maintain control.

"I've missed you, baby," she said softly. "I'm so sorry I had to leave you the way I did."

There was something in the inflection of her words, and the way she touched her hair that was purely Rachel. Having her sitting across from him was incredible, and he shook his head to clear his thoughts. He wanted to say so much. He knew she could disappear as quickly as she had arrived and he was sitting here fighting back tears like a fool. "Your leaving was my fault. I can never express how sorry I am. I've relived the whole thing a thousand times, trying to understand how it happened. And why." Against his strongest defenses the tears escaped his eyes. "If I could change places with you I would. Can you forgive me, Rach? Can you ever forgive me?"

Justin lowered his eyes and waited for her answer. He felt her hand smooth the back of his head and rest on his neck. "What happened to me was meant to be, Justin. It was no one's fault. There are plans for our lives before we're even born, and none of us has control over that.

"I've—I've always heard that, but . . ."

"It's true. I don't blame you at all."

His voice broke. "You don't?"

"No, Justin. I've never blamed you. I love you and I always will. I only came back to tell you to forgive yourself and move on with your life."

"Move on?"

"Find someone and make a good life for her and yourself, the same life you gave me. Accept that I'm happy. Truly happy. I don't want you to worry about me, and please don't feel guilty."

Justin's felt his face heat up. "I . . . I made you happy?"

She stroked the side of his face and leaned toward him. "Oh, yes," she said softly. "All women deserve to be as happy on earth as I was."

Leaning closer, they exchanged a kiss, then stared intently into each other's eyes. After a few minutes, she said, "Sweetheart, I have to go now."

"Nooo, Rachel. Will you be back?"

"I cannot come back. I only came this time to help you. Have I? Have I helped?"

"Rach, honey, please don't go yet. There's more I want to say. I've been so lonely . . ."

"But you don't have to be. Open your mind to the opportunities that are around you. Move on, Justin, and if you truly love me . . ."

"Yes?" He asked when she paused.

"You'll have a good life."

"Rachel. Rachel?" he said, putting his hands on Sophia's shoulders and turning her to him.

She looked at him intently for several seconds. "Did she appear, Justin? Did Rachel appear?"

Sniffling noises were coming from Debbie Sue. Edwina touched the inside corner of one eye with her fingertip.

Justin got to his feet, gasping and declaring, "I need air. Oh, God." He made an exit through the front door. Soon the rhythmical squeak of the rocking chair floated from the front porch.

Sophia started after him, but Debbie Sue stopped her. "Let him go, Sophia. He needs to be alone for a minute. Here," she said, going for her purse and pulling the camera free. "I filmed the whole thing. Let me show you."

Sophia sat and watched the film several times. Finally she lowered the camera to her lap and looked at the two women. "What can I do? What can I say? Shouldn't I go to him?" Looking past them toward the ceiling, she called out, "Gran Bella, please tell me what I should do."

"Gran Bella's here too?" Edwina whispered in Debbie Sue's ear. "Who the hell's Gran Bella? Damn, this place is getting too crowded for me."

"Shut up, Ed." Debbie Sue turned to Sophia. "As it stands

right now, you know Justin better than anyone in this room. Go to him."

"But you said he needed to be alone," Sophia replied.

"He needed a couple of minutes, but Sophia, he's been alone for a year. What he needs the most is someone who cares about him."

"Someone warm, with real flesh and blood," Edwina added.

Sophia smoothed her hair and clothing. "Wish me luck."

"You know you've got it," Debbie Sue said.

As Sophia left the room, Debbie Sue said no more. Edwina played with the bracelets that lay discarded on the table. Debbie Sue picked up one of the candles and drained the molten wax into its saucer.

"Can you believe Pearl Ann was here?" Debbie Sue finally asked.

Edwina shook her head. "Of all people. You might know she'd be first in line to come back."

Sophia eased the door closed behind her and stood in silence, studying Justin's profile. "Do you want to be alone?"

He looked up. "No. Please. Please join me, Sophia. I had to let my head clear a little. That was intense." He sighed. "Are you all right?"

She nodded. "Feeling a little drained is all. I don't have any memory of what just happened."

"Thank you for coming here, Sophia. Thank you for helping me talk to Rachel one last time. I needed to know she's forgiven me. I don't . . . I don't know how you thank someone for that."

"My powers are pointless if I don't use them to help others." She sat down in the rocking chair beside him.

"You've done more than just help me. You've made me laugh again. You've made me feel alive again. I'm one of the deceased people you've brought back to life."

Sophia looked directly at him.

"Sophia, I don't want to lose two wonderful women in the same night," he said. "Maybe something could become of . . . of *us*. Would you be willing to give that a chance?"

A sob escaped her throat and her hand flew to her mouth, Justin reached up and took her hand away. "It just occurred to me that I've kissed your lips twice, but I've never kissed *you*."

Smiling slowly, Sophia wrapped her arm around his neck. "There's not a ghost of a chance I'd try to stop you."

# epilogue

*D*ebbie Sue, in her eagerness to show the film of the séance to Buddy, accidentally recorded over it and instead of viewing the séance, Buddy saw fifteen minutes of Edwina painting her toenails.

Debbie Sue and Edwina made a pact to never mention to anyone in Salt Lick that Pearl Ann had been seen again. Many women in Salt Lick doubted she had ever died in the first place. Anyway, that's what they had been telling themselves when their husbands didn't come home at night.

Lone Star Oil and Gas Company made a deal with Justin, and he signed an agreement that meant substantial money would be coming his way for the rest of his life. He continued working as a firefighter and contributed heavily to Mothers Against Drunk Driving.

John Patrick remained in a coma, unresponsive for sixty-three days. When he awoke, he had undergone a 180-degree change in personality and had no memory of what had happened to him. He ceased drinking and philandering. He became a friend to all, volunteered in the church and operated a birthday-party entertainment service for children, dressing as a clown and appearing with a miniature pony. Everyone who knew him or had ever dealt with him was stunned.

Unfortunately, Felicia, who had never been treated better by anyone in her life than the reformed John Patrick, became increasingly bored with her husband's new personality. She missed his bad-boy antics and divorced him for a man who wore a gun for a living, Brad Pitt, from Odessa.

Sophia and Justin continued seeing each other for several months before they concluded they wanted to be together forever.

When the new school year began in the fall, Odessa had a new teacher in their system. The middle school's fifth-grade students were constantly astounded that she seemed to see right through them, never buying their excuses for lost assignments or for missing school because of "illness." She even had the uncanny ability to know what was in the notes passed in class without reading them.

As for John Patrick's dream of owning and operating a Billy Bob's clone, the banker he approached for loans thought it was such a good plan, he stole the idea for himself and built the biggest honky-tonk in West Texas. It became a huge success.

**A⁺**

AUTHOR
INSIGHTS,
EXTRAS &
MORE...

FROM
**DIXIE
CASH**

AND

**AVON A**

Real ghosts thrive in Texas. Dixie Cash has a friend who has researched Texas ghosts extensively and written several books of true Texas ghost stories. Here are some real events from Olyve Hallmark Abbott. If you're a ghost hunter, you might want to travel to Texas and look for these ghosts.

## The Glow Stone

The night is darker than usual. The moon has slipped behind the clouds. A faint light comes from a small bulb on a cattle barn on a faraway hilltop. That is the setting for the glowing tombstone of Veal Station Cemetery near Springtown, Texas.

The first white settlers founded Veal Station in the early 1850s on horseback, and I had trouble finding it in a car, with directions. For some reason, I hesitated to go at night, alone, in the dark. Did I say by myself?

The local newspaper editor directed me to a cordial gentleman named Steve, who gladly agreed to go with me. Not to hold my hand—just for protection in case I needed it. I had visited dozens of haunted cemeteries before, but this eerie glow thing intrigued me.

Dusk finally turned to dark, and we arrived at the cemetery. We parked the car facing west, close to the big gate, but we found it locked. (I never saw a gate I couldn't squeeze through or a fence I couldn't crawl under.) We could see the luminous stone from the car, all the way across one hundred yards to the back fence. That might not be a bad idea—not leaving the car, I mean.

But after all, we were here for a reason, *and* the pedestrian gate stood ajar.

Steve assured me he had seen the stone glow in all types of weather, even rainy. On this clear, quiet night, not a field mouse squeaked as we continued our walk. We lost sight of it for a moment or two, but on cue, brightness appeared from the far end of the graveyard.

"There!" I said. "There it is." I shivered.

We scarcely needed our flashlights. Strangely, when we approached, still several yards away, the luster disappeared. We moved back, careful not to step in a gopher hole, and the marker again served as our illumination—bright as ever.

Similar markers stood in the same family plot, but they were dark. Of course, a few decades separated the burials, and they were not from the same granite slab. It is generally accepted that if there is no scientific explanation for a phenomenon, something paranormal is at work.

Before we left, I asked Steve about the rumored apparition of a woman who roamed throughout the graveyard as if looking for something, or someone. He said, "No, I haven't seen her. I believe that's what it is, just a rumor."

I tend to agree. We'll put that one to rest. We saw what we came for, embedded the visual in our minds and climbed back into the car, suggesting aloud that any spirits not come with us. We discussed if minerals in the granite caused the glow. This tombstone may forever be a conundrum.

But wait, there's more. A couple years after my book on haunted cemeteries came out, a reporter from our city's newspaper called me. He asked if I'd give him specific instructions on how to get to Veal Station. He wanted to write an article about the phenomenon. I told him and asked if he'd like me to go with him.

"No, but thanks. I can find it."

He called again the following day. "I found the cemetery but couldn't see anything glowing." He thought he misunderstood the directions.

"Are you sure you don't want me to go with you?"

"No, I'll be fine. I must've missed a turn."

The phone rang the next afternoon. "Olyve, would you mind going with me?"

Good idea. I wanted to go all along.

The problem was, from the time I wrote the book and when the reporter couldn't see the stone like I said he could from the front gate, tree limbs must have grown and obstructed the view. I thought I saw something shining. Maybe a frog's eyes . . . or a snake's.

But after passing the tree, we saw the stone. Again, when we came closer, the glow ceased. We backed away, and then repeated the movements. Same thing.

Now I wish I could take credit for this suggestion, but I can't. My reporter friend said, "What would happen if we got down really low and walked toward the marker?"

"You mean walk like a duck?"

I admit I wondered how he arrived at that idea. So we gave it the ol' knee bends and waddled all the way to the tombstone. The glow did not stop until we got there!

For whatever we learned, it was *interesting*—a generic term which should have been more scientific. Could the little 100-watt bulb actually have caused the glow after all? The thing is, only the rough sides glow, and one side faces away from the light—it couldn't have reflected on it.

The reporter shot a great picture, an un-retouched glowing tombstone. We headed back home, and he left to write his story. I went to sleep that night, laughing to myself. I had actually walked like a duck.

I also wondered about light being a form of energy. *Incandescence* from heat. *Luminescence* from cold.

*Ghostly light?* Reflect on that.

# A Different Drummer

Why is a hotel haunted? For centuries, the belief is that a tragedy either happened there, the structure stood over a cemetery, or the hostelry simply appealed to the ghost as a comfortable place to hang his . . . his . . . well, it looked comfortable.

Occasionally, someone lived and died in a place and never wanted to leave. That may be the case with this lovely, two-story, white-frame hotel in Central Texas.

After the town of Calvert settled, it soon bustled with saloons, "pleasure houses," gambling halls, and businessmen with minds aimed toward the future . . . and pleasure houses. The town expanded, but in the 1870s, a yellow fever epidemic broke out, killing three hundred and striking down two thousand other residents. The situation looked grim.

A German named Gottlieb Dirr and his family found their way to Calvert. Gottlieb worked in the coal mines until a surprise flood occurred, forcing the mines to close. He used his baking talents and opened a bakery and grocery business. It flourished, and Dirr built the hotel as a five-room cottage in 1872 for his family of five children.

After Gottlieb's death in 1898, his widow, Hannah, showed she had a business mind of her own. She added a second story onto their house. With a few additional modifications, she was all set to open the "Cottage Hotel." Hannah knew of extra perks for her clientele. She designated a special room for "drummers," the traveling salesmen of today.

They realized right away that the hotel offered them selling opportunities. After the drummers visited the town's businesses, they returned to the "Drummers' Room," where they displayed their merchandise and wrote orders.

Fast forward to the twentieth century when a fire destroyed most of the business district. And further, into the 1980s, two brothers whom I'll call James and Fred, purchased the hotel and changed the name to the Calvert Hotel Bed and Breakfast. They shipped their own antiques from the northwest coast and created a lavish hostelry.

When I visited the Calvert, everywhere I turned I saw glorious antique furniture and accessories—a charming place in a small Texas town. From the time I researched Calvert's recent history, I knew dinner guests made reservations far in advance for Fred's delectable full-course meals and wines of their choice. They dined on white linen tablecloths, with flowers and candles. People drove for miles around for such dinner parties.

The brothers soon became aware of unusual occurrences—hearing voices with no one there and footsteps after they had retired for the night. There was something about the hotel that attracted the "other world." They told me of several incidents they had experienced.

I contacted author Trana Mae Simmons, whose Aunt Belle lived in Calvert. They shared their own experiences at the hotel. Both women are sensitive to the paranormal, so perhaps it's hereditary. On an occasion in 2004, Trana, her husband, and Belle visited the hotel, armed with cameras. Two other friends arrived soon after.

It could have been only a temporary chill, but no, Trana sensed a definite presence next to her on the settee. Belle, sitting across from her, could see the image of a small woman holding a feather duster and dressed in dated clothing. She obviously wanted to clean the room and preferred the ladies to leave. They all decided to make a hasty exit. Belle later identified the woman from a photo, as Mrs. Dirr.

They decided then to look through the rest of the hotel and take more photographs. On the way down the hall, Trana envisioned a white dog racing past, brushing against her as it ran. James told me that a white ghost dog has indeed made appearances both inside and outside the hotel. It's a small dog and will turn in a circle before running off. It might be he wanted someone to follow him. But where?

Later that same evening, when they returned for one of Fred's famous dinners, they arrived for a meeting in the former Drummers' Room. Within a few minutes, Trana sensed a female presence rushing out of the room, mumbling, "Too many men, too many men!"

After dinner, she told James of the incident. He didn't even have to think when Trana told him what had happened. He immediately said she had to be a woman named Leona. His explanation was that in life, Leona had married one of the Dirr men. They divorced, and she received the hotel in the settlement. Later, male family members took her to court to regain the hotel. They lost, but the result caused Leona to lose her liking for men there and then. Whether or not men were in the room, if Leona saw them . . . well, they were there to her. A ghost can see anything he or she wants to.

I don't know if Hannah and Leona ever run into each other on their visits to the hotel. I believe they would, but my thought is, it belongs to Hannah.

After a tour of historical Calvert homes, Belle and Trana probably expected other incidents to occur at the hotel. They retired for the evening and sometime after midnight, they heard men's vigorous voices. The following morning, James said he, too, had heard voices, but when he checked into it, he saw no one.

He could see light beneath the closed door to the Drummers' Room.

When he opened the door (with caution, of course), a phantasmagoria of small bright lights flew around, as if coming right at him, and then circled back. He watched them in amazement for several seconds before they vanished.

Since ghosts are not limited only to former humans in this

town, James and Fred, on more than one occasion, have seen that little white dog trotting in front of the hotel, then across the railroad tracks. While he should have still been in sight, he vanished. Other people in town told them the previous owner had a white dog, just like the brothers and their guests had observed. The truth is, it died years before.

A few months later, after selling the furnishings at auction, they sold the hotel and moved away. It never occurred to me the reason might have been because of the guests who never checked out.

The Calvert Hotel is now a private residence, so we can no longer experience the paranormal for ourselves.

If you visit this quaint Victorian town of antique shops, you might catch a glimpse of a little white ghost dog by the railroad tracks.

I hear he trots to a different drummer. . . .

## "Here's to Your Ghost"

The intoxicating liquid of many colors existed five thousand years ago in Babylon, China, Mesopotamia. . . . An ancient Egyptian tombstone bears the inscription, " . . . satisfy his spirit with beef and fowl, bread and beer." In taverns across Egypt, the favorite toast was, "Here's to your ghost."

According to the history of the Magnolia Brewery Building in Houston, in 1892, Hugh Hamilton founded the Houston Ice and Brewing Company, also known as Magnolia Brewery. Architect Eugene Heiner designed and built the four-story structure, which he completed in 1893. In less than two years, they brewed more than 60,000 barrels of beer annually. The one building expanded into more than ten by 1915, dispensing close to 250,000 barrels. The beer flowed like . . . well, beer.

Hugh Hamilton died long before witnessing the demise of his

company in 1950, which began with Prohibition, major floods, the Crash—all contributing to economic stress. Buildings washed away, or fortunate owners found buyers.

Eminent architect, designer, and developer Bart Truxillo bought the remaining two buildings in 1968 and restored the declining property. The history of the company shows the Magnolia Brewery Building survived, thanks to Mr. Truxillo. It is a registered Texas Historic Landmark and is listed in the National Register of Historic Places.

In 1978, beer found its way back from a long absence to the Brewery Tap. This was long after people cooled beer in cellars with ice brought from ponds, the same way they did vegetables to keep them fresh through winter.

The Brewery Tap, the popular bar that occupies the lower portion of the building, has an old-world atmosphere with large tables and an ambiance, which makes customers—many regulars—right at home. There may be others who also feel at home. We just can't see them.

It seems one specific ghost craves attention or at least wants his presence known. Lana Berkowitz, staff writer for the *Houston Chronicle*, wrote about the spirit as interacting with Kathy, the bartender, by playing "Kathy's Waltz" on the jukebox. He also teases by moving things from place to place.

Picture this: The bartender places your choice of ice-old tap beer on the bar. She smiles. You nod thanks. You pick up the glass and head for the dartboard with a friend. But something happens on the way to the back wall. A cold brush of air sweeps against your cheek.

"What was that?"

The bartender smiles again. "Not 'that,' it's who. We call him William."

The story is, there is at least one revenant resident in the Brewery Tap. The bartender had decided he really needed a name, and she thought he responded to William better than any other. Not Bill, it had to be William.

The building is the second oldest in Houston. The upper floor is The Brewery Ballroom, a formal hall, ideal for weddings, receptions, dinners—a myriad of celebrations. Who is to say an occasional spirit doesn't join the high-spirited affairs?

A paranormalist organization investigated the ballroom and captured several anomalies on camera. With so many people having worked or lived in the building when it was briefly a hotel, our ghost or ghosts of interest could be any one of them. The majority vote, however, goes toward an employee who met death in the basement years ago. He was in the wrong place when a beer keg fell down on him.

They say a cloud of light will occasionally hover high above the bar. Taking a picture at just the right time can capture an orb. For those who believe an orb is electromagnetic energy of a ghost, then William is your man.

And if not William, perhaps Hugh Hamilton never left. Maybe.

Ghostly books by Olyve Hallmark Abbott:

*Ghosts in the Graveyard: Texas Cemetery Tales*

*A Ghost in the Guest Room:*
*Haunted Texas Hotels, B&Bs and Inns*

*Texas Ghosts: Galveston, Houston, and Vicinity*

Here's one of Vic's favorite recipes. He likes to make these at Halloween to pass out to Salt Lick's ghostly trick-or-treaters.

## SPOOKY BLACK-CAT COOKIES

1 cup crunchy peanut butter
2 eggs
1/3 cup water
1 pkg. chocolate cake mix
small candy-coated chocolate candies
red hots

1. Preheat oven to 375°F.

2. Beat together peanut butter, eggs, and water.

3. Gradually add cake mix. Mix well.

4. Form dough into 1-inch balls. Place on ungreased cookie sheet. Flatten balls with bottom of glass dipped in sugar. Pinch out two ears at top of cookie. Add small candy-coated chocolate candies for eyes and red hots for nose. Score with a fork to form whiskers. Bake at 375° for 8 to 10 minutes.

Makes about 4 dozen cookies.

Edwina continues to write her Advice to the Lovelorn column in the *Salt Lick Weekly Reporter*. As she has grown wiser with time, her comments have become more profound.

*Dear Edwina,*

*My husband of thirty-seven years has become obsessed with the TV show* Dancing with the Stars. *He goes around the house in black tights with his shirt tails tied in a knot around his expansive waist, which, in reality is a beer gut. Occasionally I hear him yell, "Merengue!" or, "Paso Doble!" I don't know what those words mean, but when I hear him say them, I try to stay out of his way. I'm afraid this phase he's going through is going to destroy our marriage. Should I be patient with it and just let it run its course?*

*Anxiously awaiting your advice,*
*Dancing Without a Partner*

Dear Without-a-Partner,

You're without more than a partner. You're without a clue. This is a tough one, hon. I've got a lot of answers for you, but the picture of your beer-gutted husband in tights keeps clouding my mind. Wish you hadn't shared that.

Any-hoo, what's to keep you from joining him? Have you seen those female dancers' bodies? Dancing sure as hell hasn't hurt *them*. And when he yells those foreign words, yell them back and see what happens. You might end up in your own horizontal dance of love, if you get my drift?

You've got your "workout" cut out for you, sister.

Edwina "Got a Partner " Martin

*Dear Ms. Perkins-Martin,*

*My concomitant in marriage and I are attorneys. We once worked closely together. Six months ago she shared with me that she has chanced upon her old boyfriend from high school on Facebook. I thought that was nice, but now she's on her computer night and day, supposedly working on a difficult litigation case that could alter the state of jurisprudence as we know it. She hasn't asked for my elucidation or riposte and if she were really engaged in that endeavor, why would she stop to cachinnate or attenuate the screen when I come into the room? We haven't been intimate in months, she barely affirms I'm in the room, much less the bed, and she told me this morning we need to sit down this weekend and have "a talk." Give me your presupposition of what I should expect.*

*With profound gratitude,*
*Barrister of the Courts*

Dear What-in-the-Hell Did You Say?

I'd like to be a fly on the wall at your house this weekend. Maybe when you talk, what you say is easier to follow than what you write. I got out my thesaurus and here's what I think you said: Your wife has hooked up with an old boyfriend online and has been giving you the cold shoulder. And now you're afraid she wants to do the nasty with her old flame. Is that close?

As for the talk she wants to have, if I know women—and let's face it, I'm one of the better versions the good Lord released—she's already made up her mind and she's planning to let you in on her little secret. All the expatiation on your part will do no good. (That little thesaurus thing-a-ma-jig comes in handy.) I'll share with you what my granny once embroidered on a pillow for me: "If you love someone set them free. If they come back to you it was meant to be. If they don't, at least you've got this damned pillow to hold on to at night."

In other words, counselor, she has submitted her case and the court is no longer in session.

Edwina Perkins-Martin,<br>
Barrister of the Heart

*Dear Edwina,*

*My husband wants me to go to a fortune-teller with him. He said it would be fun and if we know what to expect, it might help us plan for the future. The problem is I know what to expect and that's a baby in about seven months. And it ain't his. He had a vasectomy four years ago after our youngest was born.*

*Should I break the news to him now or wait and let the fortune-teller do it?*

*Yours truly,*
*Expecting Something To Happen*

Dear Expecting,

I foretell that something will definitely happen. Girlfriend, you've got more problems then poor ol' General George Custer at the battle of the Little Bighorn. When he said to his Crow scout, Don't Hear Too Good, "Tell me if you see any Indians," he had no idea.

I'd tell him the truth, hon. The sooner the better. A baby on the way is mild compared to the problems he's really got. I wouldn't make it worse by letting a stranger drop the news on him.

Hoping for the best, but predicting the worst,
Edwina "Wouldn't Be in Your
Shoes for Nothin' " Martin

*Dear Domestic Equalizers,*

*Ladies, I might want to hire you but I need to know if you are a listed member with the BBB?*

*Thank you for your response,*
*Cautious Concerned Consumer*

Dear CCC,

If it makes you feel better, I'm happy to report that my partner and I are members of the BBB as well as the NRA, the DAR and soon the AARP. We also are qualified for DART (for the uninformed, that's Daughters of the Republic of Texas). My husband is a retired Navy SEAL and my partner's husband is employed by the DPS.

We're lifetime members of the One-A-Day Vitamin club, Little Meals on Little Wheels, the Just Say No Acceptance League and we give generously to Jerry's Kids. Debbie Sue still has her library card; however, mine was revoked due to an unfortunate incident in the Adult Reading section. I've got one punch left to receive a free Happy Meal and Debbie Sue and I both stand behind the USA!

Hope we get your business PDQ,
EP-M

*Ms. Perkins-Martin,*

*Please settle an argument between my husband and me. He says I think I'm always right. I say he's wrong. I'm just occasionally misinformed, which makes me right. There's no such thing as a person being always right except in my case, because I am always right.*

*What do you think? I'm right, right? I don't see how any rational person could think otherwise. So I'm right. I'm going to tell him he was wrong and I'm right. You do agree? I'm right. Right?*

*Thank you for proving my point,*
*Needing Validation*

Dear Needing Something Beyond Validation,

There is no shame in being wrong. I've tested the idea many, many times and I'm still alive and well.

There is, however, something wrong with being crazy as a loon and trying to pass yourself off as sane. We normal people have no way of knowing when you're coming and it really screws up our day, if only for a minute.

So here's something you can do that is really, really RIGHT. Tell people up front, "Hi, I'm totally nuts, do you agree?" You'll get the validation you need every single time.

No need to thank me, because I'm right,

Edwina

The following poem by the beloved Joyce Kilmer is not about a haunted house, but it could be. Dixie thinks it's reminiscent of the sadness that lived inside the home Justin and Rachel shared.

## The House with Nobody in It

### by Joyce Kilmer

Whenever I walk to Suffern along the Erie track
I go by a poor old farmhouse with its shingles broken
  and black.
I suppose I've passed it a hundred times, but I always
  stop for a minute
And look at the house, the tragic house, the house with
  nobody in it.

I never have seen a haunted house, but I hear there are
  such things;
That they hold the talk of spirits, their mirth and
  sorrowings.
I know this house isn't haunted, and I wish it were, I do;
For it wouldn't be so lonely if it had a ghost or two.

This house on the road to Suffern needs a dozen panes
    of glass,
And somebody ought to weed the walk and take a
    scythe to the grass.
It needs new paint and shingles, and the vines should
    be trimmed and tied;
But what it needs the most of all is some people living
    inside.

If I had a lot of money and all my debts were paid
I'd put a gang of men to work with brush and saw and
    spade.
I'd buy that place and fix it up the way it used to be
And I'd find some people who wanted a home and give
    it to them free.

Now, a new house standing empty, with staring window
    and door,
Looks idle, perhaps, and foolish, like a hat on its block
    in the store.
But there's nothing mournful about it; it cannot be sad
    and lone
For the lack of something within it that it has never
    known.

But a house that has done what a house should do, a
    house that has sheltered life,
That has put its loving wooden arms around a man and
    his wife,
A house that has echoed a baby's laugh and held up his
    stumbling feet,
Is the saddest sight, when it's left alone, that ever your
    eyes could meet.

So whenever I go to Suffern along the Erie track
I never go by the empty house without stopping and
 looking back,
Yet it hurts me to look at the crumbling roof and the
 shutters fallen apart,
For I can't help thinking the poor old house is a house
 with a broken heart.

**DIXIE CASH** is Pam Cumbie and her sister, Jeffery McClanahan. They grew up in rural West Texas among "real life fictional characters" and 100 percent real cowboys and cowgirls. Some were relatives and some weren't. Pam has always had a zany sense of humor and Jeffery has always had a dry wit. Surrounded by country-western music, when they can stop laughing long enough, they work together creating hilarity on paper. Both live in Texas—Pam in the Fort Worth/Dallas Metroplex and Jeffery in a small town near Fort Worth.

# BOOKS BY DIXIE CASH

### SINCE YOU'RE LEAVING ANYWAY, TAKE OUT THE TRASH

ISBN 978-0-06-059536-4
(mass market paperback)

"A rollicking debut. Authentic dialogue and a strong Texas flavor. . . . Debbie Sue and her posse are sure to keep readers laughing all the way to the last page." —*Publishers Weekly*

### MY HEART MAY BE BROKEN, BUT MY HAIR STILL LOOKS GREAT
### A Novel

ISBN 978-0-06-113423-4 (paperback)

"This big-hearted, relaxing read is as much fun as watching a Tim McGraw video while drinking a margarita with your best friend— and without the calories!" —Nancy Thayer, best-selling author of *The Hot Flash Club*

### I GAVE YOU MY HEART, BUT YOU SOLD IT ONLINE
### A Novel

ISBN 978-0-06-082972-8 (paperback)

"Nobody beats Dixie Cash for humor and inventive situations." —Linda Lael Miller

## DON'T MAKE ME CHOOSE BETWEEN YOU AND MY SHOES
### A Novel

ISBN 978-0-06-082974-2 (paperback)

"Quick witted, fast paced, and plain old fun, Cash's madcap series just keeps getting better." —*Booklist*

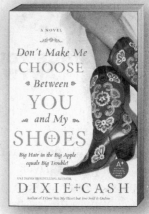

## CURING THE BLUES WITH A NEW PAIR OF SHOES
### A Novel

ISBN 978-0-06-143438-9 (paperback)

"The Equalizers must don their best big-hair thinking caps to find a way out of this cowpoke mess. Tangy and a little bit dirty—a mystery cooked up in the heart of BBQ country." —*Kirkus Reviews*

## OUR RED HOT ROMANCE IS LEAVING ME BLUE
### A Novel

ISBN 978-0-06-143439-6 (paperback)

"Belly-grabbing West Texas humor dished up with delightful relish . . . West Texas witty—smart and funny. Will keep you up late laughing!" —Joan Johnston